THE GIRL BEHIND THE LENS

Tanya Farrelly works as an EFL teacher and facilitates Creative Writing classes for South Dublin County Council. She holds a PhD in Creative Writing from Bangor University and her work has been shortlisted for several prizes, such as the Hennessy and the Francis MacManus Awards. In 2008 she was named runner-up in the William Trevor International Short Story Competition and her debut short story collection, *When Black Dogs Sing*, was published by Arlen House in September 2016. *The Girl Behind the Lens* is her first full-length novel.

Tanya lives in Wicklow with her husband and runs a monthly Spoken Word event called Staccato.

 @tanyafarrelly

Also by Tanya Farrelly

When Black Dogs Sing (a short story collection)

The Girl Behind The Lens

TANYA FARRELLY

An imprint of HarperCollins*Publishers*
www.harpercollins.co.uk

Killer Reads
An imprint of HarperCollins*Publishers*
1 London Bridge Street
London SE1 9GF

www.harpercollins.co.uk

This paperback edition 2016
1

First published in Great Britain by
HarperCollins*Publishers* 2016

A catalogue record for this book is
available from the British Library

ISBN: 9780008215118

Set in Minion by Palimpsest Book Production Limited, Falkirk, Stirlingshire

Printed and bound in Great Britain

MIX
Paper from
responsible sources
FSC® C007454

*For Tom, whose kindness and generosity
are boundless...*

ONE

Oliver Molloy woke abruptly and felt the urgent need to get out of the house. As he swung his legs over the side of the bed, he tried to rid himself of the remnants of a particularly disturbing dream, but it refused to be obliterated, even after he'd turned on the dim overhead light.

It had been almost a month since he had seen her, but every time he closed his eyes she was there. He had begun to dread the night, the time when he was most susceptible to these visitations. Mercedes had become like a cataract, something he couldn't see past, and it was only daylight that could dispel her presence and allow him to breathe normally again.

Oliver pulled on his heavy winter coat and wound a scarf round his neck. The scarf caught on his unshaven jaw, but it was unlikely that he would encounter anyone out walking in the hours before dawn. He eased the front door open. The street was quiet. A lone cat crossed the neighbours' garden and leapt onto the wall between them. It looked at him, eyes luminous in the semi-darkness, and then opened its mouth and let out a silent cry. When he didn't respond, it moved on.

Finally, a thaw had begun. For three weeks the city had been held captive by an unprecedented freeze. A layer of ice still covered the canal, but already it had thinned at the edges to reveal the murky water beneath. It trickled slowly from among the reeds as the willows wept at the water's edge and stained the ice grey. The cold crept through his leather shoes and he hurried his step to improve his circulation. Coming towards him, dressed in a grey tracksuit, breath streaming in the icy air, was a jogger. The man nodded an acknowledgement as he passed. Oliver dug his hands deeper in his coat pockets and marched on.

By the time he reached the last lock before the main road, the point at which he normally turned back for home, the sky had begun to lighten. He stepped onto the lock, crossed halfway and looked back along the canal in the direction of home. In the time that they had been together, he had never dreamt of Mercedes. Now, she wouldn't leave him alone, and every dream was an attack, a vicious recrimination. The dream from which he'd woken that morning had been the most disturbing yet. With one hand on her hip, she'd stood there, body jutting slightly forward as she told him that he was nothing without her. She'd called him a fake, said that it wouldn't take long for people to see right through him. Then she'd pointed to him and laughed, and when he looked down his body was transparent. There was nothing but a watery outline that showed where it used to be. Inside was hollow, bereft of organs; he was nothing – just like she said he was.

He shuddered and this time it had nothing to do with the cold. He walked down the opposite side of the lock and gazed into the water. There were no swans near the bridge where they usually gathered, waiting for the students from the nearby college to throw them crusts from leftover sandwiches. He supposed they'd return now that the thaw had come.

As he stood staring into the water, he became aware of some-thing caught beyond the reeds. It looked like an old coat; something that may have been discarded before the freeze came. He stared harder, eyes straining in the half-light, and then he saw something glint among the bulrushes. Gingerly, he stepped down the bank. The mud was frozen beneath his feet and he edged closer to the water, crouching as near as he dared to peer between the rushes. Where the ice had melted a man's hand rested above the water, fingers blue-white. On the second finger a gold wedding band caught the first light.

Hastily, Oliver retreated from the water's edge. He could go home, try to forget that he had ever seen the body beneath the ice. He didn't want to phone the guards; it was the kind of attention that he would rather avoid, but then there was the jogger. If he didn't report the body, somebody else would. Could he risk the man coming forward, saying that he'd seen him by the canal? Even as the thought went through his mind, he found himself dialling the number for emergency services. He couldn't ignore his civic duty, and so he waited with the dead man for help to arrive.

They took their time in coming. He guessed there was no hurry for a man whose life had already ended. He moved down the bank again and stared into the water. The body was face down, arms raised above the head as though making a plea for help. The fingers had stiffened into position and looked as though they might snap, like dead wood, if he were to touch them. Had the man fallen into the icy water and been unable to get out – or had it been an intentional act? Oliver couldn't fathom why anyone would do such a thing; there were easier ways to end it. Of course there was a third option, one that made him uneasy just waiting in the place where it may have happened. The man could have been murdered and his body dumped in the water. It wouldn't have been the first gangland killing in the area and it certainly wouldn't be the last. It made him glad he'd opted to practise family rather than criminal law. The former had its share of malevolence, but as a rule it didn't involve bloodshed.

Finally, the garda car turned over the bridge. It travelled slowly, lights off. Oliver walked to the edge of the road and raised a hand for their attention, guessing that his black coat would not stand out against the grey morning light. The car pulled up and two men stepped out. The first was an overweight man in his fifties who walked with a surprisingly swift step. The other, a young officer who looked like he was fresh out of Templemore training school, walked closely behind.

'Mr Molloy? Garda Sweeney and Garda Regan. You reported a body in the water?'

Oliver nodded and gestured towards the canal. 'It's just beyond the rushes, trapped under the ice. You can see a hand above the surface.'

Oliver stepped back and the two guards moved closer to the canal. The older man nodded like he'd seen it all before. 'We'll just take a statement from you if that's all right,' he said.

The young garda asked Oliver questions as Sweeney stood looking into the distance beyond the bridge. A few minutes later, the sound of a motor drowned out Garda Regan's voice. Both he and Oliver turned to watch as a dinghy appeared from beneath the bridge cutting a swathe through the thin ice. The crew of three men cut the motor and let the dinghy drift close to where the body was. Oliver watched, half concentrating on giving Regan his personal details, as the men broke the remaining ice and pulled the body from the water. They did it in such a way that Oliver didn't see the man's face and the corpse, murky water flowing from his sodden coat, disappeared onto the surface of the boat.

'There's a wallet,' one of the crew shouted across to Sweeney. 'Credit cards say Vincent Arnold. We'll run a check from the station, see if it matches any missing persons report.'

'Good enough,' Sweeney nodded.

'It'. Oliver wondered whether *it* referred to the body or the name on the card. Did such exposure render you indifferent to death? He'd once heard an undertaker use such a term and had been appalled by the callousness of the word. Death was a business, something that had to be dealt with cleared away.

An image of Mercedes appeared in his mind; her body limp as he'd held her for the last time. He'd been surprised at how long she'd stayed warm – so that it had taken him hours to accept that she was really dead. He'd tried to close her parted lips, but they refused to meet. At any moment, he thought, they might have started to move, to form words between tongue and teeth.

The dinghy was moving off now. Sweeney's narrowed blue eyes appraised him as he tried to rid himself of thoughts of his wife. He shifted and gestured towards the canal. 'I suppose you see this kind of thing all the time,' he said.

Sweeney shrugged and squinted at the morning light. 'Tell me, do you usually go out walking this early in the morning, Mr Molloy?' he asked.

Oliver returned his gaze. 'Only when I can't sleep,' he said.

Sweeney nodded and heaved his bulk into the passenger seat of the car where Regan was already waiting. Oliver turned in the direction of home. The garda car passed him and he raised a hand, but neither of the guards acknowledged him. He dug his hands deeper in his coat pockets, quickened his step against the cold, and found himself hoping that he wouldn't have reason to encounter either Sweeney or his colleague again.

TWO

Joanna sat on the floor surrounded by photographs and eyed each one critically. The college exhibition was to take place in a month's time, but she had been working on the collection all semester and felt that she'd taken enough shots to put together an impressive composition. The collection consisted of a series of black-and-white shots depicting brides in various guises. Joanna had picked up a wedding dress second-hand. She'd liked the slightly worn look of it, the way the lace trimming had frayed at the edges. She had wondered as she fingered the silk who had owned it, and why she'd decided to give the dress to a charity shop.

The brides stared up at her as she arranged and discarded the pictures. She picked up her favourite, an angular shot of a young woman in a bridal dress sitting on the window ledge of an empty room. The girl's reflection had been caught in the glass, her wistful expression captured perfectly in the lens. Beneath the window, a battered suitcase anticipated the girl's departure.

Joanna stood back and directed the head of the halogen lamp over the pictures scattered on the living room floor. There was a bride running down the street, her hair falling loose and her bouquet to the fore of the picture lying in a puddle on the ground.

Another showed a bride walking in a narrow street with the battered suitcase. Her back was to the camera and she held her dress up with one hand to reveal a pair of Doc Martens on her feet as she walked the street slick with rain.

Joanna smiled. The girl in the photo was a good friend, and they'd had some fun during the shoot. The girl hadn't modelled before, but her pale skin and slight frame had been exactly what Joanna had been looking for in a subject and she had finally persuaded her to do it. Joanna was just placing this photo next to the first when there was a knock at the door. She looked at the clock on the mantelpiece, which confirmed her suspicions. It was after eleven o'clock, too late for any caller. She turned out the halogen light, which she hoped had not been visible through the thick curtains, and made her way stealthily towards the window. Through a chink in the curtains, she peered out. The security light had clicked on. That, in itself, wasn't unusual, next-door's cat often set it off, but she couldn't see anyone and, just as she'd begun to wonder if she'd imagined the sound, a pounding on the knocker confirmed the presence of the late-night visitor.

Joanna crossed the room, eased the door open and stepped into the hall. She listened for any sound upstairs, but heard none. The knocking had not woken her mother. Joanna pressed her eye to the spyhole, and saw a woman standing in the porch. She wasn't anyone that Joanna had seen before, and she wondered, as the woman raised the knocker for a third time, if she had the wrong house. Exercising caution, she decided to find out.

'Who is it?' she called, mouth close to the door.

She watched as the woman at the other side paused, looking directly at the spyhole as though she too could see through to the glass, and finally spoke.

'Angela?' she said.

On hearing her mother's name, Joanna decided that the woman was no threat. She removed the chain and opened the door so that they were standing opposite one another. Joanna gauged that the woman was about her mother's age. She was quite tall and held herself in an almost regal manner.

'I'm looking for Angela. This is Angela Lacey's house?'

'Yes, but I'm afraid my mother's not here. Can I help you?'

The woman hesitated; clutching her handbag in one hand while the other remained in the pocket of her camel-coloured coat.

'Do you know when she will return? I'm afraid I've got some bad news. I must speak to her … I know it's late but … '

'I'm sorry, but are you a friend of my mother?'

The woman smiled a strange smile. 'A friend, no … I wouldn't say that. Your mother knows … well, knew … my husband.' She trailed off, eyes glistening.

'Look, would you like to come in? She … she is here. It's just that she's in bed, but seeing as it's important I can wake her.'

Joanna stepped back and the woman entered the warmth of the hall. Joanna showed her into the living room where her photographs were scattered on the floor. She saw the woman's eyes dart around the room, taking everything in. They rested on the photos.

'What's your name?' Joanna asked.

'Rachel. Rachel Arnold. You can tell your mother it's about Vince.' She was busy plucking off one leather glove as she spoke. Joanna nodded and told her to sit down.

As she climbed the stairs Joanna wondered who Vince was, and how he was connected to her mother. When she'd reached the top of the stairs she turned on the light in the landing and eased open the door to her mother's room. It was in darkness and she could hear her breathing heavily in sleep.

'Mum.' Gently, she touched her shoulder. Her mother stirred slightly and Joanna whispered to her again, louder this time.

'What? What is it?' Angela said, partially sitting up. Her voice was thick with sleep.

'There's a woman downstairs. She says she needs to talk to you about somebody called Vince?'

8

Joanna's mother sat up suddenly and pushed the duvet from her. 'Vince?'

'Yes, her name's Rachel something. She's waiting in the living room. Do you know her?'

Angela ran a hand through her hair. 'What time is it?' she said.

'After eleven … I didn't know whether to answer or not … it's so late and … do you know someone called Vince?'

Her mother stood in the middle of the room and cast about her. She picked up a blouse from the back of the bedroom chair and then put it down again. Joanna took her dressing gown from a hook on the bedroom door.

'Here – put this on,' she said.

Her mother slipped into the dressing gown and tightened the belt. She sat on the edge of the bed and stuck her feet in her slippers. 'She's in the living room?'

'Yes. I had to invite her in. She looked kind of upset … and I couldn't leave her on the doorstep … not like that.'

Her mother nodded, took a deep breath and ran a hand through her hair again to flatten it. Joanna followed her from the room. Her mother paused at the top of the stairs and she almost walked into her.

'Look, maybe you should stay here,' her mother said.

Joanna hesitated. 'Will you be all right? I mean … who is that woman? Why would she call so late?'

'Just someone from the past … please, wait in your room, Joanna. I'll explain everything later.'

Joanna nodded, but her mother didn't look at her. With one hand on the banister and the other lifting the end of her robe she hurried down the stairs.

'Rachel, you've rung me twice already. I've told you, I haven't heard from him.'

'I know. I've come to tell you … Vince, he's … he's dead.' The woman's voice wavered.

'What … what do you mean? How could he?'

The living room door closed, and Joanna crept down the stairs in an effort to hear what followed.

'They found him. This morning the guards came. They'd found his body in the canal, trapped beneath the ice. Some man out walking saw him.'

Joanna moved further down the stairs until she was almost in the hallway.

'What happened? Did he fall in? Jesus, I ... Did you see the body?'

'No ... Patrick went to identify him ... he said it was better if I didn't ... the body had been in the water for at least a week, they said. It's not how I want to remember him.'

Joanna listened, but she heard no comforting words from her mother. Instead there was silence, broken finally by the other woman. 'That's ... that's her isn't it. That's ... '

'Joanna, yes. My daughter.' Ice in her mother's voice. Then: 'Why have you come here, Rachel?'

'Because I thought you should know ... because of her ... it seems like the right thing, doesn't it? I mean now that ... '

'Now that he's gone, you mean? No, I don't think it does. She need never have known, but you've decided to see to that, haven't you? I think that's why you've come here ... to cause trouble ... some kind of revenge, now that you don't have Vince to stop you. My God ... have you been saving it up all these years?'

Joanna descended the last few steps of the stairs. She had never heard her mother so angry. She wanted to intervene, to know who the woman was, and why the death of this man should concern her. She stood in the hallway and stared at the living room door, reluctant, yet willing herself to open it.

'How could this possibly be revenge?' Rachel Arnold said. 'He's dead, Angela. Don't you get it? If you must know, then yes, there is a reason why I've come. It's because of this ... it was among his things and there's only one place he could have got it.'

'I don't know anything about it.'

The woman said something else, but Joanna didn't hear. There was silence then for a few minutes. Joanna wondered what they were doing, her mother and the woman. Were they carefully avoiding each other's eyes? Was the woman wishing she'd never come?

'What's this?' she heard the woman ask.

'They're Joanna's. She studies photography. She's putting a collection together for an exhibition.'

'They're good, very good. Did you encourage her?'

'No. Must be in the blood, mustn't it?'

'Will you tell her?' the woman said.

'I don't have much choice now, do I? If I know Joanna, she's probably already heard half the conversation.'

Joanna moved back from the door and furtively made her way up the stairs. She was trying to understand what she'd heard. She had a feeling that she knew who Vince was, but she needed to hear her mother say it. She sat on the top step of the stairs and waited to hear the living room door open. She wanted to listen to the rest of the conversation, but she didn't dare. It was unlikely that the two women had much more to discuss now that the woman had said what she'd come to say.

When the door eventually did open, Joanna withdrew into the shadows of the landing. Her mother spoke in a low voice as the woman stepped into the cold night.

'I'm sure you wish I hadn't come,' the woman said.

'Too late for that now, isn't it?'

'He's being released tomorrow. The funeral's on Tuesday if you want to tell her ... I don't expect you to come.'

'No, I'm sure you'd rather I didn't.'

The woman said nothing to deny it, and the next sound Joanna heard was the woman's shoes on the tarmac before her mother closed the front door. Joanna waited for her to call her, to say something, to explain, but there was silence from downstairs and when she looked down through the banisters, the hall was empty.

11

Slowly, she descended the stairs. Her mother was sitting in her armchair in the living room with her head in her hands.

'Are you all right, Mum?' Joanna said.

Her mother shook her head and looked at her hands clasped in front of her.

'How did you know this Vince then?'

She waited for an answer. Her mother cupped her hands to her mouth and exhaled a breath that she must have been holding. It hissed through her fingers and a sound like a sob broke from her throat.

'He was your father,' she said.

THREE

Oliver picked up one of his wife's blouses and folded it carefully before tossing it in a bin liner. He had taken all of Mercedes's clothes from the wardrobe and they were strewn in a pile across the bed and in the black bags that lay scattered at his feet. He picked up a sweater and held it to his face. It smelled of Mercedes's perfume – a rich, woody fragrance that had seemed always to linger in the room long after she'd left it. It was that scent as much as the sight of Mercedes's clothes that evoked, unbidden, the memories that tormented him. He threw the sweater in an almost full bin liner, and knotted it tightly, trapping the scent of his wife inside.

That morning, when he had opened the wardrobe to take out a clean shirt, he was accosted, as he had been every morning for the past three weeks, by the sight of Mercedes's clothes. He had decided at that moment that the only way for him to move on was to rid the house of any sign of her. Immediately after breakfast, he'd begun the clear-out. Apart from her clothes, which he would donate to a charity shop, Mercedes had owned few possessions. There was a music box that had belonged to her grandmother and a collection of porcelain dolls that she'd had since she was a child. Both had been of sentimental value to her and, because of this, he didn't have the heart to pack them away with the rest, so he left them on a shelf in the living room where they had always been.

When the phone rang, Oliver clambered across the bin liners to reach it, but then seeing the international number on the display screen, he let it ring out until the answering machine clicked in. His heart beat wildly as he heard the voice at the other end, that husky Spanish accent that had fascinated him so much in the beginning and, if he were completely honest with himself, still did.

'*Mercedes, soy yo. Te sigo llamando y llamando …* '

He got the gist of Carmen's words. She wanted Mercedes to call, they could sort things out, she said. There was a pause as she considered what to say next, and clearly deciding that there was nothing else she could say that would make any difference to her sister, Carmen hung up, leaving Oliver staring at the phone. He'd lost count of the number of messages she had left. Sometimes she phoned and hung up before the machine had kicked in. He wondered how much longer he could avoid her. He expected her to call his office any day. She had already tried his mobile, but he hadn't answered. He suspected that she wanted to speak to Mercedes before she spoke to him. It must have been killing her not knowing the result of the bomb she had dropped on her sister.

Well, he would not alleviate her anxiety. He suspected that eventually she would turn up looking for answers. Carmen was not the type to shy away from any situation. She would pay no heed to the fact that she had been the instigator – that she had been responsible for everything. He didn't trust himself to meet her. What she had done was stupid, unforgivable, and he didn't know what he might do if they met. If it hadn't been for Carmen, that horrible night would never have happened. He and Mercedes may have grown slowly apart as so many couples did, but it would not have ended like it had. He would never forgive Carmen for that.

He pressed the button on the machine and erased Carmen's message. Then he looked at the bags at his feet and decided that it would be better to leave some of her things hanging in the wardrobe. Should Carmen arrive unannounced, he would have some explaining to do if everything that belonged to her sister had vanished. It was unlikely that Mercedes would have taken everything with her so fast had she simply moved out.

Oliver untied one of the bin liners and pulled out a silk skirt. As he did so he imagined the cool swish of it against Mercedes's tanned and shapely legs. She had worn that skirt to a wedding they'd attended in Barcelona just months after they'd met. He remembered slipping his hands beneath it later that night on a beach lit only by the lights of the fishermen lined up along the shore. Her legs were bare and he had run his hands along her silky thighs and pulled her to him as the fishermen, oblivious to the lovers, stared out at the black sea and waited for the fish to bite.

Oliver's hands were shaking as he hung the skirt in the wardrobe. He hadn't allowed himself to think of his wife like that for a long time. He had resented their lack of physical contact – a sex life that seemed to have petered out before it had run its natural course. Things had been strained between them long before Carmen had said anything. He tried to justify his actions by blaming Mercedes. If she hadn't become so cold, so indifferent, would any of it have happened?

He spent the next hour sorting through his wife's things – re-hanging some of them in their shared wardrobe and packing the others away. By lunchtime, he had finished. He took the bags and loaded them into the boot of the car. He wondered if any of the neighbours were watching – prying eyes peering from behind lace curtains. He was thankful that neither he nor Mercedes had struck up any friendships with their neighbours. They were private, passed themselves off with a 'hello' or a 'nice day', but that was as far as their contact had gone. Generally, he liked to avoid people who asked too many questions about his private life, and Mercedes had shared that feeling.

It was freezing despite the thaw. Oliver felt rather low as he drove into the city to unburden himself of Mercedes's clothes, but he knew that it was the only way forward. Mercedes was gone, and his problem was far from over. There was Carmen to deal with. Not to mention the rest of Mercedes's family. Soon, people would begin to ask questions and he'd better have his answers ready.

The shop was small and had a sign over it that read Mrs Quinn's Charity Shop. He'd never been there before, but he figured that rather than going in with the stuff it'd be better to leave it outside. No point in drawing attention to himself. He pulled up close to the door and took a couple of bags out of the boot. Just as he put them down, the shop door opened and an elderly woman appeared.

'Are they for us?' she asked.

'Yes, I have a few more to go.'

The woman, surprisingly agile for her age, grabbed a bag and made towards the door. 'Bring them on in,' she said, leaving him no choice but to follow her.

When he returned with two more bags, the woman was examining Mercedes's clothes. She held a blouse up to the light and viewed it appraisingly. 'This is nice stuff. Are you sure she wants to get rid of it?' she asked.

Oliver panicked. 'My wife died,' he said quickly, thinking that would put an end to further questions.

The woman put down the blouse. 'I'm terribly sorry.' Her eyes narrowed in sympathy. There were deep lines etched at the sides of her mouth. She moved her hand as if to reach out to him and then didn't.

Oliver nodded and tried to block out Mercedes's voice in his head. *Because of you.* 'I'll just get the rest of the stuff from the car,' he said.

The woman smiled sadly, and he left her sorting through Mercedes's things, fingering the cloth, searching for any imperfections. He felt a strange sort of emptiness as he watched her examining the things that Mercedes had worn. That she would never wear again. He hadn't expected to feel that way, as though there were a void somewhere inside him.

He leant into the car boot to take out the last bag. He'd forgotten to knot it and the contents were spilling out where it had toppled over. He was shoving the clothes back in when he heard someone calling his name.

'Oliver. Oliver Molloy, is that you?'

He looked up. There was a woman hurrying across the street. He didn't recognize her at first. He stood there, at the open boot, trying to figure out who she was.

'It is you,' she said, as she got closer. 'My God, it's been such a long time!'

Finally, he recognized her, but couldn't think of her name. She was an old friend of Mercedes; someone she used to work with.

'Hi,' he said, as he slammed the boot closed. 'I'm sorry I can't remember … ?'

'Adrienne,' she said. She smiled and extended her hand.

'Adrienne. Of course, I'm sorry, like you said it's been what … three … four years?'

The woman called Adrienne laughed. She hadn't let go of his hand, and he was aware of her fingers squeezing his. 'I know, it's hard to believe … I mean … God, how are you? How's Mercedes doing?'

Oliver cast a quick look at the door of the shop. 'Yes, she's fine. We're both good … ' he said. 'And you, how are you doing? Are you still at Abacus?'

Adrienne laughed, a tinkling kind of laugh that reminded him of the C note on a piano.

'No, I left soon after Mercedes did. I don't know if you

17

remember I was studying acting at the time … well, I've been trying to make a go of it. It's difficult, of course, no money in it, but I get a bit of work doing ads and stuff … '

'Really … wow … an actress.'

Adrienne smiled and he smiled back. She had a very pretty mouth; there was a dimple at one corner and her lips were coated in a shiny pink lip-gloss. He had no doubt that this girl would get parts.

'It's so good to run into you like this. Mercedes and I should never have lost touch … we used to have such laughs. I must get your number, maybe we can arrange to meet up like we used to … '

Adrienne began searching in her bag and took out a mobile phone.

He gave her the house number and then Mercedes's mobile number. 'You won't be able to get her at the moment. She's away in Barcelona. Her father's not so well,' he said.

Just as he'd said it the shop door opened behind him and the old woman came out. Christ – that had been close. Adrienne was busy saving the numbers in her phone.

'Oh, I'm really sorry to hear that. I'll give it a few weeks then … hopefully, everything will be okay,' she said.

'Yeah, it's hard you know.' He glanced at the old woman who was standing feet away examining the display in her shop window. He thought fast of something to say to change the topic from Mercedes. 'Hey, what ever happened to that guy you used to bring round for dinner … did you?'

Adrienne started laughing. 'Norman? My God, I haven't thought of him in a long time … '

Oliver laughed. 'I could never see what you were doing with him.'

Adrienne looked away. 'Yeah, well, I didn't know either in the end.'

'And now, is there someone special?'

18

'No. I'm just concentrating on my acting … trying to make it work, you know?'

Her coppery hair fell in her eyes. She flicked it back, and when she looked up there was a moment of awkwardness. He had always thought she was attractive. The old woman, to his relief, had gone back inside. Adrienne smiled at him.

'I'm really glad I saw you. I'd better go, but please tell Mercedes I was asking about her and that I'll call her soon.'

'I will. It was great to see you.'

He leaned down and kissed her cheek. Her face turned a shade of pink to match her lips, and he wondered if he'd been right all those years ago when he'd suspected she'd had a thing for him, and if he should have taken advantage of it.

He watched her run across the road and get into a silver Renault Clio. She waved to him as she passed. He waved back and made as if he were searching for something in the glove compartment. When he was sure she was out of sight, he got out of the car, went round to the boot and brought the last black bag into the shop.

The woman was sitting at the counter now, reading a magazine. She nodded and got off the stool when he entered. 'Just put it over here, love,' she said, pointing to a pile of bags yet to be sorted. He was about to turn away when she spoke again. 'It's a difficult thing having to get rid of someone's belongings. When my husband died, I couldn't bring myself to clean out his wardrobe. I'd take out a shirt and I could smell him off it. It was like he was in the room with me. But it's better that you do it, you have to move on. She wouldn't want you mourning.'

Oliver nodded, solemnly. 'No, she wouldn't,' he said. 'She was full of life. That was the thing I loved most about her – her energy.'

He left the shop feeling strangely bereft. He got into the car and drove slowly away feeling as though he'd left something behind. He thought of Adrienne. Maybe he should've told her that Mercedes had left him. It would have aroused her sympathy and maybe they'd have acted on that spark from the past. He hated to go home to an empty house. It was lonely in the evenings and he needed a distraction; someone to keep the ghosts away.

FOUR

Joanna stared down at her mother, who refused to meet her eye. 'So all that stuff you said about not knowing who my father was – that was all lies. Why? Why couldn't you have told me?'

Angela looked past her and through the open door to where, minutes before, the woman had stood. 'I honestly thought it was for the best,' she said.

Joanna looked at her hard. 'How? I mean, all those years you said it was a one-night stand, that you didn't know what happened to the guy. Did you not think that at some point I'd find out, that we might walk into him in the street or that he'd come looking for me?'

Her mother shook her head. She was still carefully avoiding her eye. Joanna stopped pacing and stood before her.

'Mother, please – give me something to go on here. I mean, what was his name even? Vince what?'

Angela stood up and tightened the belt of her robe. 'Joanna, can we just not do this now? It's late. I don't want to talk about it. I'll tell you everything, but not tonight. Surely, you can understand … it's … it's been a terrible shock.'

'That woman, who is she?' Joanna said, ignoring her mother's plea.

Angela put a hand to her head as though it ached. 'Rachel. Rachel Arnold, Vince's wife.'

Arnold. At least she had a name – assuming that the wife had taken his. 'And did he know – about me?'

'Yes.'

'So, what was the deal then? If he knew, why could you not tell me? Why did you have to pretend?'

Her mother looked at her now – eyes tired, face drawn. 'I didn't tell you because you'd have wanted to find him. You'd have wanted to know who he was – and I didn't want that – he didn't want that.'

'Was he … was he married?'

'Joanna, please.'

'Just tell me – was he? Is that why he didn't want to know?'

'Yes. Look, keep your voice down. What difference does it make? He's gone. You heard what she said: he's dead, Joanna. Can't you just leave it, please?' Angela took a few steps towards the door.

'Leave it? Are you serious, Mum? How would you feel if you'd just found out your whole life had been based on a lie? And the person responsible was your own mother!'

'It wasn't like that, Joanna. I did it for your sake … would you rather I'd told you, and he didn't want anything to do with you? Would you rather that? It was bad enough he rejected me, I didn't want to put you through it as well.'

'Well, I think I'd have deserved the chance to find out, don't you? So, what … he got you pregnant and then went back to his wife, is that it?'

'Pretty much.'

'How did she find out?'

Angela looked up. 'I told her.'

'You … what did she say?'

'Not a lot. She listened to what I had to say and then she told me to leave. I have to admit I admired her composure. I didn't tell her in order to hurt her – I wanted her to know what he'd done. I wanted her to know that I existed.'

'And she stayed with him despite knowing?'

'It's what people did back then.'

'And that was that? No contact, nothing all those years?'

Angela lifted the end of her dressing gown and crossed the room to where Joanna's photographs lay scattered on the floor.

'He wasn't … he wasn't a bad person, Joanna. He was young, arrogant, I suppose, yes, but his intent, it wasn't malicious. He cared for me, I know that – but he couldn't leave her, it would have meant losing too much.'

'What do you mean? People do it – they do it all the time. They simply decide what's most important to them – and clearly we weren't.'

Angela shook her head. 'It wasn't that straightforward. Rachel's father was the head of the newspaper. He was the one that gave Vince his chance.' She paused, looked up from the pictures. 'He was a journalist – covered all the sports events. He took pictures, too. So, you see, you have inherited something from him.'

'But you must have hated him – he chose Rachel … she was his wife, yes, but it didn't mean he couldn't have been some part of our lives, of mine. Did he even send you money?'

'Sometimes. Cheques arrived – no note – nothing to ask me how I was doing, how you were. It was one of the conditions, you see.'

'What conditions?'

'Rachel told Vince that he would cut all contact – that it would have to be as though he and I had never met – it was that or she'd tell her father – and Vince could say goodbye to his career.'

'What – and he was okay with that?'

Angela shrugged. 'It was the choice he made. And now you know – I'm sorry you had to find out like this. I really am. I just hope you can understand, even a little bit, why I didn't tell you. Protecting you was all I ever had in mind.'

Angela had crossed the room. She put her hand on Joanna's arm, but she pulled away.

'I can't believe you expect me to accept this,' she said. 'Twenty-six years, Mum! And what's worse, if that woman hadn't come here tonight, you'd never have said anything, would you?'

'Joanna, keep your voice down. The neighbours—'

'Who cares about the neighbours? Who cares? This can never be fixed – don't you understand that? You've robbed me of any chance to know my father.'

'I'm sorry, Joanna. I know how this must seem to you now, but—'

'It's unlikely it'll seem any other way, so don't expect it to. I don't care what kind of person Vince Arnold was – and he doesn't sound like much of one – I should have had the opportunity to find that out for myself.'

They stood staring at each other.

'I'm sorry,' Angela said, again. 'What else can I say?'

'Nothing,' Joanna told her. 'Nothing you can say will put this right.'

FIVE

Oliver leaned forward at his desk and tried to focus on what the woman was saying. Her mouth was moving, but he couldn't concentrate on the words that were coming out; instead, he was hearing fragmented bits of speech floating on the air thick between them. The woman sat back and crossed her black-stockinged legs. The action caused him to shift his gaze momentarily from her face. She was not beautiful, but she gave the impression of a woman convinced by her own attributes. Her small face, framed by a thatch of dark hair, was too pointed at the chin, and her narrowed blue eyes gave her the look of a small, but fierce animal. It was her full lips, startlingly red against her pale skin, that captured his attention. And there was something else, too, something that despite their physical dissimilarities reminded him of Mercedes. He couldn't quite figure what it was, but it bothered him.

'So, what are my entitlements? I'm still his wife, so that must mean I'm entitled to half of this new house despite the separation? I mean, I'm not the one that walked out on the marriage.'

If he hadn't been feeling so ill, he may have commented on that. The fact that this woman had had an affair with her husband's friend – a lover who, from what he had gathered, had long since departed the scene – seemed to escape her memory.

Oliver pulled at his tie. She was staring at him, waiting for an answer, but the air in the room seemed to have evaporated and a nauseous feeling was rising from the pit of his stomach. Something in the atmosphere, maybe the woman's perfume, seemed to exacerbate it, and when he looked again at her expectant face he found that it was partially obscured by splotches of yellow light.

'I'm sorry, but could you excuse me for a moment?' he said.

He felt rather than saw her eyes follow him from the room.

In the men's room the nauseous feeling overcame him and he leaned on the sink with both hands and retched acid-tasting bile. Perspiration broke out on his forehead, and he loosened the knot of his tie and tried to breathe, but he couldn't calm the frantic beating of his heart. The woman who sat in his office was nothing like Mercedes. And yet in every woman that he'd met since that terrible night he had seen something to remind him of her. It would have to stop.

He examined his face in the mirror. Beneath the fluorescent light his skin was opaque and the dark circles beneath his eyes screamed of his sleepless nights. He turned on the cold tap, cupped his hands and doused his face several times in icy water. Eventually his heart resumed its regular beat, but his legs felt weak and he couldn't still the trembling in his hands. It was the panic that he felt in his dreams, but in daylight it was far more frightening.

To distract himself, he thought of the woman who sat in his office awaiting his return. It was a divorce case that he'd been working on for the past year. She was the sort of woman that he despised, intent on taking her husband for everything she could get, but he couldn't afford not to represent her. Business had been slow, and it was an easy case to win.

He took a deep breath, grabbed a bunch of paper towels from the dispenser and blotted his face dry. The woman was his last client of the day. He would simply have to get through it.

'I'm sorry about that. Haven't been feeling very well all day,' he said. His legs were still shaking as he sat back down in his leather chair. The woman leaned forward at his desk.

'So,' she said, 'what are my rights here?'

If it was sympathy he'd been after, he'd miscalculated. The woman, who seemed to have forgotten that it was her infidelity that had instigated her husband's divorce proceedings, was interested only in money. It pained him that the law, albeit to his advantage, was on this woman's side. He gave her a long, silent look in which he hoped his distaste was evident and then, putting his personal feelings aside, forced himself to enter legal mode.

When the woman had left, he closed and locked the door behind her. His partner, who worked in an adjoining office, had gone to the courts and wouldn't return that evening. Oliver sat down but, not feeling like working, he picked up the newspaper from his desk. He'd read it briefly that morning. The body in the canal had made the front page. The man, named as Vince Arnold, had worked as a sports journalist for one of the national papers. Arnold. It wasn't such a common name. He'd known an Arnold once – sat his bar exams with him at the King's Inns. He wondered if there was any connection. Putting the paper down, he typed the man's name into Google. The obituary came up. Oliver clicked on it, read: 'Sadly missed by his wife, Rachel, brother, Patrick … ' Patrick Arnold, that was it. The name of the guy he'd studied with. He'd often wondered what had become of him. Rumour had it that he'd been struck off – found guilty of fraud, something to do with a land deal. He couldn't remember the details. He looked again at the notice – the Removal Mass was to take place the following evening in a church not far from the office. Curious about the dead man, and wondering if it were the same Patrick Arnold he'd known, he decided that he would go along to find out.

SIX

'Where are you off to?' her mother asked, as Joanna sat on the stairs pulling on her boots. Joanna had barely spoken to her in the two days that had passed since Rachel Arnold's visit. Angela had been at pains to restore normality, Joanna knew that, but she wasn't about to concede. The fact that they'd always been close – more like sisters – made her mother's lie impossible to accept.

She looked up, knowing that her mother wouldn't like her answer. 'My father's funeral,' she said.

'You're not … surely, you're not thinking of going?' There was a warning tone in Angela's voice that Joanna was only too familiar with.

'Why wouldn't I? It's my last chance to see him … to know what he was like.'

'But you won't see him. The coffin, it'll be closed.'

'How do you know?' Joanna stood up, and took her heavy winter coat from the banister. She wrapped a red scarf round her neck.

'It's not possible in these circumstances. The water, it'll have bloated the body. Made him … unrecognizable. He'd been in the canal for days.'

Ignoring her mother, Joanna took her car keys from the hall table. 'Well, it's my decision and I've decided to go,' she said.

'Don't.'

A low warning that caused Joanna to stop and look closely at her mother.

'Why not? Is there something else you're worried I'll find out about?'

'No. It just won't do you any good, that's all. Look, can't we talk? It's getting us nowhere, you behaving like this … '

'*Me* behaving like this? What about you? You're the one who brought about this mess – you and your lies. Did you think I'd just forgive you, Mum? And anyway, I don't see what's so strange about going to my own father's funeral, do you?'

Angela stood blocking the door. 'I'm asking you not to do this, Joanna, for my sake. Don't go bringing that woman into our lives.'

'This isn't about you.' Joanna strode past, forcing her mother to step back from the door.

'Well you needn't expect them to welcome you,' Angela shouted after her.

Joanna ignored her. She slammed the car door and reversed dangerously fast out of the driveway.

Joanna was still seething when she arrived at the churchyard. How dare her mother attempt to stop her from going. She pulled into the car park, which was already filling up, and attempted to calm down before going inside. As Joanna sat there, she watched, from the anonymity of her car, the groups of people gathered near the church doors. Yellow light spilled from inside and illuminated the faces of men in heavy winter coats congregated at the entrance. They moved from foot to foot in an attempt to thwart the icy chill as their wives clutched at each other's arms. These, she thought, were the people who had shared her father's life.

In the street, the cavalcade of rush hour traffic passed the church gates – a procession as slow as that which would bring the dead man to his mourners. She watched them pass and felt strangely detached. Heads turned and the crowd dispersed to make way for the long black hearse as it drove slowly through the gates. It was followed by a single mourning car. The doors opened and a tall man dressed in black got out. The driver opened the door at the other side and Rachel Arnold stepped out, head held erect as she stood by and watched the pallbearers slide her husband's coffin from the back of the hearse and then wheel it into the church. Several people touched her arm, and she exchanged words with them as she passed.

Joanna waited until the crowd outside the church had entered. And, with a glance in the rear-view mirror, she stepped from the car and crossed quickly to the entrance. A man reached the door just as she did. He nodded and beckoned for her to enter first.

There was quite a crowd in the church. Rachel Arnold sat in the first pew and next to her sat the man from the mourning car. The previous night, Joanna had read Vince Arnold's obituary online. She knew that he had a brother – Patrick – and she figured that must be him. The Arnolds had no children. None, that is, except for her.

Joanna stared at the coffin and reminded herself that the man inside was her father, but she felt detached. Her feelings amounted to nothing more than a macabre curiosity about the dead man. She scanned the room, eyes moving over the rows of people that filled the church as they had once filled her father's life. As the priest droned on, she became aware of someone watching her. She turned to find the same man she'd met at the entrance staring at her. Embarrassed, she looked away, but when she turned again a moment later he was still looking. He smiled slightly and nodded. She returned his gaze, but not his smile. And suddenly the Mass had ended.

The church organ played as Rachel Arnold made her way

slowly down the aisle accompanied by the man in the dark suit. The people in her pew stood, and she joined the procession of mourners who filed out of the church to pay their respects to the widow.

When she stepped outside, she saw the man who had smiled at her. He was unshaven and wore a long black coat. He was talking to the man by Rachel's side – the one Joanna imagined was her uncle. She saw him introduce the man to Rachel, who took his hand. They talked while others idled waiting for their opportunity to pay their respects. Joanna wondered who the man was. He'd stared at her so intently in the church that she wondered if he knew her.

She waited until the crowd had thinned. Then suddenly she found herself standing before Rachel Arnold wondering what to say.

Rachel took her hand in hers and squeezed it. 'You came,' she said. 'I wondered if you might.'

Joanna nodded. 'I'm sorry for your loss,' she said. The well-used expression sounded meaningless, but she couldn't think of what else to say.

'Is your mother here?'

'No.'

Rachel looked relieved. 'I take it she told you?'

'That he was my father, yes.'

'I'm sorry that you had to find out like this. I'd have liked it to be different.' Rachel looked around. There were still some people waiting to speak to her. She kept her voice low. 'I'd like to talk to you again, Joanna – when everything calms down. You must have so many questions about Vince.'

Joanna nodded, unsure of what to say.

Rachel fumbled in her bag. 'I'll give you my number,' she said. She took out a small notebook, scribbled something, tore the page out and handed it to Joanna. The man in the black coat was standing a few feet away smoking a cigarette and talking to

Patrick Arnold. Joanna looked past Rachel to where the man stood.

'That man … the one in the black coat … who is he?' she asked.

Rachel turned to look at him. 'He's the one that found Vince. It turns out he knew Patrick, Vince's brother. I'll introduce you if you like. You should meet him, Patrick … '

Joanna hesitated. 'No. I mean – I'd like to, but another time. It's all a bit too strange right now.'

'Yes, yes, of course.' Rachel nodded her understanding.

Patrick Arnold had turned away from the man in the black coat. He glanced over, but Joanna took her leave before Rachel had a chance to beckon him. The other man stubbed out his cigarette and walked towards his car, which was parked near Joanna's. He looked up as she approached.

'I heard you're the one who found him,' she said.

The man looked at her, curious. 'That's right.'

She held out her hand. 'I'm Joanna. The man … Vince … he was my father.'

'I'm sorry,' he said. 'I'm Oliver. Oliver Molloy.' His hand was cold as he shook hers. 'I can imagine how distressing it must be … '

She shrugged. 'I didn't know him,' she said.

'Oh?'

She felt suddenly stupid, unsure why she had said that to a total stranger. A morbid desire to know the details of her father's death made her carry on. 'They said he was trapped under the ice? How did you find him … ? I mean was the body … ?'

Oliver studied her for a moment before he answered. 'He was close to the edge of the canal, just beyond the reeds. He'd probably floated down from somewhere else. His hand was above the ice, but apart from that I didn't see him … like you said he was trapped … '

'Do you think it was an accident?'

'I suppose ... don't you?' His grey eyes looked into hers with interest.

'I wouldn't know. I just ... I wondered. The thing is I didn't know he existed until last night.'

Oliver Molloy watched her, waiting for some kind of explanation. His silence forced her to speak. She was surprised at her own anger.

'My mother never told me about him ... and then last night *she* came ... ' She looked over at Rachel who was talking to a small group of people standing by the mourning car. Patrick Arnold was looking in their direction.

'I'm sorry ... that must have been quite a shock.'

'Yes.' Her uncle was still looking over. She didn't want to meet him; she wasn't ready for that. 'Look, I'd better go. Thanks ... for talking to me ... I'm sure you must think it strange. I hadn't meant to tell you all that. I'm just ... never mind.'

The man reached into the pocket of his coat and pulled out his wallet. 'Here, take my card. If you ever want to call me ... for advice or just to chat ... '

She took the card from between his fingers: 'Molloy and Byrne Solicitors' in thick black print.

'Not just legal advice ... anything at all ... sometimes it's easier to talk to a stranger.'

Joanna slipped the card into her pocket. 'Thanks,' she said.

He smiled and said goodnight.

SEVEN

Oliver closed the door behind his last client of the day and walked to the window. The evening air was punctuated by the sound of car horns as frustrated commuters attempted to escape the chaos of the city in order to return to their comfortable suburban lives. Below, the quays were blocked in both directions. Traffic inched forward en masse like some huge lumbering beast as pedestrians launched themselves in front of slow-moving cars to cross bridges whose lights burned orange in the blackness of the Liffey.

A rough-looking couple were arguing in the street. The man took a few steps towards the woman who pointed a finger in his face as he swayed and gesticulated, spilling beer from the can that he clutched in one hand. The woman lifted a hand as though she was about to slap him, but he turned away. She tugged at his arm, and he shrugged her off, raised the can to his lips and made his way back towards the boardwalk where he would probably spend the night. The names she shouted after him hung in the night air.

Oliver turned away from the window, disgusted by the fact that he had wanted the man to strike out. He wanted him to lose his patience with the woman; the fact that he hadn't rendered him, Oliver, the inferior of the two. If he had walked away, none

of it would have happened. Mercedes would, at that moment, be making dinner in their house across the city – the house that he couldn't bear to return to each evening; instead, choosing to stay late in the office, replaying the events again and again in his mind, tormenting himself with the possibility of an alternative outcome – one that might not have been so devastatingly absolute.

Mercedes had been in the kitchen that day when he arrived. A rich aroma of cooking spiked the air. She didn't answer when he shouted hello, and he assumed she hadn't heard him and continued up to the bedroom where he kicked off his shoes, undid his tie and pulled on a warm fleece over his white shirt. When he went back downstairs she was putting dinner on the table.

They talked about their day. He didn't notice anything strange in her behaviour; she hid it well. Then she began to tell him about a guy in the office at work who was having an affair with a French girl in her department. She cursed him. She didn't blame the girl, she said; she was smitten and couldn't see that he was never going to leave his wife for her.

'I suppose the only thing she can be blamed for is being foolish. What do you think?' she said.

Oliver shrugged and told her he'd seen that kind of case so many times. Of course the law would say that the man was wrong; the mistress wouldn't come into it, and the wife, well, she'd try to take the man for every penny she could get. They always did.

'I'm not talking about law; I'm talking about lives. I mean … who's to blame, the husband or the girl? What if I were the wife, for example, who do you think I should take it out on, you or the girl that you seduced?'

It was then that he went on his guard. 'Look, not everything is black and white,' he said.

'Isn't it?'

'No, you don't know these people, their situation.'

35

'Ah, but I do.'

Mercedes's eyes flashed as she spat the words, and he knew that she'd found out. He should never have believed that Carmen would keep quiet. She was too like Mercedes: a straight talker. She liked to get her own way, but she lacked Mercedes's morals. Carmen didn't care whose lives she destroyed to get what she wanted, and she knew that her sister was likely to forgive her in time.

Mercedes had stood up and instinctively he did the same. She walked round to his side of the table, drew her tiny frame up to its full height and slapped him so hard that his cheek stung.

'Why did you do it?' she said. 'Why the fuck did you have to do it, and with Carmen. You … you think you're so above it all, above everyone, but you're weak. Can't you see it? You're just like the rest of them. Dangle a piece of bait and you're hooked. It's pathetic.'

He tried to apologize. He told her that, yes, he'd been weak at that moment. Hell, they hadn't had sex for the last couple of months. What did she expect him to do? He realized as he said it that his apology with its counter-accusation was probably not the best tactic, but he couldn't help but try to push some of the blame onto her. It was his only mechanism of defence.

'So, you don't think your sister had any part in this?' he snarled. 'You don't think that her coming round here when you were away, dressed like a … like a fucking prostitute had anything to do with it? I mean, what man with blood in his veins wouldn't, for Christ sakes? She was screaming for it!'

Mercedes hit him again. This time it wasn't just a slap. She pummelled and kicked him, and he tried to grab hold of her wrists to stop her, but she bit his hand so hard she drew blood. He knew that he should've taken it, but something inside him just snapped. Mercedes lashed out, her fist catching his jaw. He stumbled backwards, and then lunged at her. His hands were round her throat as he pushed her down onto the sofa. She

36

struggled and he pressed down harder to prevent her from hitting him again. He was appalled and aroused by the violence, and the more she tried to free his hands from her throat, the tighter he clenched them. When she finally stopped struggling, he released her. He thought that he had merely tired her out, stopped her from attacking him. Wasn't that what he had set out to do?

Oliver's hands were shaking from the memory as he tidied away the files on his desk. He jumped when the door opened and his partner, Colin Byrne, appeared in the doorway.

'Is there something you're keeping from me, Oliver?'

'What?'

He froze at the open cabinet.

'Is business better than I figure, because I'm beginning to think you're hoarding all the clients for yourself. You've been here late every night.'

'Ah. No, it's not that,' Oliver said. He hesitated, returned the files to the drawer and locked it. 'To be honest, Colin, I've been having a few problems. Mercedes and I haven't been getting along.'

'Wouldn't it be better to go home then and try to sort it out?' Colin asked.

'It might if there was somebody there to sort things out with. She's gone away for a while – I'm not sure for how long. So, I'd rather be here sorting some stuff out, anything rather than sitting in that house thinking about her.'

Colin didn't ask questions. He was tactful, and when Oliver didn't offer any more information he took his cue to leave.

'She'll be back,' he said, touching Oliver's shoulder before going home for the night.

The truth was Oliver couldn't stand being in that house. He'd begun to take the phone off the hook in the evenings so that he didn't have to listen to Carmen Hernandez's messages. Sooner or later he knew that he would have to come up with something to put Carmen off for good. He'd considered sending her a letter.

He'd even spent time copying Mercedes's handwriting in order to send Carmen a note that said she never wanted to see her again, but then he'd given up. He knew that it wouldn't be enough, that there had to be something else, but without Mercedes he couldn't think of anything else. He could say that she had left him. Carmen would believe that, but he knew that Mercedes's disappearance would motivate her family to contact the police – and he wanted to avoid that for as long as he possibly could.

Oliver was about to leave the office when there was a long buzz on the intercom. He looked at his watch. Could Colin Byrne have forgotten his keys? Cautiously, he crossed to the window and looked down into the street. A man in a dark-coloured coat stood below. He didn't recognize him until the man stood back and looked up at the window. Curious, Oliver lifted the intercom and told Patrick Arnold to come up to the office.

EIGHT

Joanna's mother was seldom home. At first, she thought her absence an attempt to avoid her but, when she thought about it, her mother had been out a lot recently, even before Rachel Arnold's visit. She hadn't asked Joanna about the funeral nor had Joanna volunteered any information about it. What she had decided to do was take Rachel Arnold up on her invitation in order to find out about her father.

She stood outside the front porch of the Arnolds' house and leaned on the bell. It buzzed, a sharp, insistent sound. There was movement in the hall, and through the amber glass next to the front door she saw a figure move down the hallway, and she braced herself for the meeting. The door swung open, but instead of Rachel Arnold, Joanna found herself face to face with the man she had seen at the funeral – the one that Rachel had told her was Patrick.

Joanna stammered, disconcerted. 'I'm here to see Rachel.'

Patrick Arnold seemed to scrutinize her. 'Joanna, isn't it? I saw you the other night at the church, but you disappeared before I'd a chance to say hello. I'm Patrick, your … Vince's brother.'

He extended his hand; it was warm as it gripped hers. He had been about to say 'your father' Joanna mused, but had thought better of it. She wondered how close this man had been to his brother – if Vince had confided in him all those years ago about the affair with her mother. He stood back and Joanna stepped into the warmly lit hall, acutely aware that she was entering her father's house.

She glanced round. Both walls and carpet were a deep cream colour. A large Monet print hung above the stairs, and a man's navy sports jacket lay draped across the banister. She wondered if it was Patrick Arnold's, or if it had been her father's. Patrick led her into the living room, and she resisted the urge to touch the coat as she passed.

Rachel's expression as she entered the room was a mixture of pleasure and surprise.

'Joanna, I'm so glad you've come. I see you've met Patrick.'

He stood by the fireplace looking slightly amused but he didn't say anything. None of them did, they stood round in the bellowing silence until Rachel finally spoke.

'Odd meeting like this, isn't it? But then it's been an odd few weeks. It's hard to know where to begin. Thank you for coming the other night. I wasn't sure you would but I imagine she's told you everything, your mother?'

'She told me some things.'

Rachel's blue eyes were not without sympathy. 'It must have been a shock to find out like that. I'm sorry.'

Joanna straightened. 'That's what Mum said. Bit late to be sorry now though, isn't it? It seems no one wanted me to know.'

Rachel didn't deny that. 'And what *did* she tell you?' she asked.

'I know about my mother's affair … that he didn't want anything to do with me when he found out, that you forbade contact.' The words cut even as she said them, the wounds deeper than she'd thought.

'Well, I should have known she wouldn't leave that out.' There was anger in Rachel's tone, but she checked it. 'I don't suppose

40

she told you that I wanted to adopt you, bring you up as our own.'

'What?'

Rachel nodded. 'Vince and I had been trying for a child for a number of years – then he had the affair with your mother and … well, she refused to give you up, of course. Why wouldn't she? I hated her. She had Vince's child and I didn't. How fair was that? So yes, I told him if he had any part in your life, our marriage was over. I suppose you think that was selfish … maybe it was, but it would never have worked. I wasn't about to be part of any triad. I was his wife.'

Patrick, having stood by listening, spoke suddenly. 'So you see it wasn't that easy … for anyone, not for my brother either.'

Joanna felt light-headed. She wished her mother had told her everything and not left her open like this. She turned on Patrick Arnold. 'Oh, it seems it was easy enough. He cut himself off – never bothered to find out anything about me – his only child. Just as well he didn't have any others, isn't it? If that's the kind of father he was.'

This was aimed at Rachel, who looked taken aback by her sudden anger.

'I'm sorry, Joanna. And I don't blame you for being angry. I'm not going to pretend that it isn't my fault – all our faults – it must seem everybody conspired against you. We did think about you … I wondered if he'd one day want to find you. I knew where you lived; your mother was in the phone book, so he knew it too. And it seems he did wonder because I found this among his things.'

Rachel crossed the room and took a book from the shelf. As she did so, Joanna saw a silver-framed photo of her father on a cabinet; it was the same photo she'd seen when she'd typed his name into a search engine the night that Rachel had come to the house. Vince Arnold smiling into the camera at what looked like a racetrack. He wore a white shirt open at the neck and a sports jacket, his hair was thinning, eyes creased with laughter lines as he squinted into the sun. Most of the national newspapers had printed the picture next to the article reporting his death. A tragic accident, they had said – Arnold was the latest victim of the biggest freeze to have gripped the country in almost forty years.

Rachel returned and Joanna found herself looking at another picture, which Rachel held out to her.

'This is the reason I went to your mother's house that night. I thought that maybe she knew something; that she'd had some contact with him before his disappearance, but she denied ever having seen it.'

It was a picture of Joanna on her confirmation day, posing outside the church in a little skirt suit that her mother had bought her for the occasion. There were many like it in the family album at home.

'Where did he get this?' she asked.

Rachel shook her head. 'I've no idea. I thought maybe you could help me to find out?'

Joanna looked at her. 'Well, it couldn't have been my mother; she said she hadn't seen him in years.' Even as she said the words, she knew that it was the only possible way such a picture had come into her father's possession. She looked at Patrick and again wondered how much he knew.

'Did you know my mother then?' she asked him.

'No, I was just a kid. Vince didn't exactly want me hanging around back then.'

'But you knew … about me?'

'Yes, he told me one night … he was upset.' He glanced at Rachel Arnold, giving Joanna the impression that he didn't want to say too much in front of her.

Joanna looked at Rachel, unable to decide whether she should hate this woman for making her father disown her, or feel some allegiance to her as another victim of her parents' deceit. If she were to find out anything about her father, she decided, she had better keep her resentment in check. These people were her only link to him. Family by blood if nothing else; at least, Patrick was. She looked at him, curious, wondering if he bore any resemblance to Vince. She looked again at the picture Rachel had given her. 'I'll ask her about it,' she told her, putting the photo in her bag.

NINE

'Business must be good, Ollie.' Patrick Arnold strolled around Oliver's office, and then paused, where Oliver had stood only a moment before, to look down onto the quays.

'No shortage of divorces right enough,' Oliver said. 'But I assume that's not what's brought you here?'

Patrick gave a short laugh. 'No, but I might be putting a bit of business your way.'

'Oh?' Oliver sat on the edge of the desk and scrutinized Patrick Arnold. Time had been good to him. It must have been, what, fifteen years since he'd seen him?

Patrick crossed the room and put his hands on the back of the swivel chair in front of Oliver's desk. 'My brother owed a lot of money. In fact, he was deeply in debt. Gambling – dogs, horses, anything that moved he put money on it. Six months ago he took out a life assurance policy. I expect there'll be questions asked: you know what these insurance companies are like; they'll use anything they can find to get out of paying.'

'Are you saying your brother's death might have been suicide?'

Patrick shook his head. 'No, but they might start poking around, trying to make it seem like that. There's no way Vince killed himself. We just got the result of the autopsy and it says he died of heart failure from hypothermia, not drowning. Ever heard of someone freezing themselves to death?'

'Still and all, seems a bit strange, doesn't it? That he'd take out an insurance policy, and six months later he winds up in the canal.'

'That's what I'm saying, Ollie. There's no way they'll let something like that get past them.'

'And why do you reckon he decided to take out the policy?'

'Loan sharks. He'd borrowed money from a lot of sources, and not all of them legit. I'm guessing he was afraid of what they might do if he didn't pay up, and that brings me to the next question – there are several parties who might come looking for what they're owed and Rachel's worried that she'll have to pay them. She's already been getting calls from some bookie that Vince ran up a debt with.'

'Back up a second and let me get my head around this. You're saying that your brother took out life assurance because he was concerned about some dodgy characters he owed money to. And you're also telling me that the autopsy said that Vincent died of hypothermia – that there was no water in the lungs?'

'Not enough, it seems, to make drowning the primary cause of death.'

'So do you suspect any foul play here? Hypothermia could have happened anywhere. Who's to say your brother wasn't dead before his body even hit the water? I assume there's to be an inquest?'

'Yeah, but really we don't suspect anything like that. I reckon Vince fell through the ice and couldn't get out. He couldn't swim and, remember, the canal was frozen over; it wouldn't take much for you to lose your bearings down there and lose sight of the place you'd gone down, particularly if you panicked.'

'In which case, you would drown,' Oliver said.

'I'm not a pathologist, Ollie, I don't know. Maybe he died on the ice, and ended up in the water when it cracked. A lot of people were fool enough to go walking on it. We'll have to wait for the result of the inquest to know for sure. In the meantime, we're hoping you might look after the insurance end of things – and the loan sharks. I'm assuming that since some of these loans weren't legit Rachel won't have to shell out for them.'

Oliver shook his head. 'It sounds like there wouldn't be anything legally binding, but it might be safer if she just paid them. These are not the kind of people you want to rub up the wrong way, Patrick. Your brother knew that. As for the insurance – I'd need to see the policy before I could give you any advice on it. The inquest will hold things up, but then probate tends to put everything on hold for months anyway. I take it Rachel is the beneficiary of this policy?'

Patrick shrugged. 'I presume so. I don't know the details.'

'And what's the value, roughly speaking?'

'Again, I have no idea. Vince and I never discussed it. I didn't even know there was a policy until Rachel mentioned it.'

'Okay. Well, firstly, if your sister-in-law has the money, I'd pay off that bookie. Everything else can be paid from your brother's estate, provided he had one.' Oliver paused. 'If you don't mind my asking, why aren't you looking after the legal end yourself?'

Patrick smiled. 'Ah now ... don't tell me you didn't hear about that, Ollie. God knows, lawyers love to talk.'

'I heard something all right. But, like you say, people talk; you can never be too sure what to believe.'

Patrick spread his hands. 'Well, I wish I could say it wasn't true, but I got myself debarred shortly after I'd set up a practice. It's not something I'm proud of. I made a stupid mistake – got caught up in something I shouldn't have. But look, sure I'd have made a lousy lawyer anyway. Best to leave all that to pros like you. So I'll bring you that policy to have a look over. Make sure the insurance crowd can't find anything amiss. Rachel will be relieved to have a solicitor involved. It's her I'm doing it for.

Things are hard enough for her without having to deal with Vince's financial mess.'

Oliver nodded and picked up his briefcase. 'I'm happy to help.'

He showed Patrick Arnold out of the office and down the narrow stairs. Arnold thanked him and said he'd be in touch to go over the policy.

'We must have a pint while I'm home, Ollie,' he said.

'Sure,' Oliver told him. 'Give me a shout.'

He locked the outer door and watched as Patrick Arnold hailed a cab. There was something about the whole thing that didn't sit right.

TEN

The lights were on when Joanna returned home. She expected to find her mother in front of the television, but she wasn't. When she climbed the stairs, she saw that her mother's bedroom door was ajar and the light was on. She was talking in a low voice. Joanna peered through the opening from the landing, curious.

Angela was sitting on the edge of the bed, her back to the door, talking on her mobile. 'It's not how … obviously, I didn't expect that … no. But … she's angry, what would you expect? Me?' She laughed. '… well, you weren't exactly … no, I know that. Okay, it'll be around three. I'll text you when I'm leaving. Don't worry, I won't, I have them here. Okay, I'll see you then. Bye … bye.'

Her mother ended the call, stood up and went to the window.

'Who was that?' Joanna asked.

Angela spun round, hand to her chest. 'Joanna, Jesus, you put the heart crossways in me. I didn't hear you come in.'

Joanna went in and sat on the edge of the bed. 'So who was on the phone?'

Her mother waved her hand distractedly. She'd left her mobile on the bedside table. 'Oh, it was just Pauline,' she said.

'How is she?'

'Grand, she's grand. Are you in long?'

'No, just a few minutes.' Joanna picked up the phone. 'Did you get a new mobile?'

'What?'

Joanna held up the phone. 'What happened to your other phone?'

'Didn't I tell you? It drowned. I left it on the cistern and forgot about it. Then, when I was cleaning, I knocked it into the loo. Dead as a dodo when I took it out.'

'You should have put it in a bag of rice.'

Angela took the phone from Joanna and put it in her pocket. 'Rice?'

'Yeah, it absorbs the water. If you give it to me, we can try it,' she said, following her mother from the room.

'Ah, I'd say it's too late now. Anyway, it had its day. It kept switching itself off.'

Joanna detected something edgy about her mother, probably because she'd overheard her on the phone. No doubt she'd been telling Pauline what had happened. She wondered how much her mother's old friend knew. They'd been friends since they were teenagers, so she would have known about Vince Arnold. Girls didn't keep those kinds of things from each other.

In the kitchen, Joanna watched her mother spoon cocoa powder into two mugs. It was a nightly ritual when they were both home. She was trying to decide how best to broach the subject of Rachel and the photo, and then, figuring that no time would be a good one, she simply said it. 'I was talking to Rachel Arnold.'

Her mother turned sharply. 'What, did she come here again?' she said.

Joanna shook her head. 'No, I went over there. I know what you're thinking, but I wanted to find out about him. The thing is, when I was there she showed me this.' She took the photo from her bag and held it out.

Her mother shrugged. 'What about it?' she said.

'Vince Arnold had it. She said you denied ever having seen it, but I know you must have given it to him, Mum. There're half a dozen just like it in the album downstairs.'

Angela poured hot water on the cocoa and slammed the kettle down in frustration. 'Jesus, would that woman ever keep out of our business!'

'But it is her business, Mum. And it's mine, too. You said you had no contact with him after he discovered you were pregnant, but that's not true, is it? You gave him that picture.'

'I told you, Joanna, I haven't seen Vince in years.'

'So where did he get it then?'

'I sent it to him after you'd made your confirmation. I don't know why. I suppose I wanted him to see what he was missing – what he'd have had if he'd chosen differently, if he'd chosen us. I knew there was more between us than there'd ever been between him and her. It takes some people longer than others to see their mistakes.'

Joanna's mother stirred the cocoa; she wouldn't meet her eye. It was almost as though she were talking to herself. Joanna took her mug and, cradling it in both hands, took the next step.

'She said they'd wanted to adopt me.'

Angela snorted derisively 'She didn't hold much back, did she?' She raised her mug to her lips and took a sip of cocoa, then continued. 'Rachel couldn't have children, so she decided she'd try to take mine. I think she blamed that on Vince's affair, the fact that she couldn't get pregnant, but that had nothing to do with it.'

'So what happened?'

'He called me and said he wanted to meet. I thought when I received that call that maybe he'd changed his mind; "it's about the baby," he said. Would I meet him in a café to talk? When I arrived and saw her there I nearly turned and walked back out. They were curt, both of them. She couldn't take her eyes off me.

It made me glad that I'd made the effort, even if by then I knew that a reconciliation was the last thing on the cards.

'"What do you intend to do?" he said. He couldn't look at me, not with her there, but she was doing enough of that for both of them. "What about?" I said, pretending I didn't know what he was asking. "The child ... you don't want to raise it surely?"

'"And why wouldn't I?" I said. I got mad then, told him if they expected me to get rid of it, they had another think coming, that he could run from his responsibilities if he liked, but I wasn't going to. That's when she started talking. "That's not why we're here," she told me. "We want to help. It's not easy bringing up a child on your own. People talk, and then there's the bills, it's not cheap." She went on, listing things out as though I hadn't thought of them. I watched her, wondering what it was this woman wanted, baffled by the fact that she said she wanted to help me – and then she said it. Six thousand pounds – she took a cheque book from her purse and showed it to me. She'd taken the trouble to write it out. I looked at my name in the swirly black ink – I'd get it as soon as I'd handed the baby over – nobody would ever have to know, she said. I could get on with my life; forget the whole thing had ever happened.

'Vince sat there all the while she was talking, silent – eyes lowered to the carpet. I ignored Rachel: willed him to look at me so that I might see in his eyes what he made of this preposterous suggestion, but he continued to sit there, eyes downcast – not daring to meet mine. "What's wrong," I asked him, "can't you even look at me?" "You should think about it," he said, looking past me – "what she said is right – he'd have a good life." *He* – he said. He was convinced you'd be a boy.

'I stood up then, told them both that they could keep their money – I had no intention of giving up my child. If Vince wasn't willing to leave Rachel, then he was giving up any right he had to you. Not that I had to state that – Rachel wasn't about to let him have anything to do with a child that wasn't hers too.'

Angela stopped talking – she seemed exhausted by having to go over it all. Joanna tried to absorb all that her mother had told her.

'And you didn't see them again?' she asked.

Her mother shrugged. 'I saw her on the bus once. I had you in the pushchair. She kept staring at you. I pretended I didn't know her – got off the bus two stops early and walked the rest of the way home.'

'Did you not feel … sorry for her?'

'I suppose I did sometimes. He should have left her – it wasn't fair – she'd have met someone else – we'd have been happy. But people don't always do the right thing.'

Angela stood up from her stool, rinsed her mug and left it on the draining board. She spoke with her back to the room. 'I know I can't tell you what to do, Joanna, but I'd rather you didn't see Rachel Arnold again. And it's not for what she might tell you – you needn't think that, I just don't want her latching onto you now that Vince is gone.'

Joanna said nothing. Enough lies had been told, and she wasn't prepared to commit to not seeing Rachel again. There were things she wanted to know about her father.

Awkwardly, her mother kissed her goodnight. It was the first time since Rachel Arnold had come into their lives. She looked tired, Joanna thought. When she reached the door, she turned.

'I almost forgot, Pauline asked me to go shopping with her tomorrow afternoon – she wants to get a dress. She's going to a wedding or something. So I won't be here when you get in.'

'Okay, Mum, I'll see you tomorrow night then.'

Joanna sat for a while in the kitchen, looking out into the dark, listening to her mother moving about upstairs. She thought of the solicitor she'd met at the funeral and went out to the hall to check her coat pocket to see if she still had his card. She took it out and looked at it. She had a sudden urge to see the place where the man, Oliver, had found her father's body. She decided that she would call him the following day when her mother was not around.

ELEVEN

'So where exactly were you when you saw him?'

Oliver pointed down the bank towards the lock. 'Just there,' he said. 'I'd crossed over and come down the other side.'

He watched as the girl, Joanna, moved towards the water's edge. She knelt close to the damp earth, lifted the camera and began to photograph the scene. She zoomed in on the reeds where he told her he'd spotted what he'd thought was a coat. She asked him to describe as clearly as he could what he had seen – the position of her father's body and how the rescue team had removed him from the water. She moved back then and took some shots of the lock with the reeds in the foreground. He heard the sound of the shutter opening and closing repeatedly until she rose and walked stealthily onto the lock to point her camera at the murky canal beneath. It was coming on for four in the afternoon and the light had begun to fade.

Oliver took the opportunity to observe the girl as she stood there, eye to the lens, her attention focused entirely on the camera. She was quite striking, but in a different way altogether from the Hernandez sisters. Her auburn hair hung loose over her shoulders, and her skin was so pale that it appeared almost translucent. He wondered how old she was and guessed that she was perhaps mid-twenties. She had told him as they'd walked along the canal road about how she was the fruit of Vince Arnold's early infidelity. He would have been, what, late twenties when he'd had the fling with Joanna's mother? According to the papers, he was fifty-four when he died.

Oliver had not told Joanna about Patrick's visit. He'd arranged to meet him that evening in Brogans' pub, and he'd decided to tell him that he couldn't take on the legal work he'd offered him. Given Patrick's record and the circumstances in which Vince Arnold's insurance policy had been taken out, he wanted no involvement. The last thing he needed was to become embroiled in a potentially dubious insurance claim. Patrick could find some other patsy to look after that one. His gut told him to stay clear.

The girl had finished taking pictures. She put the cover back on the lens and retraced her steps down the bank.

'Do you reckon it was an accident?' she asked.

Oliver looked at her, at her pale skin and eyes the colour of storms. 'The family seems to think so,' he said. There was no point in telling her about the autopsy result, raising questions in the girl's mind. She was still trying to get to grips with having discovered the identity of her father.

'Rachel said that you studied with Patrick?'

'Yes, it was a long time ago now.'

'Is he a solicitor, too?'

'No. He hasn't practised in a long time. He … well, to tell you the truth he was struck off. I asked him about it when we were speaking. He was quite frank, said he'd done something he shouldn't have and got himself debarred.'

Joanna nodded. 'Did he tell you anything else? Did he say anything about my father?'

Oliver hesitated, and then decided that it might be better to tell the girl the truth. She would hear it anyway, he assumed, from Rachel or Patrick if they were to keep in touch. 'He mentioned that your father may have run up some debts. He was

55

a sports journalist, I believe, and it's not unusual for people involved to fall into the trap. Betting is a tempting game. I've seen men lose everything over it.'

'Do you think maybe he ... that he might have taken his own life? People often do, don't they, when they have problems like that?'

Oliver shook his head. 'It did occur to me when Patrick told me, but I asked him and he said no. They think that Vince was simply unlucky, another victim of the freeze.'

They had started walking, left the lock and reeds behind. Oliver pointed towards the camera. He wanted to change the subject and to get to know something about the girl.

'You like taking pictures?' he asked.

She smiled. 'This probably looks a bit strange, macabre even. But yes, I take the camera most places, never miss an opportunity. I'm doing a degree at the moment in the IADT.'

'That's the art college?'

'Art, yes. What – you don't see photography as an art form?'

Oliver laughed. He knew that she was trying to bait him, make him say the wrong thing. 'I'm sure it is. I never thought much about it.' They were nearing the point where he turned off for home. He thought about the house and if there was anything there that he might not want the girl to see. He had an hour or more before he was to meet Arnold and, despite the circumstances, he was enjoying her company. 'I live just round the corner,' he said. 'Do you fancy continuing this conversation over coffee?'

The girl hesitated, but then agreed.

'Maybe you can show me some of your pictures,' he said. 'Convince me that it's art.'

She laughed. 'Not on this, I can't. It's your traditional wind-on camera, nothing digital going on here. I've got to develop these in the darkroom.'

'Wow, people still use those things?'

'Mostly only photography students, to be honest, but I love it.

Some professional photographers still do it this way, but it's more expensive – the money you have to spend on solutions and stuff makes it a costly hobby.'

'And is that what it is – a hobby?' Oliver asked.

'For now it is. Obviously, I'm hoping it'll pay the bills one day. Otherwise, there wouldn't be a lot of point in investing all this money in a degree course. At least that's what my mother says.'

'Doesn't she approve?'

Joanna shrugged. 'I think she finds the arts a bit whimsical. She'd have been happier if I'd gone on to study something more practical – business, or law maybe – like you. What area do you work in?'

'I practise family law: divorces, custody cases, nothing too exciting.'

They had reached the house. The girl waited as he turned his key in the door, and he wondered again if there was anything lying around that shouldn't be. 'I hope you'll excuse the mess,' he said. 'A man on his own tends to let things go … '

She followed him down the hall. When they entered the living room he saw her eyes travel quickly around, taking everything in. He followed her gaze – there was nothing particular in this room to suggest a woman's presence. He had removed all evidence of Mercedes – packed everything away where he didn't have to see them. Joanna took the camera from round her neck and carefully placed it on the coffee table. He asked her if she'd like tea or coffee, and she followed him into the kitchen and sat at the breakfast bar while he scalded the pot and put the teabags in. He felt very conscious of her presence and wondered what to do or say next.

'So what do you do for fun?' she asked him.

'I sue people.'

She laughed. 'No, really,' she said.

He turned to her, smiling. 'You're right, that's not so much fun, but it's all I seem to have time for lately.'

He steered the conversation away from himself by asking her about her course.

'I'm putting together a portfolio at the moment,' she told him. 'We're having an exhibition in a few weeks' time.' She paused and then jumped up from her stool. 'In fact, if you're really interested, I can show you the shots. I have them saved to a USB. It should be in my bag.'

'Great, I'd love to see,' he told her. 'You go get it, and I'll take the tea into my office. It's just through here.' He took the two mugs, placed them on the desk and booted up his computer. Joanna went out to the living room to retrieve her bag.

They were standing side by side in the small room watching the slide show of her photographs when the phone rang.

'Aren't you going to get that?' Joanna asked him.

'No, let them ring back,' he said. 'I'm sure it's nothing that can't wait.'

He closed the office door on the ringing lest the answer machine should kick in.

TWELVE

Joanna arrived home to an empty house. Her mother had not yet returned from her shopping expedition with Pauline. She decided that she would process the film on which she'd taken the canal bank shots that afternoon, but it was just as she had that thought that she remembered she'd left the USB stick containing the photos for her college presentation in Oliver Molloy's laptop. She looked at the clock. She needed that USB for her class the next day. She had two choices: she could either scan the photos again, which would take a lot of time, or she could go back to Oliver's for the stick. She didn't have his home phone number so she would just have to take the chance on his being home.

Joanna drove slowly past the row of terraced houses until she came to Oliver's. There was a light on in the front room, but it went out just as she turned off the engine. Perhaps she had just caught him before he went out, she thought.

She was about to get out of the car when the front door opened and a woman stepped out. The woman pulled the door behind her and walked swiftly down the path and crossed the road just in front of Joanna's car. She couldn't say why but, instinctively, Joanna shrunk down in her seat. She didn't want to be seen sitting in her car outside Oliver's house, even though she was doing nothing wrong.

She'd had a clear view of the woman as she'd crossed in front of the car. She was dark-skinned and dark-haired, and definitely didn't look Irish. She wore a leather jacket, a short skirt and knee-high boots. If Joanna had had her camera, she'd have felt compelled to take her picture, but she'd left it in the darkroom back at the house. She continued to watch the woman until she grew small in the distance, then she vanished altogether. Joanna wondered if she'd hailed a cab at the side of the road.

She looked at Oliver's house. There was a single light on in the hall, but otherwise no sign of life. She wondered if the woman was his girlfriend and was surprised that with that thought came a pang of disappointment. For some reason, she had assumed that he was single. She supposed it was his quip earlier about 'a man alone tending to let things go'. She wasn't his wife, then; but he was an attractive man and she shouldn't have been surprised that he might have just as attractive female callers.

After a sufficient time had passed since the woman's departure, Joanna got out of the car and made her way up the driveway. She rang the bell, a musical ding-dong, and waited. There was no sound within. She rang the bell again, but still there was silence. Oliver must be out, she thought, and in that case, the woman she had just seen leaving had either been there when he left, or she had her own key. Joanna sighed and traipsed back down the driveway. As she did, she saw a glove on the path. She leaned down to pick it up. It was a red wool glove that the woman must have dropped on her way out. Joanna put it back where it was, closed the gate behind her and got back into the car.

She wondered what to do. She could wait, but there was no telling what time Oliver might return. And what if the woman returned instead? She didn't want to make trouble. She would just have to wait until tomorrow to get the USB back. There was nothing for it but to go home and begin scanning her photos again.

Joanna gathered her collection of photos and took them up to her room to scan. Her mother had still not returned home. The landline rang when she was about half an hour into the work and she went to her mother's room to answer the extension. It was her mother's friend, Pauline, asking to speak to Angela.

'Mum? No, she said she was going shopping with you. Oh really? Maybe I got that wrong, then. She said something about going to buy a dress for a wedding, that wasn't with you? Okay, Pauline. No worries. I'll tell her to give you a call.'

Joanna put the phone down, puzzled. She was sure her mother had said it was Pauline she was meeting. A few minutes later, she heard her mother come in. She went into the landing and shouted down the stairs.

'That you, Mum?'

'No.' It was her mother's customary reply.

Joanna went downstairs. 'Pauline just called,' she said. 'Did you not say you two were going shopping together today?'

Her mother looked up. 'What?'

'Pauline, I thought you said you were meeting her today but she's just been on the phone.'

'No, I said I was meeting Helen.'

'Really? I was sure you said Pauline.'

'Oh, maybe I did, I meant Helen.'

Joanna looked at her mother's lack of shopping bags. 'Did you not see anything you liked?'

Her mother shook her head. 'I wasn't really looking for anything – I just tagged along. Did you get yourself something to eat?'

'No, I was out. I was thinking of maybe ordering something in. Do you fancy it?'

'No, I'm okay, I grabbed a bite with Helen earlier. Get yourself something.'

61

Joanna nodded. She wasn't sure she believed that her mother had mixed up the names of her two friends. Certainly, she knew she hadn't misheard. But if she hadn't gone shopping, where had she been? Rather than confront her about it Joanna decided to let it go. Maybe it was something and maybe it wasn't; her mother's lies had broken all trust between them. She missed the closeness they'd shared before Rachel had dropped her bomb. The distance wasn't helped, she knew, by her own omissions. She would have liked to tell her mother about the afternoon she had spent with Oliver Molloy, about him taking her to see the place where Vince's body had been found, but she wouldn't. She would hide the fact and the photographs she'd taken from her mother because she knew that if she told her she wouldn't understand.

THIRTEEN

Oliver's meeting with Patrick Arnold, supposedly for old times' sake, came to a sudden close when he said that he couldn't take the job. Oliver excused himself on the pretence of a heavy workload that wouldn't permit him to take on even the most insignificant case. And insurance companies, as Patrick knew, could be sticky. Arnold had brought a copy of the policy with him, and he insisted that Oliver take a quick look to ensure that the document itself was in order. There was one thing of note that Oliver observed, and which he continued to think about on his walk home. There were two beneficiaries to the policy; the first, as expected, was Rachel Arnold, but the second was the dead man's daughter, Joanna, who was set to inherit fifty thousand euro. Oliver wondered if the girl knew about this. He suspected she didn't, nor was she likely to find out until the result of the inquest came through – provided they found that Arnold had died a natural death. Would she welcome the money as some form of acknowledgement, albeit too late, or would she see it for what it surely was: an attempt on Vince Arnold's part to assuage his guilt?

Oliver's preoccupation with the Arnolds was cut short on arrival at his house. The garden gate was open, which in itself was not unusual, but halfway up the drive there was an object on the ground. He stooped to pick it up. It was a woman's small, red knitted glove. He put it to his nose and inhaled the unmistakable woody scent of perfume that had been caught in the fibres. He tried to think if he'd ever seen Mercedes wearing such gloves, and then he told himself not to be ridiculous. They were the size of her hands, yes, but wasn't she cold as he'd laid her in the ground, wasn't her body, unquestioningly, lifeless? And a fragrance, a perfume, meant nothing. The same scent was worn by millions of women around the globe, and was very likely to be used by sisters. There was only one explanation, but it did nothing to comfort him, Carmen Hernandez had come looking for answers.

Oliver put the glove on the hall table. Carmen's visit came as no surprise. He'd known, after all those unanswered phone calls, that eventually she'd turn up. And she wasn't the kind of woman to be shrugged off, particularly when she was on the scent of something. He cursed his stupidity in ever having become involved with her. But, catastrophically, he had and now he had to deal with the consequences: a dead wife. And, if he didn't tread carefully, an immediate police investigation.

He needed to think of a way to convince Carmen that Mercedes never wanted to see her again. If he knew what had been said between the two sisters, how Mercedes had reacted to Carmen's betrayal, it would be easier, but unfortunately, Mercedes hadn't revealed that. He imagined Carmen trying to convince Mercedes that she'd told her for her own good, even making out that she'd seduced him simply to show her that she couldn't trust him. Mercedes was always too ready to protect her little sister, but would she have forgiven her for this? Or would she finally have seen Carmen for the manipulator she was?

When Oliver entered the living room he left the light off. He didn't want to risk another visit from Carmen before he'd had a chance to think things through. He could still smell the perfume from the glove and was surprised by its potency. It was the Chanel he had bought for Mercedes's birthday. Oliver took the glove and put it in a drawer. Then he washed his hands to rid himself of the scent that evoked a myriad of memories. He turned on the television, sat and watched the world news in an effort to distract himself, but it didn't work. His mind kept returning to the imminent visit of Mercedes's sister.

He thought of the first time he had met Carmen Hernandez. Mercedes had invited him to Spain for her parents' silver wedding anniversary. They had been going out for almost six months and Mercedes had already moved into the house in Grove Road. Something which she'd kept from her devout Catholic family. She had forwarded them her new address, as her mother kept to the old habit of writing letters, but she'd said nothing to reveal the fact that she was living with Oliver. Such an admission would only have resulted in an apoplectic episode on the part of both her churchgoing parents. Knowing this, Carmen had, over the anniversary dinner, questioned Mercedes about her new lodgings – her dark eyes sparkling with mischief as Mercedes answered evasively while managing not to tell outright lies.

That night Mercedes had crept from the bedroom that she and Carmen shared, and had spent the night with Oliver in the guest room next door. He had been aware of the probability of Carmen hearing their lovemaking through the wall. He'd said as much to Mercedes, but she didn't care. She said nothing would wake Carmen she was such a heavy sleeper, and he had to admit that the thought of Mercedes's younger sister lying in the dark, listening, secretly excited him. Carmen had made a wry comment over breakfast the following day, asking if anyone had heard strange noises in the night. She was rewarded by a glare from Mercedes, which seemed to add to her amusement. She had turned her red-painted smile on Oliver and winked at him.

Oliver had ignored Carmen's interest then, her blatant flirting. Mercedes had never paid attention, used as she was to her sister's precociousness. Only three years separated them, but Mercedes had seemed much more mature than her sister. There was a wild, almost feral wantonness about Carmen, which had both fascinated Oliver and made him wary, but clearly not wary enough. Carmen had got her way in the end, and at a price far greater than any of them could have anticipated.

Oliver switched off the television. He tried to think rationally. Carmen had come, not because she thought that any harm had befallen Mercedes, but because her sister had not answered her calls. He would tell her that Mercedes had been livid when he came home that evening, that she'd already packed her things and had left that night saying that she never wanted to see him again. It would please Carmen to think that it was over between them. And if she thought there was any chance of taking her sister's place, it might dissuade her from looking for Mercedes. He would be furious in the first instance. Then gradually he would lead her to believe that she might benefit from her sister's departure.

Oliver stood up. He was tired and he decided that he would go to bed, read a little, and try to put Carmen from his mind. The next few days would take all his energy and cunning. He went into his office to turn off his computer and noticed that the Arnold girl had forgotten her USB stick. He hoped she didn't need it for anything urgent. As it was, he didn't have her number to contact her.

He sat at the desk and checked his emails. And then, out of curiosity, he opened up the files stored on Joanna's USB. She had several photo albums, including the one she'd shown him, saved on the device. He clicked on one entitled 'Artistic Self-Portraits'. The first shot was of a girl's abdomen with a flower lying on top. Intrigued, he clicked on the next. It was a portrait of Joanna sitting astride a high stool. Her back was to the camera, her long hair swept wildly around her as she stared coquettishly over her naked shoulder at the lens. Another was a close-up of her face and bare shoulders, titillating the viewer with the unseen. She wore heavy eye make-up, and her lips looked pale. All of the shots were in black and white. Intrigued, Oliver closed that folder and opened another marked 'Burlesque'. Various women appeared in this collection, mostly wearing some combination of top hats, tail-coats, fishnets and stilettos. They were coloured shots this time – the women wore deep red lipstick and dared the photographer with smouldering eyes. Joanna herself appeared wearing elbow-length black gloves and holding a cigarette holder. Her eyes were an astounding shade of green. Vince Arnold's daughter certainly had a flair for erotic photography. Oliver copied some of the photos onto his laptop and saved them. He spent some time wondering about the Joanna in the photos and what kind of lover she would make. Removing the USB and putting it in his coat pocket, he decided it might be fun to find out.

FOURTEEN

Joanna ordered a drink and glanced around the Porterhouse pub, which was unusually busy for a Tuesday night. She hovered near a small table where two men looked near-finished their pints and, when one rose, put on his leather jacket and told her with an appraisingly look that the seat was all hers, she settled down to watch the door and wait for Oliver Molloy.

She had phoned his office that morning to arrange to retrieve her USB stick, and he had agreed at once to meet her. She had listened for any semblance of wry amusement in his voice when she mentioned the forgotten device, but she heard none and assumed that he had not looked at any of the files saved there. A part of her had hoped that he would be curious enough to look, but maybe not everybody was as much a snoop as she was. Oliver worked on the side of the law, after all, and probably had ethics.

Just then the door opened, Oliver came in, briefcase in hand, and looked around the bar. Joanna stood and waved to get his attention. He smiled when he saw her and weaved his way across the room.

'I hope you haven't been waiting long. Would you like a drink?'

'I'm grand, thanks,' she told him, lifting her glass of wine.

He took off his heavy winter coat and put it on the back of the chair. Beneath it he was wearing a smart grey suit, white shirt and tie. And, on his left hand, Joanna looked for and found, a slim gold wedding ring. How had she managed to miss it last time – or had he simply forgotten to put it on? She wondered how it tallied with his quip about living alone and resolved to somehow bring it up during their conversation.

Oliver put his pint of Guinness on the table and then searched his coat pocket. 'Before I forget,' he said, producing the USB and handing it to her. 'I found it in the computer last night but, unfortunately, I didn't have your number.'

Joanna nodded, but said nothing about her return visit to the house or of her sighting of the young foreign woman. She would find a different way to get the information she wanted.

'I hope it wasn't too much of an inconvenience,' he said.

'Not really, I had to scan the wedding pictures again, but there wasn't anything else on it I needed.' She cast him a furtive glance. He was smiling and she wasn't sure if she imagined it or if there was a spark of mischief in his eye. 'There are some other pictures on it, from other photo shoots I did.' She twirled the USB and leaned forward. 'I don't suppose you looked?'

Oliver took a sip of his pint, and licked the froth from his top lip. 'No, what are they of?' he asked.

Was that a smirk as he put down his glass?

'Well, there's one file of self-portraits, arty kind of shots.'

He raised an eyebrow. 'Arty in what manner?' he asked.

She smiled and shook her head. 'You missed your chance to find out.'

Now he laughed openly. 'Maybe I did,' he said. 'And on the other hand … '

Joanna swatted his arm. 'You did, didn't you?' she said.

He lifted his glass. 'A lawyer has a dictum – never write anything down if you can say it, and never say anything if you can nod. If possible, don't nod.'

'Claiming the fifth, eh?' she said. 'I hope you liked what you saw.'

He laughed again, but refused to be drawn in.

When she noticed he was nearing the end of his drink, she offered him another. 'I hope I'm not keeping you from anything?' she said.

When he said no, she took her purse, feeling his eyes on her as she made her way to the bar.

'I meant to say, I was very impressed with your pictures, the wedding ones, I mean.'

'Oh yeah?' She set his pint down in front of him.

'Particularly the one with the bride in the Doc Martens. Very grungy!'

She spotted her chance and took it. 'Would you have thought that if your wife turned up in a pair of the Docs on the day?'

His expression darkened. He glanced at the gold band on his finger. 'It wouldn't have been her style,' he said.

'Have you been married long?'

He hesitated. 'I'm separated. My wife left me a little over a month ago. You probably noticed there was nothing well, womanly, in the house. She just took all her things, upped and left.'

Joanna touched his arm. 'I'm really sorry … I didn't mean to … ' So who was the woman she'd seen coming out of the house? She fought the urge to mention it. Was it his wife, returned to pick up her things while he was out – or some other conquest? If she mentioned it now she would look too interested.

'That's okay. You weren't to know.'

'All the same, I feel like I really put my foot in it. Do you miss her?'

'Sure. It's different being on your own. Mercedes and I were always fighting, but we had our good times, of course. I'm just sorry it ended the way it did – we had a massive row and she walked out.'

'Mercedes?'

'Yes, she was … is … Spanish.'

Spanish. It must have been her. Was he unaware that she had been back? Maybe she ought to tell him, but it was too late to mention it now. She would seem like a snoop, a spy. 'It hasn't been long, maybe she'll come back?' she said.

Oliver shook his head emphatically. 'No. It's over for good this time.'

'What makes you say that?'

'Well, to tell you the truth, I don't want her back. We said things, things that can't be unsaid … and even though it's difficult, I know it'll be better in time. I haven't really been out since it happened – this evening's been nice. I've really enjoyed it, up to the point where you had to ask me about my wife, of course …'

Joanna put her hand to her mouth. 'Oh God, I'm so sorry.'

'Nah, I'm teasing you. Kind of. It's all very raw right now, but I'll get over it.' He drained his glass. 'Right, I suppose we'd better go. By the way, those photos – they really are … intriguing.'

He grinned as Joanna punched him in the arm.

'Having the conversation we've just had, this might not seem the right time to ask, but I think maybe you'd better give me your number. Just in case you come round and leave any of your other belongings in my place.'

'Ha! You think, do you?' Joanna gave him the number, conscious that something had started between them. 'And yours?' she said, taking out her phone. She frowned at the screen. She had a missed call from Rachel Arnold. She checked the time – it had come in about an hour before.

'Something wrong?' Oliver asked.

'A missed call from my father's wife. I wonder what she wanted.'

'Will you call her back?'

'Yes – there are things I'd like to ask her. Anyway, your number?'

Oliver called out the number and she punched it into the

phone, distracted now by Rachel's call. She hadn't got back to her about the picture. She wondered what she would tell her about it – the truth, she supposed. There was no reason not to.

FIFTEEN

Oliver whistled as he turned his key in the lock. He didn't know if it was the girl's buoyant mood that had been catching, or if he had turned a corner somewhere inside his head, but the dread of homecoming that had been so prevalent on recent nights was absent as he pushed open the front door and stepped into the darkened hall.

He reached for the light switch, removed his coat and hung it on the end of the banister. As he sat on the stairs, undid his shoelaces and kicked off his shoes, he contemplated that it was the first good day he'd had since the night he and Mercedes had argued. He didn't know if Joanna was wholly responsible for his improved mood, but he vowed that he would call her again soon.

Oliver kicked his shoes under the stairs and looked in vain for his slippers. He walked in his stocking feet towards the living room, but when he reached the entrance he stopped dead without knowing why. There was something there – a presence – blocking the doorway. He reached out a hand and felt nothing, but the feeling did not go away, and a cold shiver ran the length of his spine. It was then that he also noticed a smell of smoke and he began to worry that there was a problem with the heating or that he had left something switched on. Thwarting the palpable presence between him and the living room, he stepped through the doorway. Suddenly, he noticed a red ember glowing in the blackness of the room and the acrid smell of smoke became stronger.

'Good evening.'

He fumbled for the light switch, his heart thumping in his chest, and when he turned the light on, stinging his eyes and illuminating the room, the sight of Carmen Hernandez sitting in his armchair smoking a cigarette greeted him.

'What the hell are you doing here? How did you get in?'

'That's not a very nice way to say hello, is it Oliver?'

Carmen tapped her cigarette into an ashtray by her side and crossed her perfectly shaped legs. She dangled a key in her right hand and smiled at him. 'I had it from last time, remember?'

He crossed the room and snatched the key from her fingers. 'What are you doing here? Why didn't you call first?'

'I did. I called and called, but the phone is always busy. Where is Mercedes? I've tried calling her mobile too, but she doesn't answer.' She looked around the room as though Mercedes might appear at any moment.

'I don't know.' He spoke quietly, trying to remember how he'd decided to play it. It had to be anger in the first instance – that is what she would expect, and given how he felt about her sudden appearance it wouldn't be difficult.

'You don't know?' She raised one eyebrow. 'What? Has she left you?'

She got up and began to walk around the room. She stopped a few feet away from him and waited for an answer.

'What do you think?' he said.

'I think yes, but she'll be back.'

'Why did you have to tell her?' he said. 'Or was that your plan all along? What did you think would happen? That you could take her place? Because, believe me, that will never happen. You're nothing like Mercedes.'

'And that's why you wanted me.' Carmen's red lips parted in a smile. 'If it were me, I'd want to know. Mercedes is my sister. I was thinking of her. She deserved to know the truth.'

Oliver felt his anger rising. 'The only one you were thinking of was yourself,' he said. 'Does it surprise you that she doesn't answer your calls? I'd be surprised if she ever spoke to you again. What kind of sister are you anyway? I'm not the only one to blame in all this. You were there, too. In fact, you were the instigator of the whole thing. It's your fault that she's gone. She'd never have known if it weren't for you. She'd be here now.'

Carmen had walked to the window to stare out into the darkness. 'What happened?' she said. Her reflection in the window looked worried. Her fingers crept over the glass, tracing a senseless pattern.

'She went crazy, that's what happened. You know Mercedes. She couldn't believe we'd done that to her. She said that she never wanted to see you again.'

The reflection looked disturbed. 'She said that?'

'Yes, but don't worry, she didn't make any excuses for me either.'

'Sure, but what did she say about me?'

Oliver shrugged. This was his opportunity to fabricate it. He would give her enough reason to believe that Mercedes's failure to answer her calls was a natural consequence to what had happened.

'She said that she was going away and that I needn't bother trying to contact her, she'd have changed her number. I asked her if she intended to return to Spain, and she said no, that as far as you were concerned she hoped she'd never have to speak to you again. She couldn't believe how you'd betrayed her. She said that she hated you, hated both of us.'

Carmen wasn't smiling now. She lit another cigarette, hand shaking. 'We must find her.'

'What for? What can you tell her that she doesn't already know?

Accept it, Carmen, she wants nothing more to do with either of us.'

Carmen let the curtain fall, and turned from the window. If anyone had seen her through the glass, he thought, they would have mistaken her for Mercedes. She was the same height, had the same tiny frame and dark hair.

'Look, maybe it was stupid, me telling her. If I'd known that she was going to leave like this, I wouldn't have. When I told her, she was angry, yes, but I thought she'd come round. You know what we're like. I didn't think she'd go off … Where do you think she's gone?' She stopped talking to bite on one scarlet painted thumbnail.

He was glad to see that he'd unnerved her. Now was the time to pull back a little. He didn't want to push her into doing something drastic.

'I honestly don't know. I've tried calling people, friends, but no one has seen her. Maybe if we give it time, she'll come back like you said.'

'I'm not leaving until I find her.' Her eyes challenged him, and he shrugged.

'I want to find her, too. I've been going mad since she left. I don't know where else to look, to be honest. I've tried all of her close friends. They haven't heard from her, or at least that's what they've said. I suppose, if she were with them she'd have instructed them not to tell me. This is what she wants, isn't it? Us going crazy worrying about her.'

'I'll call them. Maybe they'll tell me.'

'I don't think so. You're as much a part of this as I am. All we can do is hope that she shows up, or at least contacts us.'

Carmen sat back in the armchair and drew on the cigarette. She held the packet out to him, and he shook his head.

'Where are you staying?' he asked.

She exhaled; smoke curling from her glossy lips. 'I thought I might stay here.'

Oliver looked at her. 'You can't be serious. I mean, you can't. What if Mercedes did come back? Can you imagine how she would react if she found you here?'

Carmen laughed. 'Don't worry. I'm staying at a hotel,' she said. 'You, you're like a clock, so easy to wind.'

She shifted in the chair, and as she did so her skirt rode up to reveal one tanned thigh. He could have her now. He felt like doing it in anger. He could show her who was in control, but he resisted the temptation she posed. It was what she wanted. It was what she'd wanted from the start, but he had preferred Mercedes's subtleness to her sister's palpable sexuality.

'You should go,' he said.

'Don't worry, I didn't intend staying.' Carmen tapped her cigarette on the plate she'd been using as an ashtray and stood. Her coat lay across the arm of the chair, and she held the cigarette between her lips as she put it on. 'I'll come tomorrow. You can give me whatever numbers you have.'

'I'm working.'

'What – all night?' She brushed against him as she passed.

'Look, it's probably better if you don't come here. I'll call you,' he said.

Carmen's eyes flashed. 'Don't think you can get rid of me. I came to find my sister, and I won't go until I know where she is.'

Oliver stood at the living room window and watched her retreat. The sound of her heels clacked on the pavement, and he hoped that the neighbours would see her and assume that she was Mercedes. The room smelled of cigarettes. He emptied the plate of ash into the fireplace and opened the window. A rush of icy air entered the room, and he welcomed it. Her appearance had left him shaken. How would he convince Carmen to leave without having seen Mercedes?

SIXTEEN

Joanna walked down a busy Grafton Street towards Bewley's café where she had agreed to meet Rachel Arnold. The country may have been in recession, but you wouldn't think it to look at the sea of surging bodies out for the last of the sales. Outside Brown Thomas, she managed to fall out of the horde to stand for a while and watch a young woman with pink-tipped hair busking outside the store. She took her camera from her coat pocket and took a few quick snaps of the musician before dropping some coins in her case. Ambivalent feelings about meeting Rachel slowed her steps. She didn't want to betray her mother, but she did want to find out more about the man who had been her father.

Rachel was already there when she arrived. She half-rose from her seat and waved, almost upsetting the cup and saucer in front of her. She steadied them with an unsteady hand, and cleared away the newspaper she'd been reading. As soon as Joanna was seated, a waitress approached. Joanna ordered, and then observed Rachel as she too told the girl what she wanted. Despite her carefully applied make-up, Rachel Arnold looked worn. Dark smudges encircled her eyes and told of lack of sleep. Instantly, Joanna felt sorry for her. What must it be like to suddenly lose your life partner, particularly when there were no children to fill the void?

After exchanging a few niceties that, unsurprisingly, didn't include asking after her mother, Rachel jumped right in.

'Did you ask about the photo?'

Joanna nodded. 'Mum said that she sent it to Vince after I'd made my confirmation, so it was a long time ago.' As she said the words, Joanna felt a stab of guilt, but she was not betraying her mother, not really; it was only a picture, after all, sent well over a decade before. 'It was the only time as far as I know. She said there had been no contact in years.'

'She could have just told me that.'

Joanna shrugged. 'I think it still smarts … what happened. She doesn't like to talk about it. Seeing you after all that time, hearing that he was dead … she went on the defence. You'd probably have done the same thing.'

'Maybe.'

'What was he like? I don't mean what did he look like, I've seen pictures; I mean what was he like, as a person?'

Rachel didn't answer immediately. She looked beyond Joanna at nothing. 'Well, I don't want to just list things, but he was clever, passionate – maybe too much so.'

'How do you mean?'

'He was obsessive about things, about people even. He'd meet someone new and get totally smitten; they'd become inseparable for a while until, eventually, Vince would tire of them.'

'You mean my mother?'

Rachel shook her head. 'No, I mean anyone. Everything was a fad. The same with activities; he'd throw himself into something, become totally consumed by it, and get bored of it just as quickly. The more difficult it was, the more he wanted to conquer it.'

Difficult. Had her mother been difficult? Is that what he'd set out to do, to conquer her? Joanna saw the waitress coming towards them with the tray. 'What kinds of things?' she said, before the girl could interrupt.

'There were so many, let me see … riding. Horse riding. He didn't like heights; he was terrified when he started. A few weeks later, he was doing jumps. He was still terrified; he just refused to give in. As soon as he'd managed to get around a circuit a few times without falling off, he stopped. Maybe that'll give you some idea of what he was like. Bullheaded.' Rachel smiled, a sad nostalgic smile.

Joanna could see that it was for his stubbornness, his utter perseverance, that she loved him. Rachel had continued to talk as the girl served them. Now she paused to butter a scone and spread it with dollops of jam.

Joanna leaned towards her, eager for more information. She hadn't come to question Rachel about the triangular relationship between Vince Arnold and the two women. She wanted to know who her father had been, what it was that had drawn her mother to him. 'His brother, Patrick … are they alike?'

'Not really. He's equally charming, persuasive, but there was more of an edge to Vince. He was more determined. Patrick is … ' She paused, looking for the word. 'I don't know; I never really feel that I know him. He's not the sort of person I'd confide in. I feel slightly bad saying that; I probably shouldn't. He's been incredibly helpful during the past week. He came back from Italy when Vince went missing, he's been living there for the last few years, and he's stayed on to sort things out. Legal things. It was he who identified Vince's body, I … I couldn't do it. To see him like that … I couldn't bear it.' A tremor in her voice, eyes watering over. She sipped her tea, attempted to recover herself. 'You know you look like him. You've the same eyes.'

Joanna thought of the pictures she'd seen on Google. Did she resemble Vince? She hadn't thought so. Maybe when he was younger, or maybe it was just what Rachel wanted to see. What did she really think – sitting there, talking to her husband's only child? She certainly didn't come across as hostile. Maybe it helped her to talk about him; it didn't place him so immediately in the past. Joanna wondered what she thought of the mess Vince had got himself into, the gambling debts that Oliver had told her about. She didn't want to bring it up directly, that would be to admit that Patrick had told Oliver who, in turn, had told her. She didn't want to become involved in some kind of family dispute. 'How do you think it happened?'

Rachel looked up sharply. 'The accident?'

Joanna nodded, sipped her coffee.

'Despite what I said about Vince wanting to conquer things, water was the one thing that beat him. He never learnt to swim, was terrified of putting his head under the water.'

'So, why would he have been down there … at the canal?'

'Oh, he didn't mind walking by water; he just didn't like being in it. When I think of it, it's the worst kind of death he could have imagined.'

'They say it's not that bad. That it happens quickly. The police, I presume they don't think there was any foul play involved?'

Rachel paused, the scone to her lips. 'God, no. The autopsy said he died of cardiac arrest brought on by hypothermia. You land in water that cold and the shock is enough to kill you. There'll be an inquest, but it's just a formality.' Rachel was silent for a moment, but then she smiled. 'He'd have liked you, Joanna. You'd have had so much in common, I think. Did your mother tell you he was into photography? There are scores of albums at home – pictures that he took travelling, and at sports events. If you come to the house some day, I'll show you.'

Joanna smiled. 'I'd like that,' she said. She couldn't help but like her father's wife.

SEVENTEEN

Oliver took Mercedes's phone from the drawer in his desk. He had switched it off the night that it happened. He had considered sending Carmen a text message, but then he remembered that the telephone company could ping it to find out where the message had been sent from. A client had told him that once. He'd had a friend who worked in a service provider trace a message sent from his wife to prove that she was in a place other than where she said she was. He'd have to take a trip out of town in order to send a message to Carmen. Then there was a second problem. The sisters always communicated with each other in Spanish. He didn't trust that his Spanish was good enough to construct a perfectly fluent message, nor did he have faith in the accuracy of any of the translation sites: he knew from translating Spanish to English when he'd attempted to decipher conversations that Mercedes had with her sister when they spoke on the phone. No, he would have to send the text from Mercedes to himself. That would temporarily keep Carmen at bay. It would be the weekend, though, before he had a chance to get away. He put the phone back in the drawer and locked it.

To distract himself, he thought about Joanna. He'd enjoyed their flirtation in the pub that evening. He took his own mobile from his pocket and decided to send her a text. He'd like to meet her, but it would be no harm to build up a little anticipation first.

He typed, and then sent the message.

Any more pics?

A few minutes passed before the phone blipped.

What did you have in mind?

Hmm. Artistic self-portrait?

But you've seen those ones already ;-)

He stared at the phone. What to write next?

Did I? Afraid I've more of a kinaesthetic memory.

Silence. Hmm. Maybe she wasn't ready for that.

Oliver was at the bottom of the stairs when the doorbell rang. He stopped dead. Carmen had already phoned several times, and he knew from the voice messages she'd left that she wasn't happy. That unhappiness had probably been upgraded to a smouldering rage the moment he'd taken the phone off the hook, and now she was out there, nothing but the front door and a few feet of hallway separating them.

The bell went again. Oliver remained perfectly still, thankful that he'd confiscated the key from Carmen the night before. The net curtain on the hall window rendered him invisible from the outside; he just hoped that it wouldn't occur to her to crouch down and look through the letterbox, or to cup her hands and put her face against the glass. He was ready to move if she should do so; with one swift movement he would wedge himself against the hall door out of sight.

He was barely breathing when the figure outside moved, but what he saw from his place at the foot of the stairs was not the svelte form of Carmen Hernandez, but Joanna, striding towards the gate. Hurriedly, he opened the door.

'Joanna.'

She turned as he called her name. 'Hey, I'd just given up.'

'Sorry, I was in the middle of something, come on in.'

He stood back, and Joanna stepped into the hall. He caught a scent of something as she passed close to him, not the woody scent of the Chanel that he'd got the other night, but something fresh, citrus.

'Hope you don't mind me stopping by, I ran out of credit.' A sly smile.

He laughed. 'No, it's great to see you.'

'I just had coffee with Rachel Arnold.'

'How did that go?'

'Yeah, good. My mother said she'd prefer if I didn't see her, but I'm glad I did. She told me some stuff about my father, gave me a better idea of who he was.'

Oliver nodded. 'She's probably afraid you'll take Rachel's side. It's understandable. Tea?'

'No, I'm good.'

She followed him into the living room. He pulled the curtains lest they be disturbed. She sat next to him on the sofa.

'Can I ask you? You know Patrick Arnold; what kind of man is he?'

Oliver thought for a moment. How much should he tell her? He'd already told her about Arnold being debarred, so why not tell her the rest. 'I don't know him that well,' he said. 'We studied together, but I didn't exactly hang out with him. That said, he paid me a visit in the office the other evening.'

'What did he want?'

'He wanted me to look over your father's insurance policy. He's afraid he might have problems, what with the circumstances of your father's death. You see Vince only took out the policy six months ago.'

'That's pretty strange, isn't it?'

'That's what he figures the insurance crowd will think. You see they don't pay out on a suicide.'

'Is that what he thinks happened?'

Oliver shook his head. 'Not at all. He reckons it was an accident.'

The girl looked relieved. He wondered what difference it would make to her if she thought her father had taken his own life. How might that affect a person, being the child of a suicide? If the insurance company knew about his debts, they would surely try to make a case of it. Oliver wondered if Patrick were covering anything up. It seemed rather likely. A man runs up several debts, owes money to the wrong kind of people, and then takes out an insurance policy for a hundred thousand to bail out the wife.

'I told Arnold I was too busy to take anything on.'

'Oh?' She looked at him, curious.

'Yeah, I thought it best not to get involved. There is one thing, and I don't even know if I should tell you this, but you'll find out eventually. The policy names two beneficiaries: Rachel Arnold, obviously, is one – but the other is you, Joanna.'

Joanna's eyes widened. 'Me? Are you sure? Why would he … ?'

'I was surprised too when I saw it, but when you think about it, it makes sense – the guy obviously wanted to make up for the past.'

'Maybe, but he knew the money would only come to me after his death. Surely, if he was in that frame of mind, he'd have made some kind of effort to know me when he was alive.'

'There's no telling why people do the things they do. Sometimes, they don't know the reasons themselves. Maybe he was afraid.'

'Did Patrick say anything else about it? I mean, does Rachel know? She didn't say anything.'

'Hmm. She might be in for a surprise. Patrick is the executor of the will. Unless Vince discussed it with Rachel when he had the policy drawn up, there's no reason she'd know anything about it yet. Nothing will happen until after the inquest. I suspect, as Patrick does, that the insurance company will be out to find any loophole they can. But if Patrick's right and your father's was simply a tragic death, you're set to come into a fairly substantial amount of money.'

'How much?'

'Fifty thousand.'

'Wow.' Joanna was quiet.

'It's nothing less than what you deserve. Think what it costs to bring up a child.'

She nodded. 'I wonder what my mother will say.'

'Well, it would buy a whole lot of phone credit.'

Joanna laughed and swatted him. 'It's nice here,' she said. 'Quiet.'

He'd moved closer to her while she was talking. Now he took her hand.

'I know the timing's not great on this, and if you don't want anything to happen, I totally understand, I'm just recently separated and there's all that stuff going on with your father, but I really like you, Joanna. And if you think you might feel the same, well … it'd be great. If not, I suppose I've always got those photographs.'

Joanna started to laugh. She hadn't pulled her hand away. Nor did she back off when he kissed her.

EIGHTEEN

Joanna was woken by a loud banging. Disoriented, she reached for the bedside lamp but, instead, her hand found warm flesh and she remembered that she was not in her own bed. Disturbed, Oliver moaned and turned on his side. She shook him gently.

'There's someone at the door,' she whispered.

'Hmmm?' Suddenly he sat upright. 'Sssh. Don't make a sound,' he said. The covers were pushed back and he climbed out of bed.

'It's her, isn't it?' Joanna said. 'It's Mercedes.'

Oliver didn't answer.

She heard him rummaging in the dark, then the rustle of him pulling his clothes on.

'Don't worry,' he said. 'She's not getting in.'

'Doesn't she have a key?' Joanna was halfway out of bed at the thought. Maybe she ought to get dressed, ready to hide if necessary.

'No. No, she didn't take it.' His voice a whisper in the dark.

Joanna fell back against the pillows. Oliver had moved to the window. A shred of light entered the room as he lifted a corner of the curtain to peer down into the garden.

'I can't see anything,' he said. He dropped the curtain and the room was plummeted into darkness again.

Joanna heard him open the bedroom door. 'Where are you going?' she said.

'It's okay, just stay here.'

The door closed leaving her alone in the dark. She shivered, pulled the covers up around her. What was he doing? She hoped he hadn't decided to answer it. What if the woman suspected that there was someone there and forced her way upstairs? Joanna's boots were in the living room. She should've brought them up, but how was she to know that someone would call in the night? And anyway, what kind of hour was this to come knocking? Surely, if she wanted to talk to him, she could have done so at a normal time. Maybe she was drunk, which really spelled trouble. Joanna listened for any sounds from downstairs, but she heard none. A few minutes later, Oliver reappeared in the doorway.

'It's okay. She's gone,' he said.

'Did you answer?'

'No. no.' He climbed back into bed. 'I'm sorry about that.'

'It's not your fault,' Joanna whispered, but the woman turning up like that had put her on edge. Maybe she had been hasty in believing that his marriage was over. Clearly, there were unresolved issues.

'What do you think she wanted?'

'Who knows? It's three in the morning. Whatever it is, I'm sure it can wait.'

She lay there listening to him breathing, wondering what it was that was going through his head. 'Are you sure it's over?' she said.

'Yes. You needn't worry about that.' He leaned across and kissed her.

She kissed him back, tried to forget about the woman at the door. She hoped it wasn't just a one-night thing; something he would say had been a mistake. But she was here now and it was what she wanted.

Some time later she woke needing to go to the bathroom. Silently, she slipped out of bed and made her way across the landing. A full moon lay beyond the frosted glass of the bathroom window and illuminated the room in its milky light. The tiled floor was cold beneath her bare feet. On the back of the bathroom door hung a pink bathrobe which she guessed belonged to Mercedes. She took it down and held it to her face before slipping it on. It smelled of some expensive perfume. She pulled the cord on a small fluorescent light above the mirror and blinked until her eyes adjusted. In a cabinet to the right of the mirror there was moisturizer, nail varnish remover, hand cream, things that belonged to Mercedes. Joanna wondered why she hadn't taken them with her. Had she left in such haste? A loofah hung in the shower. She was sure that if she looked closely enough she would see Mercedes's long dark hairs clogging the bath. She closed the cabinet door wondering if Oliver Molloy was truly over his wife. She turned off the bathroom light, and then stood in the landing, listening. There was no sound from the bedroom. She crept quietly down the stairs, felt her way into the living room. She fumbled for the switch, her eyes adjusting slightly to the darkness. When she turned it on, the room was as they had left it. Her boots lay on the floor near the sofa. She looked around the room, then got up and began to walk around, stopping to look at things. There weren't any photos. Had he taken them away? Most people had photos. Perhaps it was too difficult just to look at his wife. On a shelf above the television stood an old music box. She picked it up and opened the lid. A ballerina began to twirl accompanied by the sound of tinkling music.

'What are you doing?'

She jumped at the sound of his voice and snapped the music box shut. He stood framed in the doorway in his dressing gown.

'My God, you scared me,' she said. He was looking at the music box in her hand, a strange expression on his face.

She put the box back on the shelf. 'I couldn't sleep, so I came downstairs. I hope I didn't wake you.'

'I don't sleep really,' he said. 'Insomnia, it's a curse.' He rubbed at his eyes.

She wanted to cross the room, put her arms around him, but something stopped her. She wondered if he thought she'd been snooping while he was asleep. Maybe she should have stayed in bed instead of walking around the house at night. It was only then that she remembered she was wearing Mercedes's robe. No wonder he'd looked at her so strangely. She fingered the cotton, began to apologize.

'I'm sorry. You must've thought … I just found it hanging on the bathroom door. It was cold … I shouldn't have … '

Oliver shrugged. 'It doesn't make any difference,' he said. He scratched his head. 'Do you want something to drink – hot chocolate maybe?'

'Yeah, great. I don't think I could sleep.' She felt uncomfortable now in Mercedes's dressing gown. What was she thinking putting it on? So stupid. She heard him move about in the kitchen and went back upstairs to get dressed.

He looked surprised when she reappeared in the living room fully clothed. 'Are you leaving?' he said.

'No, I was cold. But I can, if you want me to?'

He put down the mugs. 'No, I don't want you to leave. Why on earth would I want that?' He smiled, pushed her hair back and kissed her.

'I'm sorry,' she said.

'What for?'

'The robe, it was stupid. I didn't think.'

'Don't worry about it. I was a bit surprised, that's all.' He sat down and sipped his hot chocolate. Joanna sat next to him. 'How would you feel about going away this Friday night? I've a bit of business to do up in Belfast. We'd have to leave in morning?'

'I'd love to. I've actually never been.' Joanna relaxed, thankful that his mood had changed again. A weekend away would be perfect, give them a chance to spend time together without the risk of intrusion by his ex-wife.

NINETEEN

As soon as Joanna had left, Oliver called Carmen. He didn't mention her visit in the early hours of the morning and neither did she. To keep her off his back, he agreed to meet her at the Westbury Hotel where she told him she was staying. She'd insisted on him giving her numbers of some of Mercedes's friends in Dublin, and he'd scribbled down a few names and numbers of close friends he'd already called in the days following Mercedes's death.

He spotted her immediately as he entered the lobby. She was sitting at a table reading a magazine, a glass of red wine before her. She'd probably seen him already and had averted her eyes from the entrance as soon as she'd seen him step inside the revolving door. He imagined her crossing her legs into the pose in which she now sat, her whole demeanour an affectation for his benefit. She flicked through the pages of the magazine with disinterest and failed to look up until he'd spoken.

'Sorry, I'm late.'

Carmen paused, one perfectly manicured fingernail poised to turn the page. 'Do you have the numbers?'

'Yes. I've contacted most of them already, but there are a few people that you could call.'

Oliver took the slip of paper from his wallet and held it out to her. Carmen closed the magazine and scanned the numbers. Then she looked up.

'Where were you last night?'

He was surprised by the even way in which she asked him. He'd been bracing himself for fireworks as soon as they'd met. He watched her face for any sign of suppressed anger that might threaten to erupt and was surprised to see none. This was an impressive display of selfcontrol on Carmen's part.

'I stayed at my father's. I've stayed there a few times recently. It's more for myself than for him, I suppose. I can't stand to be at home when she isn't there.'

Carmen played with her wine glass. 'You miss her then?' she said.

'You know Mercedes. The place is dead without her.'

The waiter came and Oliver asked Carmen if she wanted a drink. She refused. Her glass was almost full and so he ordered a Guinness for himself, and wondered what lay behind Carmen's cool façade. The Guinness came and he took a frothy sip. At first he hadn't intended staying, but it had occurred to him that Carmen could be of use. And since she wasn't being volatile he thought that it might be a good opportunity to show his willingness to unite in their quest to find Mercedes. It would be the only way to placate her.

There was another reason why he decided to stay and share a drink with Carmen; he felt that he ought to take advantage of her seemingly genial mood. That morning he'd had a call from the human resources manager in Mercedes's job. This time the woman had left a message to say that she didn't want to pressurize Mercedes at such a difficult time, but they needed some indication as to when she might return. The call had given him an idea which could strengthen his alibi should the police investigate Mercedes's disappearance, but in order for it to work he had to persuade Carmen to help him out. If she agreed, she would also make herself his unwitting accomplice.

'I got a letter from Mercedes's job today. They said they wouldn't keep her position open for her any longer if they didn't hear from her soon,' he said.

'She hasn't been at work?'

Carmen paused with the glass halfway to her damson-stained lips.

'She had taken time off. She hates that job, but it seems she hasn't been in touch with them about returning. I was thinking, maybe you could call them. You sound just like her. I don't want her to lose her job even if she doesn't like it. Not because of me, of what we've done. They're still paying her at the moment, but they'd have grounds to fire her if she just falls off the face of the earth.'

'But why, why wouldn't she have contacted them? Something's happened to her. It must have.' Carmen bit her thumb distractedly. 'I think we should call the police,' she said.

Oliver shook his head. 'I don't think that's necessary, Carmen. Don't you think I'd have called them if I did? I know Mercedes. She's seething. She's hurt and she's angry, but that's all. There's so much going on that it obviously didn't enter her mind to call. Maybe she doesn't intend coming back. But whatever the reason, we should keep her job open for her while she's deciding what to do. Will you call them? It would give her more time?'

Carmen shook her head. 'I don't know, Oliver. It could just make things worse. What if she calls them and they discover it was all lies? Then they'll fire her for sure.'

'It's a risk. I know that, but I think we should do what we can to keep it open for her. Mercedes is smart. If they manage to contact her, she'll go along with it. I know her.'

Carmen nodded and cradled her wine glass in both hands, the stem dangling between her fingers. She eyed him over the rim. 'I suppose you hate me. You think this is all my fault?'

'I wish you hadn't done what you did, but it can't be undone. We just have to get on with it.'

He wondered how many drinks Carmen had had. Her eyes were slightly glassy, glittering like black gems amidst the whites of her eyes. He often thought that she possessed an almost masculine aggressiveness. He pitied the man that would become involved in a power struggle with Carmen. He was unlikely to escape unscathed and, with that in mind, he knew that she would make a better ally than an adversary.

Her glass was almost empty. She was watching him closely, and he waited for her to speak.

'I never saw you as a match,' she said. 'I thought Mercedes would marry a Spanish boy. There was someone … '

She said it to provoke him. But rather than take the bait he leaned in towards her.

'Naturally. We all have our history,' he said. 'But tell me about yours.'

Carmen laughed and swirled the liquid in the end of her glass. 'Ah. My history. My history is not so interesting,' she said. She put her head back and drained the glass. Her neck was long and slender.

'I doubt that.' Oliver waited, watched her smile into the empty glass.

Her teeth were perfectly white between her wine-stained lips, but Carmen was not beautiful. Her mouth was too wide, her lips slightly too full. She was an imperfect model of her sister and she knew it.

'You made the right choice with Mercedes,' she said.

'There was never a question about choice.'

'No?'

'No.' He watched her face, saw her eyes flash with annoyance.

She leaned forward in her chair. He could see the tanned flesh of her breasts as she crossed her arms beneath them, accentuating her sexuality. Every move Carmen made was calculated. He had never met a woman so aware of her body and the power it yielded.

'I saw the way you looked at me. You're doing it now. You can't help yourself, you're a man.'

Oliver laughed. 'Do you think every man wants you?'

She shrugged. 'At first they do. Then they want something else, something new.'

She was drunker than he'd thought. 'And what do you want?' he said.

'I want another drink. How about you?' She signalled to the waiter nearby.

'I should probably get going. I've a meeting with a client in the morning.'

'Oh, one more won't hurt. You don't want me drinking alone here, do you?'

Oliver smiled as he stood up. 'I don't think you'd be alone for too long, Carmen.'

'No? Then maybe we should go to my room. We could get them to send our drinks up.'

She rose, walked round the table and stood too close to him. She put a finger to her lips and swayed slightly. 'Don't worry. This time I won't tell anyone,' she said.

Oliver smiled. He could smell her perfume, the same perfume that Mercedes had worn, and he remembered how the scent of it had lingered. The concerned husband was the best card to play now that he had Carmen partly on side.

'If it weren't for Mercedes, I'd be tempted, but the most important thing now is to get her back.'

Carmen reached up and he held her wrists to prevent them from snaking round his neck.

'I think you've had a little too much to drink. You'll regret it in the morning.'

'*Je ne regrette rien.*'

Carmen swayed and he put out a hand to steady her. He walked her to the lift and when the doors opened he guided her inside.

'Which floor is it?'

'I'll only tell you if you come, too,' she said.

'I'll take you to your room, but then I'm going home.'

They stood in the corridor and Carmen searched in her bag for the key. As soon as she'd swiped it in the lock and pushed the door open, Oliver said goodnight, kissed her lightly on the cheek and made his way towards the lift. He had to convince Carmen that he was serious about finding Mercedes, and sleeping with her, tempted as he was, would not do that.

TWENTY

Joanna was excited about Belfast. The invitation had calmed her fears about Oliver regretting spending the night with her. Mercedes turning up had served a purpose: it was a reminder to her to take things slow. He liked her, she knew that, but it would take time for him to recover from the break-up with his wife.

When she got home, her mother was dragging a large sack down the stairs. She puffed and swiped a hand across her forehead.

'What's that?' Joanna asked.

Her mother took a deep breath. 'Clothes. I'm doing a clear-out. It's been a while. You'd be amazed at all the stuff that accumulates.'

Joanna laughed. 'At the rate you buy stuff, not really. Do you want a hand?'

'Yeah, there are two more bags on the landing. Maybe you could run them down to the clothes bank for me later?'

'No probs.' Joanna skipped up the stairs two steps at a time to get the bags.

'Where did you get to last night?' her mother asked.

'I stayed at a friend's. Well, more than a friend actually.'

Her mother looked up, interested. Joanna had decided to tell her about Oliver, not the full story because it would worry her, but she was doing her best to get back to how they'd been before and that meant no more secrets.

'Where did you meet him, college?'

Joanna hesitated. 'No. He's … he's the man who discovered Vince's body. I met him that night at the funeral. He gave me his number and we've met up a few times. His name is Oliver.'

Her mother frowned. She hadn't expected her to be happy about how she'd met Oliver, but it would be worse if she'd omitted it and it came out later.

'Well, I don't know what to say. I suppose people do meet in the strangest circumstances. What does he do, this Oliver?'

'He's a solicitor.'

'And why was he at the service – does he know the Arnolds?'

'Not exactly. Not Vince anyway, but he knows the brother, Patrick. Apparently, they studied law together. Have you ever met him?'

Her mother shook her head. 'As you can imagine, Vince wasn't exactly taking me round introducing me to his family.'

'Oliver said that Patrick was debarred from practising. He committed some kind of fraud.'

Her mother reddened. 'Did he? Well, like I said, I don't know him. So, tell me about this Oliver, how old is he?'

'I don't know. Older than me.'

'Not married, I hope?'

'No. Well, yes he was but he's separated now.' It was Joanna's turn to colour.

'Do you know that for certain?'

'Yes.'

'Why? Because he told you?'

'No, because I've been to his house. Do you think he'd have brought me to the house if he were still living with his wife?'

Joanna was angry. Her mother knew nothing about the situation. She had no right to question her like this. She was sorry she'd decided to say anything.

'Look, just because he found Vince that doesn't mean you have to take an instant dislike to him.'

'Dislike? I don't dislike him. I haven't even met him. It's you I'm worried about, Joanna. You get taken in by people sometimes.'

'What? I made one bad judgement and now you think I'm likely to be taken in by every man that comes along. God, you must think I'm naïve.' Joanna stood up and paced the room.

'Joanna, you're taking this the wrong way. Oliver might be a very nice man. I just don't want to see you getting hurt again.'

'If I get hurt, that's my problem.'

She was glad that she hadn't mentioned anything about Mercedes. If her mother knew how recently they had separated she would definitely have something to say about it.

'It's this tendency of yours to go for older men. They have a lot more experience than you, Joanna. They … they know how to manipulate people.'

'Like Vince Arnold, you mean. You think everyone's like Vince Arnold, don't you? That's why you were so against Michael. Now I understand. All the time it was Vince that you were thinking about. Well, Oliver isn't my father, Mum. Sure, things mightn't work out. You take that risk in any relationship. I wish you could just give people a chance.'

'I can see why you might think that. Of course, it made me cautious, but this isn't about me, it's about you, Joanna. It took you so long to get over Michael. I know he wasn't married, but he was too old for you. You need someone your own age.'

'I prefer older men. That's not a crime, is it? They have more to say. And they don't play stupid games like guys my age. I don't set out to meet them, it just happens.'

Joanna looked away. She could feel her mother's eyes upon her, but she refused to return her gaze.

'I'm not against you, Joanna. Please, don't think that. I'd love you to meet someone, someone that's going to look after you.

But don't go rushing into anything with this man. You barely know him. Be careful, that's all I'm saying.'

Joanna stopped chewing on the corner of her nail and looked up. Maybe her mother did only have her interests at heart. She couldn't help but think that she was trying to turn her off Oliver because of the link to the Arnolds.

She had been contemplating bringing up the insurance policy, but she figured she'd said enough. She didn't know what her mother's reaction would be to Vince leaving her the fifty thousand euro. Would she be pleased, or would it seem a buy off: the same as the money they'd offered her all those years ago for her baby.

'Right, I think I'll run those bags over to the clothes bank for you,' Joanna told her mother. 'Is that the lot?'

'For now, yes.'

Joanna nodded. 'Oh, and Mum, I won't be here for the weekend. Oliver's taking me to Belfast. We're leaving in the morning.'

'Already? That's a bit fast … '

Joanna's eyes narrowed, and her mother raised a conciliatory hand.

'Okay, okay. I get it – back off. Just bear in mind what I said, love, won't you? Don't let your heart run away with you.'

TWENTY-ONE

Oliver had asked Joanna to book a hotel in Belfast. The room would be in her name and he would pay for it in cash. There would be no evidence that he had ever been in the city. They'd arranged to meet at Connolly Station to take the ten o'clock train. He'd told her he had a meeting at noon, and planned to disappear to an Internet café where he would access Mercedes's Facebook account. He wanted to be sure to leave a trail that would place her in the city.

When they'd booked into the hotel, a spa hotel, which Joanna had got a deal on, he gave her money and told her to book herself in for whatever treatment she liked. She kissed him and asked him if he was sure and then, delighted, phoned reception to book an appointment. He left her changing into a white robe and slippers, and took the lift to the ground floor where he asked the receptionist to direct him to an Internet café. The girl showed him a map of the city and circled the spot where the café was. He thanked her and stepped out into the crisp morning.

Belfast was grey even in the white winter sunshine. Oliver carried a case into which he'd put a sheaf of papers along with the mobile phone that had belonged to Mercedes. As soon as he was a few hundred metres from the hotel, he took the phone out, switched it on and dialled into the voicemail. The automated voice told him there were twelve new messages. He pressed the phone to his ear to hear above the din of traffic. He heard his own voice asking Mercedes to call him. Then a number of messages from Carmen urging Mercedes to return her calls, her words so hurried that he could barely keep up with her Spanish. There was a voicemail from the HR woman in Mercedes's job too. It had been left a few days before and he wondered whether Carmen had called her that morning. If she had, she had undoubtedly implicated herself in her sister's disappearance.

When he'd finished listening to the messages, he sent Carmen a text.

No me llamas mas.

Keep it simple, he didn't want to run the risk of making a mistake. 'Don't call me anymore' would, of course, have the opposite effect on Carmen, and so he switched the phone off again as soon as he'd sent it.

In the Internet café, he opened up Mercedes's Facebook account. Luckily, she had been totally open about her passwords. If you had nothing to hide, she said, why be secretive? He scrolled down through the newsfeed, stopping occasionally to click the 'like' button under photos that her friends had posted. He replied to two messages from work friends enquiring about her whereabouts to say that she'd taken time off for personal reasons. That should be enough to keep them at bay for now. He then sent himself a message to say how disgusted she was by him, so that the location of the message would register as Belfast. It wasn't hard to do: he'd repeated some of her final reproaches to him. It was a message that, when he showed it to her, would truly put Carmen off the track.

Oliver opened his wallet and took out Mercedes's debit card. He'd had a sudden thought. If he booked a Eurolines ticket to take Mercedes from Belfast to Glasgow, there was nothing to say that she hadn't left the country. His heart thumped as he typed her details onto the site. He booked the ticket for two days' time.

He looked at his watch. He'd been gone an hour already. It was time to get rid of the mobile and get back to the hotel. He went into a newsagent's, asked for twenty Silk Cut and ninety pounds sterling cashback. The assistant didn't even glance at the card as he placed it in the machine. When he left the shop he dropped the cigarettes in a bin.

He strolled down to the quays, Mercedes's phone in his jacket pocket. When he was sure there was no one around, he leaned over the railing and dropped it in the water. In seconds it was submerged. He had to be sure there was nothing that the police could trace back to him.

He turned and walked back in the direction of the hotel. He switched off his own phone, sure that Carmen would try to ring him too when she got the message. He walked slowly, going over his actions in his head. Had he covered everything? He thought so. There was nothing more he could do now but try to convince Carmen to call off the search for her sister.

He thought of Joanna waiting back in the hotel room. She was a nice girl, and she'd been through a lot. He didn't want to mess her around. Was it right that he had brought her? He hadn't had the nerve to make the trip alone. Joanna could make him forget – at least, temporarily. There was a tremor in his hands. He needed to get it together before he got back to the hotel. He stopped off at a bar and ordered a brandy. His feet stuck to the carpet as he made his way to a darkened corner. The place reeked off stale beer. He was a killer – a person he'd have taken pleasure in sending down. Now he had covered his crime – and, he hoped, covered it well enough never to be caught. Eventually, there would be an investigation – one that he figured he would have to instigate. A concerned husband would surely report his wife missing after a number of weeks of failed contact. He sipped the brandy and considered his next move. Today was the last day anyone would have heard from Mercedes. As far as the police were concerned, she boarded a ferry for Glasgow and hadn't been seen again.

In a few weeks' time it would all begin again. Carmen would get restless. Mercedes's friends would begin to ask questions. He would have to play the role of concerned husband and report his wife missing before her sister had a chance to. It would mean keeping Carmen close – knowing her every move; ready to act before she did.

TWENTY-TWO

Oliver had been gone a long time. Joanna had come back from the spa expecting him to have returned, but still there was no sign. She crossed the room to look out the window, but there was no view, just a yard where some cars were parked. She drew the curtains and bounced onto the king-size bed. She was in no hurry to get dressed; he would be back soon, and her intention was to seduce him.

When he returned he seemed edgy. 'Sorry, I didn't think that would take so long.'

He kissed her and she tasted alcohol. He pulled off his tie, shrugged out of his suit jacket and threw it on a chair.

'I'll tell you what, I'm going to have a shower. I need to get out of this suit. Makes me feel I'm still working. You stay right there.' He pulled her to him, and kissed her again, but tension showed in his face.

She wondered if the meeting hadn't gone so well. He'd definitely been drinking. She took off the robe, slipped into the sexy red underwear she'd bought for the occasion and lay on top of the bed. She heard him run the water in the bathroom as she waited for him to return. When he came out, he stood there for a moment and looked at her.

'I want to remember you just like this,' he said.

For some reason his words sent a cold wave through her. 'Remember? You don't have to remember. I'm here right now.' She laughed, nervous.

He leaned over her on the bed, took both her wrists and raised her arms above her head. She was trapped now. He could do what he liked to her. For a moment she felt panicked; she didn't know him that well after all.

'Oliver.'

He silenced her, his lips on hers, tongue probing. Then he released her wrists, and ran his hands over her body, exploring. She wondered how many lovers he'd had and guessed that the answer was many. He kissed her neck, her breasts – examining every crevice. He put his head between her legs and she opened them wider lifting herself up to him.

'Jesus.'

He knew how to touch a woman.

Despite herself she thought of Mercedes. He had done these things to her, touched her like this. And she, what had she done to him, for him? In another place, she thought she'd have been free of Oliver's former lover, but instead she felt an affinity with the other woman. When she sat astride him, eyes closed, moving against him, she imagined she was Mercedes and the thought shattered any inhibition she might have felt. Mercedes was beneath her skin, closer now than she was to Oliver, and it was almost with violence that she moved on top of him, hair swinging wildly in his face until they climaxed at almost the same time. Breathless, she looked down at him and laughed. He brushed her hair back.

'God, I'll have to take you away more often,' he said. He ran a hand over his face. He was soaked in sweat.

Joanna rolled off him and, laughing, padded to the bathroom. 'Won't be long,' she said.

She stood under the buzzing fluorescent light and examined herself in the mirror. Mascara was smudged beneath her eyes.

Her face was flushed and her hair was charged with electricity, so that she resembled something wild. She did the best she could to restore normality, but her make-up was in her bag in the room, and so she dampened the corner of a towel and rubbed at the creases beneath her eyes where the make-up had settled, and dampened her hair down with water. When she opened the bathroom door, he stirred, lying as she had left him on the bed.

'God, I was almost asleep. What time is it anyway?'

Joanna crossed to the window and pulled one of the curtains back to check her watch. It was four in the afternoon and already the light outside had faded. She switched on a light by the bed. 'I guess we should get something to eat, I'm starving.'

'Mmm, in a minute.' He pulled her into the crook of his arm.

An hour later, they were walking the city streets. The edginess from earlier had left him and he held her hand as they walked. She guessed he wasn't afraid of meeting anyone he knew in this city. She hoped that in the future they could do this in Dublin. Her mother must have felt the same when she'd met Vince Arnold. They would never have had the opportunity to walk hand in hand like other young couples. Instead, she'd had to settle for clandestine meetings in hotels. It must have made her feel frustrated, being hidden away; a shadow in the background of Vince's life.

They strolled through the streets, glancing in shop windows, looking for a good place to eat.

'It feels a million miles from home here, doesn't it? I don't just mean because of the red post-boxes or buses, if you listen to the people. Some of them have such accents it could nearly be another language they're speaking.'

'You know, a few years ago, a group of young activists were arrested for painting the post-boxes in the north back to their original green,' he told her.

Joanna laughed. 'Are you serious?'

'They said they were doing An Post a favour for when the country would be united. It's not an impossibility, you know; if enough people north of the border wanted it, it could happen. It's in the Good Friday Agreement.'

'Can't see it ever happening though, can you? I mean it would have huge economic implications.'

Oliver shrugged. 'I wouldn't rule anything out.'

He stopped to look down a side street off the main thorough-fare. 'Let's go down here for a minute. There used to be a little shop here … I want to see if it's still … yep, there it is.' He tugged at her hand and brought her down the narrow street where a faded sign read 'Harry Hall's Bookshop'.

Oliver ducked through the door and Joanna followed. Instantly, they were met by the musty smell of old books Joanna had loved since childhood. There were old and not so old books – covers varying from faded pink and green hardbacks to the creased but still glossy covers of recently read romance novels. Oliver ran his fingers along the books' spines clearly in search of something, while Joanna allowed her eyes to wander across the handwritten signs that differentiated genres. She wandered over to the crime fiction section and took down a book by John Connolly. Her eyes scanned the shelves and soon she'd amassed a pile of books: Hughes, Hunt, Nesbø, Le Carré. She took them to the cash register where Oliver had already finished making his purchase, and the old man at the desk smiled as she complimented the range of books the small shop had.

When the old man had carefully placed the books in a red-and-white striped bag, they left. Oliver stopped outside the door of the shop and pulled a book out of his own bag.

'I got you something,' he said.

Joanna looked at the cover, where a naked woman whose head was unseen sat in a Victorian armchair by a window. The title was *Henry and June* by Anaïs Nin.

'I think you'll like it,' he told her.

Joanna thanked him, looked quickly at the blurb on the back of the book and put it in the striped bag with the others.

That night, after they'd made love again and Oliver slept, Joanna slipped from beneath the covers, sat on the toilet seat beneath the buzzing fluorescent light and read of Anaïs Nin's obsession with the writer Henry Miller and his enigmatic wife. She likened it to her curiosity about Mercedes and wondered if Oliver was aware of it. Is that why he had bought her the book? She wished they could stay in Belfast. Oliver had seemed more at ease as the day wore on, and she liked him like that.

TWENTY-THREE

Oliver had been home less than an hour when the doorbell rang. He'd put Joanna in a taxi at the station knowing that there was every chance Carmen Hernandez would turn up. Now, she was on the doorstep struggling with her umbrella. When she'd managed to put it down, she walked past him into the hall. Rain dripped from the umbrella and left dark spots on the carpet surrounding her feet, but she didn't seem to notice.

'Where have you been? I spent all of yesterday calling you.'

'I thought I told you not to come to the house.'

'Well, I got a message.' Carmen looked around for somewhere to put the umbrella. He took it from her, opened the front door again and left it outside. Rain blew in on an easterly wind. Carmen lifted her hair from beneath her jacket collar and threw it over her shoulder. He closed the front door and turned to face her.

'You mean from Mercedes?'

'Of course Mercedes. Why else would it matter?'

He spread his hands – tried to look eager. 'And what did she say?'

'Nothing, just that I shouldn't call her.'

'What – that's it? Nothing else?'

'Naturally, I tried calling her immediately, but she'd switched off again. I tried I don't know how many times. Always the same – the customer you are calling … blah … blah.'

She followed him into the living room where he'd got a fire going when he'd come in. It spit and crackled, the flames throwing shadows round the room.

'Well, as it turns out, you're not the only one to get a message.'

'What – you heard from her too?'

'Mm-mm. Apparently, she's in Belfast.'

'Belfast? How do you know? Did she say that?'

'No. She sent me a message on Facebook. She probably didn't think about the location coming up. I'm sure she'd prefer to have us going crazy wondering where she is.'

'What did she say?'

Oliver shrugged. 'How much she despised me. You can read it if you want. I know you probably won't believe me otherwise.'

Carmen took her jacket off and hung it on the back of a chair. She didn't sit down, but crossed the room to stand before the fire. 'What, and you didn't think to call me? What have you been doing? I've been trying to contact you since yesterday afternoon.' Her tone was sharp, impatient.

'In court. I've got a big case on at the moment. I crashed out last night as soon as I got in. You should have left a message. I'd have called.'

'When? Next week? Besides, your phone's off.'

'Is it?' He took the phone from his pocket, made a show of switching it on.

Carmen shivered and moved closer to the fire. 'Look at me. I'm completely wet. I hate this country. I don't know how Mercedes could choose to live here.'

Oliver shrugged. 'You get used to it.'

She slipped out of her shoes and wriggled her feet. 'Maybe I could change into something of Mercedes's?' she said.

Oliver hesitated. 'She took most of her clothes, but there are a few things in the wardrobe.'

'I'll go up and take a look,' she said.

Oliver put a hand on her arm to stop her. What if she saw something she shouldn't? He couldn't think of anything offhand, but it was a risk he wasn't prepared to take. Carmen looked up at him, curious.

'Stay here. I'll get you something,' he said.

As Oliver climbed the stairs, he thought of all the clothes he'd taken to the charity shop. He was glad that he had left some of them. Carmen would see it as a reason for Mercedes to return. He opened the wardrobe. The short silk skirt hung just inside the door. The fabric slid between his fingers, cool against his skin. He took it out, then decided against it, and instead took a pair of jeans from a hanger. He closed the wardrobe and went downstairs.

Carmen was sitting at the fire. She had peeled off her stockings and her bare legs were outstretched. If he narrowed his eyes a little, she could have been Mercedes sitting there. She looked up as he entered.

'I hope these are okay,' he said.

She stood up and he handed her the jeans. She started to unzip her skirt and he turned away before he heard the fabric fall to the floor.

'So chivalrous,' Carmen said.

He ignored her sarcasm, waited until he had heard her zip up the jeans before he turned back to her. 'Can I get you something warm to drink? Hot chocolate? Or whisky maybe, I wouldn't mind one myself.'

Carmen shrugged. 'Why not?'

They sat opposite each other and sipped the hot whisky. He'd put an extra shot in each and he wondered if it might go to her head. Carmen seemed calmer now. She cradled the hot mug and stared into the flames.

'I should never have told her. It was stupid,' she said.

Oliver nodded. 'You know I won't disagree with that. So why did you?'

Carmen shrugged. 'I don't know.'

'You must know.' His voice was gentle, coaxing.

She looked at him, eyes glittering black in the firelight. 'Don't you know? I've always wanted what Mercedes had. When we were children, Mercedes always seemed to get everything she wanted. They didn't notice me. It was always Mercedes. She was the best at everything.'

'Who didn't notice?'

'Anyone that mattered. At school she always got the highest grades. She was the most talented, the most beautiful.'

Carmen stopped talking.

'But you're beautiful,' he said. He watched her reaction, saw that his comment had disarmed her.

'But you want Mercedes,' she said.

'True. But you're different, and you should be different. I don't know what it's like to experience rivalry like that. There was just me. I didn't have any brothers or sisters.'

Carmen put her mug on the fireplace. She leaned forward in her seat. 'How old were you when your mother left?'

'Seven, almost eight.'

'And you never heard from her again?'

Oliver shook his head. 'No. I spent years wondering what had happened to her. Then I just stopped. She'd walked out, so why would I want to find her?' He stood up. He knew that Carmen had heard his history from Mercedes, but it was not a story that he felt like retelling. He didn't want or need Carmen's sympathy. 'Look, when you're finished, I'll give you a lift back to the hotel. I don't want to risk having you here. Imagine how it would look if she did turn up.'

'Do you want her to?'

'What kind of a question is that?' He pretended to feel needled.

Carmen put her shoes on and stood up. She stood close to him; put her hand on his arm.

'Oliver. We don't have to be enemies.'

He didn't answer. He had succeeded in softening her. It was a start, something that would have to count in the weeks of Mercedes's supposed silence. It was only after he'd dropped her off at the hotel that he remembered he hadn't shown her the Facebook message. It surprised him that she hadn't insisted on seeing it. Still, that would keep for another day.

TWENTY-FOUR

Joanna pulled up outside Oliver's house and cut the engine. He wasn't expecting her, and she was relieved to see his car in the driveway. Lights shone in both the hallway and behind the closed curtains in the front room, and she imagined him and the kind of welcome she might get before she'd even undone her seatbelt. In Oliver, she'd found a kind of sanctuary. She felt that, no matter what she told him, he wouldn't judge her. And it was with this feeling of jubilant anticipation that she stepped from the car and arrived at his front door.

Joanna raised her hand and was about to ring the doorbell when the sound of voices inside made her quickly withdraw. She crouched closer to the door to listen; careful, as she did so, to keep out of view of the hall window through which she might be spotted. The first voice she heard was Oliver's, but she couldn't make out what he said. The voice that answered was a woman's. Then there was a bump and a door closed muting the voices within before she could make out what they said. She'd heard enough, however, to know that Mercedes had returned.

Stepping back from the front door, Joanna glanced at the window. The curtains were drawn, but a light shone through a slight gap where they hadn't been closed tight, and she ducked as she passed the hall window and stepped into the sodden grass beneath the sitting room window. Slowly, she uncurled her body, so that her eyes were just above the level of the windowsill. She was hidden from the view of passers-by with the help of a hedge that ran the length of the garden wall, but from Oliver's neighbours' garden she would be clearly visible. She prayed that no one would see her peeking through the window into his front room.

The chink in the curtain offered her a restricted view. She saw the woman she had seen coming out of the house that day pass the window and move towards the fireplace, but she couldn't see Oliver. She strained to hear words between them, but the woman appeared to be alone in the room. She stretched her hands towards the fire. Instinctively, Joanna reached for her camera. Oliver must have re-entered the room then, because the woman said something, then reached round to the back of her skirt, unzipped it and let it fall on the floor at her feet. The woman smiled; Joanna raised the camera, adjusted the zoom and clicked the shutter once, but she didn't see what happened next. Instead, her attention was wrenched from the scene unfolding beyond the glass to the something that had brushed up against her legs in the dark. Startled, Joanna jumped backwards, knocking over a potted plant as she did so. She dived for cover behind Oliver's car as the disgruntled black cat miaowed its disapproval after her retreating form.

Joanna could hear her heart thump as she waited for the front door to open, but minutes passed and nothing happened. The cat hopped onto the neighbours' wall and, bored now by its findings in Oliver's garden, it vanished down the other side. Gripping her camera, thankful that she hadn't dropped it in fright, she rose and made her way, crouching, along Oliver's car towards the garden gate. She kept one eye on the window to ensure that nobody had looked out through the curtains, but they remained as before; the chink revealing nothing, only to those who put their faces or lens to the glass – something that she now had no desire to do.

Having reached her car without being apprehended, Joanna fumbled the keys into the ignition and drove away from the kerb. Only when she was out of view of his house did she turn the headlights on. It didn't take much to make sense of what she had seen through Oliver's window. She wondered when Mercedes had returned, and when he would tell her. Anger caused a pulsing behind her temples; mostly, it was anger at her own naivety. Her mother was right: it had been too soon to get involved with him. Sure, he'd said it was over, he might have even thought it was, but it was her willingness to become involved with him that annoyed her most. She thought she'd learnt something from her experience with Michael, but sadly she'd proven that theory wrong.

The sight of Mercedes undoing her skirt and then standing in her stockings by the fire had caused her stomach to lurch. She was glad that she hadn't seen what happened next. She didn't need to. Damn Oliver anyway; he'd completely led her on.

How could she be sure that he'd even told the truth about his wife leaving him? She might simply have been away, and he'd taken the opportunity to have a fling. Though he wouldn't be that stupid surely – bringing her to the house for the neighbours to see? No – it was more likely that he and Mercedes had reconciled despite his protests. Maybe her mother was right: he was no better than Michael with his false promises.

She hadn't allowed herself to think of Michael in a long time. She'd heard that he'd got married just a year after they'd split up, and her only feeling was one of pity for the woman that had got involved with him. He wouldn't be faithful to any woman. He just didn't have the capacity for it. She remembered how he'd denied it, talked himself round in rings until he realized that there was no absolution for what he'd done. She'd read his emails; it wasn't something she was proud of, but when he'd started sitting up half the night on his computer she'd begun to suspect that something was wrong. And then she'd seen them, the emails that had been sent back and forth between them – a woman that he'd met in an Internet chat room – a woman that he had arranged to book into a hotel with in Brussels, a trip that he'd told her was work-related. It was pathetic, but she was glad that she'd found out before it made her life pathetic, too. She'd told him never to contact her again. He'd sent her a text message six months later, which she'd promptly deleted, and didn't give him a thought again. Well, that wasn't entirely true. She wondered, sometimes, what he was doing, with the voyeuristic curiosity that people reserve for past loves, but it was just that. She had no desire ever to see him again.

She was relieved when she got home to find that her mother was out. The urge to confide in her would be too much, and she didn't want to prove her right, not because her mother would glean any kind of satisfaction from it, far from it, but because she didn't want to admit her own foolishness.

Joanna took off her coat and flung it on the sofa. She needed to distract herself; she wasn't going to wallow. The weekend in Belfast had been ideal; that was what hurt so much. She'd had a glimpse of what life could be like with Oliver. No, not with that Oliver – but with the person she'd thought he was.

She sighed and picked up her camera. She had rolls of film to develop – those pictures she'd taken at the canal bank the day that he'd shown her where he'd found the body. Had it only been two weeks before? Rachel Arnold's visit really had turned her life upside down.

In the darkroom she rolled on the film, then carefully removed it from the camera and began slowly and meticulously loading it into the spiral. She placed it in the development tank, quickly added the developer and turned it upside down a number of times. It was a tricky process that had taken her months and cost her many good photos to perfect. She thought about the pictures on the film inside the tank, the stark shots of the canal she'd taken, reeds to the foreground, dark body of water beyond – the lock that Oliver Molloy had crossed the morning he'd found her father's body. She emptied the developer from the tank and repeated the procedure with the stop and fixer solutions. When enough time had passed she lifted the lid and ran the tap to wash the film. She sat on her stool by the tank and thought of the running water cleaning the solution from the spool, washing clear the image of Oliver Molloy's enigmatic wife. The photographer in her wanted to see the shot – the image stolen. She didn't doubt it would be an interesting one.

Ten minutes passed. Carefully, she removed the spiral from the tank and began to unfurl the film. The canal bank shots were there – and the shot of Mercedes. She was turned side-profile; Joanna remembered her exact position: one hand reaching round to the back of her skirt. If it hadn't been for that cat, she'd have found it hard to drag herself away from the window – an onlooker at a car crash about to witness carnage but unable to turn away from the scene. It was as well she hadn't witnessed it; the images were clear enough in her head without having the physical evidence to torment her. Gently she hung the unfurled film, attached weights to the end and left it to dry. Printing would be another job, one that would require more time and uncompromised attention. She stifled a yawn, removed her gloves and, for that evening at least, closed the door on the darkroom.

TWENTY-FIVE

Oliver didn't have to avoid the phone anymore now that he'd spoken to Carmen Hernandez, and so when it rang he picked it up without hesitation.

'Hello, would it be possible to speak to Mercedes Hernandez, please?'

Fear. A momentary pause. 'Who's speaking?'

'This is Caroline Clarke, HR manager at ITS. Is that Oliver Molloy – Mercedes's husband?' The tone bright but officious.

'Yes, what can I do for you?'

'We're just calling to check in with Mercedes, Mr Molloy, to find out when she intends returning to work. Is she available?'

Mind racing. Calling to check in. Hadn't Carmen called them? He'd have to play innocent, feign surprise that Mercedes had not been in touch with the company. 'I'm afraid not. She's actually gone away for a few days. I'm sorry, but didn't she call you? She said she was going to do it several days ago.'

A pause, shuffling of paper, an elongated 'Noooo. I'm afraid we haven't spoken to Mercedes in a number of weeks, Mr Molloy. Is there a mobile number we could get her on, perhaps? It's just, we need to know when she intends coming back to work.'

Carmen. He'd asked her to call them. Why hadn't she done it?

120

'Yes, yes … just a moment and I'll give it to you.' He called out Mercedes's number, thought of the phone at the bottom of the water. 'The number you have called is not reachable.' Would never be reachable again. 'I'm very sorry about this, I'm sure she meant to call you. She hasn't been herself lately.' Depression, anxiety – common reasons why people disappeared. What luck that Mercedes had taken time off before it happened, that she'd been to the doctor and had got a sick note saying she was not fit for work due to stress. It wasn't true, well it was – partly. She hated that job, had decided over the Christmas holidays that she wasn't going back. He'd persuaded her to take some time out instead; it was his idea that she get the sick note. She could continue to get paid while she looked for another job; it would give her time to decide what it was that she wanted to do. She could get away with it for months, he'd told her.

'Okay, Mr Molloy, thank you very much. And when you speak to your wife, could you mention that I called, in case I don't manage to get through to her. It's very important that she contacts us directly. We haven't had a doctor's certificate from her in over a week. I know that you brought one in previously but I'm afraid she must bring the next one in herself. Company policy, I'm afraid.'

'Okay, Yes, I'll tell her.'

Now what? Mercedes's doctor had given her the certificate for a week. He'd prescribed her pills to help with anxiety. Oliver had taken a chance on requesting the second medical certificate on her behalf. The doctor was reluctant. He'd sat the other side of the mahogany desk and asked Oliver how Mercedes was doing. Oliver told him that she was better, that the pills were helping but she felt she needed more time off. Grudgingly, the doctor tore a sheet from the pad on his desk and extended her sick leave by a further two weeks.

'I generally have to see the patient,' he'd said. 'I'll give you the note, but if she needs anything further, she'll have to make an appointment herself.'

'Of course, I understand.'

Oliver had taken the note, folded it and put it in his jacket pocket. He'd hoped the doctor hadn't noticed the slow panic rising inside him. When he got home, he'd searched Mercedes's bag for the small jar of Xanax and took one himself. Those little white pills had got him through several bad moments in the past few weeks.

Carmen. She had said she would phone the job. The question was why hadn't she? Had she been clever enough to know that he was trying to implicate her – did she sense that something wasn't right? He needed to find out. After tomorrow there would be no point in Carmen calling them. Mercedes would supposedly be on the ferry from Belfast – a call from a number in the Republic would only complicate things. He'd tell her to leave it be. The fact that they'd both heard from her and that she was okay meant that she could take care of it herself.

He thought of Carmen's visit the night before – the somewhat mellowed attitude, her conciliatory tone as she left. 'We don't have to be enemies.' What could they be – allies? Had she started to consider the possibilities that her sister's absence presented, better still, that the end of their marriage posed – or was it a ploy? Why hadn't she insisted on seeing the Facebook message that he'd claimed Mercedes had sent him? How had that become suddenly so unimportant? One thing was for certain, he would have to be careful around Carmen. He had set out to placate her, to get her on side, but how could he be sure she hadn't the same objective in mind? Mercedes's sister was sharp – one wrong move and she would be onto him. Carmen would have her own agenda, of that he was sure – but if he misread it, if she succeeded in leading him down a false track, it would mean the end of everything.

TWENTY-SIX

'You can't deny it, Angela. Your signature is right here on the form.'

Joanna heard the voices as soon as she entered the hall. They hadn't heard her come in, and she crept close to the living room door to listen.

'I want to know how long you'd been back in touch with him and how? Was that the first time you'd seen him?'

A mocking exclamation. 'What? Do you think we were carrying on behind your back all those years?'

'Come on, Angela, just tell me the truth. You've nothing to gain from hiding anything, do you? There's no point in one-upmanship. And besides, what's Joanna going to think when she finds out you've lied to her?'

'Lied to me about what?' Whatever it was they were talking about this time, Joanna wanted to hear it directly.

The two women looked up, startled, when she appeared in the doorway. Something akin to satisfaction crossed Rachel's face.

'Joanna, I didn't hear you come in,' her mother said.

'Evidently.' Joanna looked from one woman to the other. 'What's going on?'

Rachel Arnold waved a piece of paper at Joanna.

'Let me deal with this,' her mother said, angrily.

Joanna took the paper from Rachel's hand before her mother had a chance to intervene. It was a form. 'Change of Beneficiary' the title read. 'What's this?'

As she asked the question she scanned down the page, saw her own name and details written in an unfamiliar hand. She knew before her mother said anything that it was connected to the insurance policy Oliver had told her about. At the end of the paper, two signatures – the first: Vincent Arnold's, and the second, her mother's. She looked up.

'Mum?'

Her mother waved a hand as though it were no big deal. 'Your father made you a beneficiary to his insurance policy.'

'Yes, I see that.' Joanna glanced at the form again. 'But this was only three months ago. Why didn't you tell me? I don't mean about the money – I don't care about that. I asked you straight out if you'd had any contact with him over the years, and you downright denied it.'

'Well, I didn't, not over the years.'

'You saw him three months ago – you signed this.' Joanna waved the form before her mother in anger. 'I don't see any reason for you not to have told me that when we talked about it, when you told me about him.'

Rachel Arnold looked at Angela expectantly. Her mother cast about her looking for something to say.

'I should have, I suppose. It didn't seem relevant at the time. I … when you told me, I wasn't thinking straight.' This was directed at Rachel Arnold. 'Vince was in touch. He phoned me one afternoon, said he wanted to talk to me about Joanna. I didn't want to meet him; it had been a long time. I didn't want to dredge it all up again. He insisted; said it was important, that if I didn't meet him, he'd contact Joanna himself. Naturally, that was the last thing I wanted, so I agreed to meet.'

'Where?' Rachel asked.

'Here, one morning when Joanna was at college. He'd brought that with him.' She indicated towards the form in Joanna's hand. 'He said he wanted to make you a beneficiary to his life insurance, Joanna. I asked him if he was sick; why else would he turn up after all these years talking about life insurance. He laughed and said no, it was nothing like that.'

'So what was it like exactly?' Rachel's tone, impatient now.

'He said he was sorry for what had happened, for what he'd done. He wanted to do something, anything, that might make up for it.' Angela's words were directed at Joanna.

'Did he explain why? I mean it seems a little strange, doesn't it, that after all those years he'd suddenly developed a conscience?' Joanna said.

Her mother shook her head. 'Naturally, I asked him that. He said he'd been thinking about it, and about you, Joanna.' She turned to Rachel. '*The girl*, he called her, didn't even remember her name. It was too late to make up for things, Vince knew that – but he figured that some day, when the time came, he could contribute something.'

Rachel looked from one to the other of them. 'So three months ago he changed his insurance policy and now he's dead. It doesn't seem right, does it? Like he'd somehow tempted the gods.'

Angela nodded. 'That night, when you came to the house, the first thing I thought was suicide. That he must have come here to put his affairs in order.'

'Insurance companies don't pay out on suicides,' Joanna said.

Her mother nodded. 'I thought of that then; it wouldn't make sense. And Vince wasn't stupid; he'd have been aware of that. No, if that were his intention he could have just given me a cheque for you, or deposited the money in your account.'

'He didn't have any money,' said Rachel.

'What?'

'Vince was broke. He'd gambled everything away – there was nothing to give.'

'Nothing?' Joanna could see that this news had taken her mother by surprise. But then there was no reason why Angela would have known anything about Vince's finances.

'Nothing. He'd borrowed money, he owed several creditors, and not all of them legitimate either.'

'Did you tell this to the police?' Joanna asked.

Rachel nodded. 'They know about it.'

'And they don't suspect, I mean if he owed a lot of money? There's the possibility that something might have happened to him, isn't there? That one of these, these loan sharks … '

'They've already said they don't suspect anyone else was involved. It was simply a tragic accident.'

'Well, there you have it,' Joanna's mother stated. 'They know what they're talking about I'm sure.'

'But what about the insurance policy?' Joanna insisted. She turned to Rachel. 'You said before, it seems an odd thing that Vince decided to change his policy just months ago—'

Joanna's phone went before she could finish her sentence.

'I'm sorry,' she said, pulling the phone from her pocket.

Oliver Molloy's name flashed on the screen. She pressed the reject button and put the phone on silent. Distracted, she turned back to her mother.

Angela had spread her hands. 'It's a coincidence,' she said. 'Of course you could say it looks strange, but life is full of strange coincidences. You two make it sound as though you're looking for some kind of mystery to solve. Look, Rachel, there's nothing else I can tell you, like you say, it's all there. He added Joanna to the policy, and I witnessed it. That's it. Not good news for you, I suppose, you've lost a substantial sum of money, but it's far less than what my daughter deserves.'

Rachel's voice was even. 'I don't begrudge Joanna the money.

If he'd discussed it with me, I'd have signed that form myself. He didn't need to come to you.'

Angela raised her head defiantly. 'So why did he then?'

Rachel sighed. 'Don't play games, Angela.'

'Maybe he wanted to see me … to … '

'Bit late for that, don't you think? Vince made his choice years ago. It's obvious I've wasted my time coming here.'

Angela looked as though she were about to make some retort and then stopped.

'Mum, if there's anything else you've not told me, I'd like to hear it. I don't care about Vince's money. If you want it, Rachel, you can have it. We can forget he ever amended that form. I've got along fine without it up till now.'

Rachel shook her head. 'He wanted you to have it, Joanna. I want you to have it.'

Angela gave Rachel a look, spread her hands and crossed the room to show that the meeting was over. 'There is nothing else,' she said. 'I've told you both everything.'

After Joanna had shown Rachel Arnold out, she rounded on her mother. 'Why all the lies, Mum?'

'Oh, please, Joanna, haven't we just had this conversation?'

'You could have told me though – about the insurance policy. As it happens, I already knew. Oliver told me.'

'Oliver?'

'The man I'm seeing, the one who found … '

'Yes, yes, I know, but what's he got to do with it?'

'Patrick Arnold asked him to take a look over the policy, to make sure there was nothing amiss, nothing that the insurance company could latch onto to get out of paying.'

'Patrick asked him?'

'Yeah, they know each other from years back … '

Angela nodded, but chewed her lip distractedly. 'Well, let's hope that will be an end to it,' she said. 'I'm sick of hearing about the whole thing.' She went to leave the room, but then turned when she'd reached the doorway. 'And, Joanna, I really would appreciate if you kept your distance from Rachel Arnold. She'd like nothing better than to make trouble between us.'

Joanna didn't answer. Her phone had started up again, vibrating silently in her pocket.

TWENTY-SEVEN

Oliver had phoned Joanna twice the night before but she still hadn't called him back. He'd texted her too, a quick 'everything okay?' message, but not a word in reply. He sat down at his desk and looked out at the traffic crawling along the quays and decided to try once more. Clearly, there was something up, probably related to the Arnolds.

The phone rang a number of times before he was greeted with a rather curt 'hello'.

'Hey. You're a hard woman to catch. Did you get my messages?'

There was a pause before she breathed 'yes' down the line. It was matter-of-fact and she didn't add anything to it. Something had changed in her tone. He didn't know what it was but, curious, he continued.

'I'm sorry I didn't have a chance to call before; things have been a bit crazy, but I was wondering if you'd like to meet for dinner tonight?'

'Tonight?'

'Yeah, if you're busy, we can do it another time … '

A pause. 'No – that's all right. What time?'

'Say seven o'clock? There's a nice little Italian place by the canal, Nona Valentina. Do you know it?'

'Sure.'

She wasn't exactly talkative, maybe she was in the middle of something. 'Is that okay then – seven o'clock?'

'Yeah, it's okay, I'll see you then.'

Sound of the dial tone as she hung up. Oliver looked at the phone, puzzled. Something must definitely have happened to put her in such a strange mood. She'd barely said a word. He wondered if she'd changed her mind. Maybe she'd decided he was too old. But they'd had a good time in Belfast, hadn't they? She couldn't have changed her mind as quick as all that. No, it was probably about Vince Arnold.

Oliver looked at his watch. It was coming on for five. There was still time to go home, shower and get changed. He picked up his keys, locked the office and made his way out to join the steady stream of people making their way home. Whatever it was that was bothering Joanna, he'd make her forget it.

Dressed in jeans, white shirt and a navy linen blazer, he entered the restaurant. He'd splashed on a good amount of the Prada cologne that Mercedes had bought him for Christmas, and the way that the waitress was smiling at him he figured that he must have made some impression.

'Table for two, please?'

He followed the Italian girl to a table by the window.

'You would like something to drink or you want to wait?' she asked.

'I'll wait, thank you.'

The girl inclined her head briefly and smiled, a dimple showing at the left corner of her dark red mouth. He watched her retreat, hips swaying hypnotically in her tight black skirt, and he couldn't help but think of Carmen Hernandez. She had the same sultry looks, dark hair curling to her shoulders.

Only two other tables in the restaurant were occupied: at one, two middle-aged women were deep in conversation, while at the other an elderly couple ate in silence, looking as if they'd run out of things to say some years before.

Oliver looked out the window. A man jogged past, breath streaming in the icy air as he made his way along the bank. It reminded him of the morning he'd found Vince Arnold's body, and he wondered if it was a good idea to have chosen somewhere so close to the scene. He hadn't really been thinking. It was close to home, and he hoped that Joanna would want to come back to the house with him after.

A few minutes later, he saw Joanna's red Peugeot pull into a parking space by the bank. She got out, wrapped her scarf tightly round her and hurried across the road, unaware of being watched. When she entered the restaurant a moment later, Oliver noted how serious she looked. She glanced around and, seeing him, she made her way across to the table. He stood up and kissed her on the cheek, but she didn't smile.

'It's good to see you. You look great,' he said.

She busied herself taking off her coat and scarf and draped them across the back of her chair.

'How've have you been?'

She shrugged. 'Oh, you know, busy.'

Just then the waitress appeared with menus and reiterated her offer of drinks.

'A bottle of house red, I think?' He looked at Joanna.

She nodded. 'Sure, that's fine.' She picked up the menu and began to scan it.

He had the feeling that she didn't want to meet his eyes, and he wondered again if she had changed her mind about seeing him. He decided to come straight to the point. 'You seem preoccupied. Is everything all right?'

'I don't know, is it? I was surprised when you called, I thought maybe your wife had come back.' Her tone was defiant.

'Mercedes … no. Why would you have thought that?' Suddenly he understood. She must have seen Carmen at the house. It would explain why she hadn't answered his calls, why she was acting so cold now. He leaned forward in his chair and looked directly at her. 'Okay, look, Mercedes did come by. She came over to pick up some of her things, but that's not why I didn't call you. I was busy with a case.'

'So you had a chance to talk then, sort things out?'

'We talked, yes, but that's all. Nothing's changed. We're not getting back together. In fact, Mercedes made it quite clear that that wasn't what she wanted.'

'Did she?'

Oliver leaned forward in his chair. Her attitude was beginning to irk him. He wondered exactly what she had seen. He'd prefer if she'd just come out and say it.

'You saw Mercedes at the house, didn't you? That's why you're being like this, but I assure you I was going to tell you. I invited you here for dinner, Joanna, because I wanted to see you. I'm not in the habit of spending time with people that mean nothing to me.'

'She called by for her things, nothing else?'

'I told you, that's it.'

'Funny, because I called by on Wednesday night and I saw her … Mercedes, she was standing by the fire, undressing. Did she leave you at all, Oliver, or did you think you'd just have a little fun while your wife was away on a trip. Is that it?'

'No … '

The waitress appeared with the wine, saving him from giving an immediate answer. Joanna stood.

'I'm not sure we'll be needing that,' she said, turning to the girl.

'It's okay, just put it here,' Oliver told her. 'Joanna, please, I can understand why you're upset, but just give me a minute to explain.'

She was still standing. 'Go on then.'

He tried to take her hand, but she pulled away. He glanced around the room. 'At least sit down for a minute.'

Reluctantly, she did so.

'You remember what it was like on Wednesday evening?'

'What do you mean?' Her eyes narrowed.

'Well, you were out in it, so I assume you remember it was raining?'

'Yes.'

'Mercedes had walked from the bus. She was soaked when she arrived, and I went upstairs to get her something to wear. She took off her wet clothes in front of the fire. But obviously you felt you'd seen enough at that point not to stick around to see what happened next.'

Joanna took a sip of wine. 'What – you expect me to believe that?'

Oliver spread his hands. 'It's true, Joanna. Nothing happened that night. She got changed, we talked and she collected some of her things. End of.'

Joanna didn't answer.

'Look, if you don't believe me, come back to the house right now and I'll show you. I was going to invite you back anyway – I'd hardly be doing that if my wife was at home now, would I?'

Joanna sighed. He could see that she wasn't sure whether to believe him or not.

'I'm not lying, Joanna. I swear. Nothing happened – in fact, nothing has happened between Mercedes and me for quite some time. But if you don't believe me, maybe it's best that we forget the whole thing.'

The waitress was watching them from behind the counter. She hadn't dared approach to take their order.

'I was sure you'd sorted things out,' Joanna said.

'Well, we didn't. How did you see anyway?'

'I heard voices and I looked through the window.'

'You looked through the window?'

She turned red. 'Yes.'

'And do you usually go around spying through people's windows?'

'No, look, can you blame me for being suspicious? There was a woman undressing in your living room.'

He shook his head. 'Which you wouldn't have seen had you not been snooping.' He could see she was on the point of getting up to go again, so he stood before she had a chance to do so. 'Look, there's no point in continuing this conversation. Either you choose to believe me or you don't. I'm not going to spend the evening arguing about it. Come back to the house with me now and we can settle this – or don't. I like you, Joanna, but I'm not about to beg.' He signalled to the waitress to pay for the wine. 'We'll take this with us,' he said, lifting the uncorked bottle.

Joanna put on her coat. 'Okay,' she said. 'Show me.'

He followed her out into the night.

TWENTY-EIGHT

When Joanna awoke, she found herself alone in Oliver Molloy's bed. She sat up, looked at her watch and found that it was just after nine o'clock. She thought of the events of the night before. She'd been unsure about going back to the house with him, but she'd wanted to see for herself that Mercedes had moved out. He'd led her upstairs as soon as they'd got in, flung open the wardrobe and asked her if she believed him. She did. Only a few items of Mercedes's clothing remained, but that didn't mean he hadn't slept with her that night.

They'd argued further. At one point he asked her to leave, but when she'd been about to oblige he asked her to rethink – said he was sorry that she'd misinterpreted what she'd seen and that he wanted her to stay. Finally, because he seemed so upset, she agreed. They'd spent most of the night making up for their argument.

Now, she got out of bed, pulled her clothes on, and opened the door to the landing. She peered through the banisters, but there was no sign of Oliver, only the drone of the radio. Leaving the door ajar so that she might hear his approach, she returned to the bedroom and opened the wardrobe. Just as she had seen the previous night, few hangers remained with Mercedes's things. They swung and clanged together when she disturbed them: a couple of blouses, a short silky skirt that had fallen or been flung on top of a row of shoes. Why had she not taken everything? An excuse, she wondered, to return again; the tie not entirely severed. Joanna stooped down to pick up a pair of red stilettos with peep-toes. The heels were newly repaired, and she sat on the side of the bed and slipped one on. It fit perfectly, but it was higher than she was used to wearing, and when she put on the other one and stood she wobbled slightly before the mirror.

She examined her reflection in the glass. The red shoes were beautiful, too stylish for her skinny jeans. She thought about Mercedes and the type of woman she was – the type of woman on whom red stilettos never looked overdone. Joanna pulled her auburn hair back from her face. She wondered if Oliver compared them, if he favoured his wife's sensual style to her more youthful simplicity. Mercedes had not left behind many possessions, only a hairbrush lay on top of the dresser, and yet her very essence seemed to linger in the room. Joanna picked up the brush, looked in the mirror that Mercedes must have looked in every day, and ran Oliver's wife's brush through her hair. With a sigh, she slipped off the red shoes, automatically threw the brush into her bag and wondered what it would be like to be the kind of woman who wore heels in the daytime.

Oliver looked up as she entered the kitchen. Seated at the table, he'd been reading the newspaper and drinking coffee.

'There you are. I have some coffee on,' he said. 'Can I make you some toast?'

'It's okay; finish your own. I'll get it myself,' she said.

'There's bread there. You'll find jam and cheese in the fridge, whichever you prefer. Or if you want there's cereal, but there isn't much milk.'

Joanna poured herself a coffee. She loaded two slices of bread into the toaster, and tried not to think about Oliver's wife and how she must have done this every morning while he drank his coffee.

'Have you classes today?' he asked.

'Not until the afternoon. I'll go home first, get showered and changed. And you – work?'

'Yeah, but I don't have to go in for another hour.' He smiled. 'We okay now?' he asked.

She nodded. She still didn't know if she believed that he and Mercedes had not slept together, but she certainly wouldn't be having breakfast with him if there was any likelihood that his wife might walk in. He must be sure that Mercedes was not about to turn up.

After breakfast, she left – breezed out, telling him to have a good day. She'd pull back a bit, take her mother's advice and not be so trusting. Besides, looking too eager never worked. She had to remind herself of that sometimes. She was too honest, didn't believe in playing foolish mind games, and she expected other people to be open too. Recent events had taught her not to trust anyone – not when the people closest to you were capable of such terrible lies.

It wasn't yet eleven o'clock when she got home. There wasn't a sound in the house. Her mother, she assumed, was still in bed; she was generally a late riser. Joanna made coffee and took it with her into the darkroom. She took the three trays and filled each with solution. The negatives were still hanging where she'd left them. Carefully, she took them down and slotted one into the enlarger, the one which held the image of Mercedes Hernandez. She adjusted the focus until it was clear, then set the timer, blocking sections of the image as it was burned onto the paper. As she lifted the image with the tongs and lowered it into the tray of developer, she thought about the money she would get from her father's life insurance policy. She'd meant it when she'd said that Rachel could keep it, but now that she knew Rachel wanted her to have it she began to entertain thoughts of what she could do with a sum of money like that. She swished the liquid in the tray, turned the picture with the tongs. She could put a deposit on an apartment with that money, although she knew that the bank wouldn't give her a mortgage until she started working. She swished the liquid and turned. With any luck she would secure a job in the not too distant future. The course was coming to an end in a matter of months and already she'd begun looking to see what sort of job she might apply for. After turning the paper a number of times, the image began to appear.

Joanna gazed into the solution, watched as the image of Mercedes developed slowly before her eyes. Dark hair, tangled to her shoulders, white blouse, short skirt – hands poised to undo the zip. Appalled and fascinated, she watched, an unwilling yet enthralled voyeur. She took the picture with the tongs, removed it from one tray and placed it in the next. She allowed it to soak for a further thirty seconds, and then placed it in the fixer tray. She had just done that when she heard a noise outside. It sounded like the hall door opening, probably her mother checking for post.

Joanna watched the clock. When enough time had elapsed she took the picture from the tray, washed it and placed it on the small mounting wall. She used a squeegee to remove the excess water from the print, and then stood looking at it for a moment. Mercedes made a striking figure. Joanna thought again what an interesting model she would make with her sultry Spanish looks. Beyond the darkroom, she heard her mother move about. She removed the latex gloves, binned them and followed the sounds to the kitchen.

Her mother was standing by the counter making coffee. Joanna was surprised to see that she had her coat on. Her bag was lying on the table too, as though she'd just come in.

'You're up and about early, aren't you? Did I just hear you come in?'

Her mother turned, surprised. 'Oh, I nipped down to the shops. We were just out of milk. Fancy a coffee?'

'No thanks, I had one already when I came in.' She didn't

mention that there had been plenty of milk then; enough anyway not to necessitate an urgent visit to the shops.

Her mother spooned coffee into the cafetière. 'Are you long in?'

Joanna shrugged. 'A while. I was just doing some test prints. I thought you were still in bed. I'm just going to go up to my room; I have a few things to get ready for college this afternoon.'

'Okay.' Angela took off her coat, sat down with a magazine and her coffee.

Joanna wondered as she climbed the stairs if her mother really had gone out to the shops earlier. Could she have been out all night, and if so, where? She glanced into her mother's room. The bed was made, everything immaculate. There was nothing unusual in that. Her mother always made the bed as soon as she got up.

Joanna went into the bathroom. She checked the shower, no droplets of water – her mother's towel was dry, and her toothbrush was conspicuously missing from the cup.

TWENTY-NINE

Oliver felt disgruntled about Joanna spying on him. He couldn't be sure that she believed his story about Mercedes only having returned for her things either. And if she thought there was something going on, there was every probability that she would go looking for proof. That was not the kind of person he could afford to have around him right now and that was a pity because he liked her. He'd surprised himself by getting upset at the thought of her walking out – but he hadn't been himself since the accident. There were times when he couldn't bear to be alone with his thoughts, and Joanna was a distraction from the Hernandez sisters and the mess he'd got himself into. He'd just have to be more careful in the future.

It had been two days since he'd heard from Carmen. Her silence made him wonder what she was up to. Could she have returned to Spain without having said anything? He doubted it. He thought of her last visit, her hand on his arm and her voice soft. 'We don't have to be enemies, Oliver.' What she'd said was right: at least, not overt ones. He didn't trust Carmen one bit, and with that in mind he decided to find out what was behind her silence.

The phone rang several times before she picked up.

'Carmen, it's Oliver. Are you at the hotel?'

A stifled yawn. 'No, I checked out. I'm at a flat.' Her voice groggy like she'd been asleep.

He paused for a beat. 'A flat?'

'Yes, a short-term let. It works out less expensive than the hotel.'

'I see. Well, I'm just phoning to see if you'd like to meet. I was thinking about what you said the other night, and well, you're right, we don't have to be enemies.'

Silence.

'Carmen, are you still there?'

A moan, another yawn. She was definitely in bed. He pictured her stretching like a cat.

'*Si*, I'm here,' she said. 'Where do you want to meet?'

He thought for a moment. He wanted to see where she was staying exactly and for how long. 'Well, if you give me the address, I could come over. Where are you?' He grabbed a pen as Carmen called out the address. 'I'll be about half an hour,' he said. Carmen, surprisingly uncommunicative, hung up. Maybe she wasn't well, he thought. She'd sounded very vague, or at least distracted.

The flat was on the third floor of a redbrick building close to the city centre. The entrance door was ajar and he let himself inside. He pressed the button and waited for the lift. A few minutes later, when there was no sound of it rattling its way towards the ground floor, he decided to take the stairs. He looked at the numbers on the doors of the flats. Down the hallway a door opened and a guy came out, shrugging into a leather jacket as he walked. His head dipped slightly in acknowledgement as he passed.

The numbers increased as Oliver continued along the corridor. He paused at the door from which the guy in the leather jacket had emerged. Number twenty, Carmen's flat. He tapped on the wood. There was the sound of shuffling inside. The door opened and Carmen ushered him into a narrow hallway. Through an open door he could see an unmade bed. Clothes lay scattered on the floor. Carmen hadn't wasted much time in making the place her own.

'Who was that?' Oliver asked.

'Who was what?'

'The guy I just saw leaving.'

Carmen smiled. 'Just a guy,' she said.

She sat at a small table by the window and tapped a cigarette from a tattered box. The air already smelled of cigarettes despite the 'no smoking' signs that he'd seen in the corridors of the building.

'To what do I owe this pleasure?' she said, as she flicked a lighter and held the flame to her cigarette.

'I thought I'd show you this. I forgot the other night at the house.' He clicked the Facebook app on his smartphone, opened up the message from Mercedes and handed it to Carmen. 'I don't suppose you've heard anything else?' he said.

She shook her head. 'Doesn't look like she'll come back any time soon, does it?' She blew smoke at the open window, drew her legs up to her chest. She was wearing tight blue jeans and a sweater that hung off one shoulder. She flicked her ash onto a saucer. 'I've been thinking. I should go to Belfast; maybe I can find her.'

This caught him by surprise. 'To Belfast? But you heard what she said; she doesn't want either of us to contact her. Besides, it would be impossible. How would you find out where she was staying?'

She held the phone out to him. 'I could make some calls,' she said. 'There can't be that many hotels in the city. If I could talk to her, maybe I could get her to listen.'

'You saw the message, Carmen. She doesn't want to listen. You'd be wasting your time.'

She stood up, drew on the cigarette and exhaled to the side. 'So what, that's it then? You're not even going to try? You give up so easily, you Irish men.'

She had one hand on her hip and was staring up at him intently. She reminded him so much in that moment of Mercedes. He shrugged, and tried to still the panic rising inside him.

'I can't force Mercedes to come back. Going after her like that would just drive her further away. You know her, she's stubborn. The only thing to do is give her time to cool off.'

'Well, you do what you want. I'm going to find her. Maybe you don't deserve her to come back if you give up so easily. Maybe I did you a favour making you a free man.'

'Don't be absurd.'

There was a fire in her voice that made him want her. It was the same fire that he'd seen in Mercedes. He wondered how and if he could get it under control. 'Look, Belfast is a big place. You'll probably never find her.'

'It doesn't matter; at least I'm doing something.'

Oliver wondered again about the guy in the leather jacket. Where had Carmen met him? The jealous feeling that gripped him at the idea of her with someone else surprised him.

He watched her flick the cigarette, sweater hanging provocatively off her tanned shoulder, and he thought of that night they'd spent together. It was the only night that he and Mercedes had been apart since they'd been married, and Carmen had been a willing substitute. Mercedes hadn't had any qualms about leaving her sister and husband alone together when she'd left that morning. She'd gone to Cork to attend a training seminar for work. It was only one day. Carmen had spent two weeks with them sleeping in the spare room, and he had to admit there were nights when Mercedes had turned away from him that he had thought about Carmen sleeping beyond the wall.

Carmen had been a different kind of lover to Mercedes. She had no inhibition. There was urgency in her mouth and hands that was exciting and, sometimes, painful. She'd teased him the next day about telling Mercedes, but when she returned they acted as normal – at least he thought they had. Mercedes asked him if they had argued. When he asked her why, she said that she'd detected tension between them, that he had answered Carmen sharply when she'd spoken to him that day. He said they'd had a minor disagreement, but that it was nothing to worry about. Carmen was just being her usual provocative self. He was relieved when, a few days later, Carmen had returned to Spain without having said anything about what had happened between them. He had no idea that several months later she would decide to tell her sister the truth.

He looked at Carmen now, determined to go to Belfast to find her sister. Had she lost interest in him since that night? Had she got what she wanted, a fait accompli? He changed his tone, determined to win this fight. 'Maybe I'm starting to accept the fact that Mercedes is not coming back,' he said.

Carmen exhaled, not bothering now to turn her head to the side; the smoke stung his eyes.

'And what will you do if she doesn't?' she said.

'Carry on, I guess. There's nothing else to do.'

Carmen stubbed the cigarette on the saucer. Her feet were bare, no bra strap showed beneath the sweater. He wondered if she'd dressed hurriedly as soon as the guy had left. Had she been pulling on her jeans as he'd knocked? He took a step closer, gave a short laugh.

'You know I admire your ferocity?'

He reached out and brushed a strand of hair from her face. She didn't flinch. Her eyes stared into his, but he couldn't read her expression.

'Do you think if it were the other way round Mercedes would look for you?'

'Of course she would. We're sisters.'

He wound the strand of hair around his finger. 'You weren't too eager for her to come back that weekend though, were you? I haven't forgotten, you know. In fact, I've thought about it a lot.'

Carmen put a hand up to stop him playing with her hair. 'What are you doing?'

'Nothing that we don't want,' he said, taking her hand and placing it to his lips.

He ran a thumb along her throat. She eased her head back and he caressed the nape of her neck. When he kissed her, her mouth was hot and tasted of cigarettes. He thought of the guy in the leather jacket and he wondered if she'd just had sex with him, but he didn't care. He wanted her. He wanted to feel the ferocity of her lovemaking that he'd felt that night. He pulled Carmen towards him and she yielded. Seconds later she was on top of him on the sofa, tugging at his belt. He put a hand on hers to stop her.

'The bedroom,' he said.

She stood, took his hand and led him to the room, where he pushed her down onto the already tangled sheets.

THIRTY

Joanna observed her mother closely over the next few days, but there was nothing unusual in her behaviour. If anything, she seemed warmer, more like herself than she had been since Rachel Arnold had dropped her bombshell that night. She was hiding something, of that Joanna was sure. There was the furtive phone call when she'd said she was talking to Pauline and then said it was Helen, the shopping trip that hadn't happened, and now the fact that she had stayed out all night. There was only one answer: she had met someone but didn't want to say.

Joanna could understand that. She knew how cautious her mother had been since her experience with Vince Arnold. It was evident from the advice she'd given her about Oliver that she didn't believe in rushing into things, so she wasn't about to go telling her prematurely about some man she'd met, particularly if it was early in the relationship.

She thought back. When had her mother's absence from the house become obvious? She had been busy herself for the last few months preparing for the photography exhibition, so she couldn't quite tell. She'd certainly been missing a lot in the two weeks since Rachel had turned up. And as far as she knew that was the first time her mother had stayed out all night. That must mean that things were getting serious.

Joanna was happy for her mother. She hadn't been involved with anyone since Vince Arnold, and now that Joanna knew the circumstances surrounding her birth she could see why. Her mother was still a young woman, fifty years old. She was in good shape and very attractive. Joanna used to think it amusing growing up, the attention her mother got from men. Angela usually curbed it with an icy stare that they would laugh about later. Even some of the boys from school had crushes on her.

She wondered where her mother had met this man. At the gym, maybe, or the amateur drama club she'd got involved in last year. She didn't act, didn't dare to, she said, but she enjoyed working backstage, helping with the set, or sometimes doing the line call. Whoever he was, Joanna prayed that he treated her well and that he knew how much her mother deserved it.

The photography exhibition was to take place at the end of the week. Joanna was mostly happy with her collection of Runaway Brides. She'd been toying with the idea of inviting Oliver, but she didn't want to call him; she was determined to wait until he contacted her. Hopefully, by that time it wouldn't be too late; for all she knew he might already have other plans.

That morning she was free. Her mother had already gone out, left her at the breakfast table eating toast, calling out that she'd see her later. Joanna decided to take a trip into town. She needed to pick up some materials in Evans Art Supplies, and she didn't feel like getting down to work straightaway.

She had picked up what she needed and was strolling back down Capel Street towards the quays when she saw her mother through a café window. She was still wearing her gym clothes, and her sports bag was at her feet, but that wasn't what interested Joanna: it was the dark-haired man sitting opposite her mother who looked vaguely familiar.

Joanna stopped walking in order to observe them, but there was nowhere really that she could stand without looking conspicuous, and she was terrified that her mother would look up and find her staring in at them. She crouched on the pavement and pretended to rummage in her bag for something as passers-by veered around her. Now that she had a better view of the man, she realized that it was Patrick Arnold. Shocked, Joanna continued to observe them. What was her mother doing drinking coffee with her father's brother? More to the point, she'd said she didn't know him. Another lie? It seemed there was no end to them.

People were beginning to look at Joanna. She couldn't search endlessly in her bag hunkered down on the pavement. She needed to make a decision. She could either go into the café, feigning surprise at meeting them, or she could wait until they came out – follow them and see what happened next. She got up slowly, glancing at the café window again, and crossed the street. She entered a bar on the corner of Capel Street, and took a seat that was close enough to the window to enable her to see the pair when they left the café. The waitress approached and asked her if she could get her anything. Joanna ordered a Coke and settled down to wait.

She thought about her mother and Patrick Arnold. Surely, he wasn't the one she'd become involved with. No, it couldn't be that. But what then, and why would her mother have pretended never to have met him? She thought of their body language when she'd spotted them through the window. Did they look close? She couldn't tell. Maybe she should have just marched in and asked them what they were doing, but they might not have told her the truth. She thought about what Oliver had told her about Patrick – struck off as a solicitor for committing fraud. Did her mother know that? And Rachel, his own sister-in-law, what was it that she had said – that he wasn't someone she would trust. Joanna truly hoped that her mother wasn't about to be burned by Vince Arnold's brother.

She'd been sitting in the bar for about fifteen minutes when she saw Patrick and her mother go by. Quickly she grabbed her bags and prepared to follow them. They were stopped by the traffic lights waiting to cross over to the Liffey. Joanna stopped to look in the window of a music shop until the pedestrian light turned green, and then, keeping a moderate distance behind, she followed them. They strolled down the boardwalk; Joanna stayed on the opposite side of the road, careful to keep them in sight. They walked apart, no hand beneath her mother's elbow, no arm round her shoulder. That at least was good. They walked the length of the boardwalk until they'd reached O'Connell Bridge and then crossed to the Southside. Joanna paused to examine the contents of a stall on the bridge, and then continued her pursuit. The pair turned left, continued along the quays, past the immigration office, and finally, turned right into Tara Street station. Joanna paused, trying to decide whether or not she should follow. She could do it, board a different carriage to see where they got off, but it might be difficult, and so she decided to leave it. She was glad she did because, a moment later, Patrick Arnold reappeared without her mother and began to walk back along the quays. Joanna turned her back to him as he passed and looked into the river. So, it was her mother who had taken the train, but where to? She didn't ever have reason to use the Dart as far as Joanna knew. She thought of the stations along the line: Howth to Greystones, north to south. Where was her mother bound?

Joanna turned and walked back towards the Luas stop in Abbey Street. As she walked she thought about the possible reasons why her mother might have met with Patrick. If it wasn't a relationship, then it had to be something to do with Vince. She thought of the insurance policy. It was Patrick who had approached Oliver to make sure that everything was in order with it. Her mother had signed the beneficiary form that Rachel had brought to the house. They were the only three who knew that Joanna had been made a beneficiary – that was until Rachel had found out. Joanna turned this over in her head, tried to match up the facts, but there were too few of them. Maybe Arnold was trying to get his hands on the money, but she couldn't see how her mother might aid in that. She and Rachel were the beneficiaries after all. Joanna was so preoccupied pondering the permutations that she didn't see the man standing just feet from her at the Luas stop.

'Joanna?'

She turned to find herself looking up into the face of Patrick Arnold.

THIRTY-ONE

When Oliver awoke, Carmen was standing by the bed sorting through some clothes and throwing things into a bag.

'Hey. What are you doing?' he said.

She didn't look up. 'I'm going to look for my sister. Are you coming?'

He sat up, swung his legs over the edge of the bed and picked up his jeans from the floor. 'I don't think that's a good idea.'

Carmen continued looking through the garments which lay in a pile at her feet. She picked up a skirt. One of his socks had become entangled in it and she pulled it free and threw it on the bed.

'Maybe you're right. It's better if I go alone. I have to talk to her. Maybe she won't listen, but at least I'll have seen her and know that she's all right.' She folded the skirt and put it in the bag.

Oliver pulled his clothes on. He put a hand on Carmen's shoulder but she ignored it, zipped up her bag and left the room.

He listened to her moving around the living room. She was feeling guilty about last night. He could tell by her brusque manner. He'd hoped that what had happened might change her mind about looking for Mercedes. If she had wanted to be with him so badly, wouldn't she be happy that Mercedes was no longer here? He wondered if he'd misjudged her. Maybe she had wanted to sleep with him again in order to vindicate why she'd done it to begin with, but instead it had served only as a reminder that they were the cause of what had happened. Either that or she'd found it a disappointment this time.

Oliver went into the bathroom and threw water on his face. Carmen was in the kitchen. He heard the surge from the tap and the water in the bathroom ran cold. He wondered what he could do to prevent Carmen from going to Belfast, but Belfast wasn't the problem. It didn't matter if she went there and returned without having found her sister. In fact, if she went away for a few days it would give him more time to think of a plan to end her search for Mercedes.

He walked into the living room. Carmen's sports bag was on the sofa. The aroma of freshly brewed coffee wafted from the tiny kitchen of the flat. He sat down at the table by the window and looked down at the grey street below.

'There's coffee if you want it,' she said.

He nodded. 'Sit down, I'll get it,' he told her.

She didn't object. She sat down with her cup of coffee, and he got up and went into the kitchen. When he returned she was sitting in the seat he'd vacated, staring out the window smoking a cigarette. It occurred to him that he had never seen Carmen not smoking, and he wondered briefly how many she went through a day.

'When are you leaving?' he asked.

'As soon as I'm finished.' She sipped her coffee and tapped her cigarette on the saucer that was already full of last night's ash.

'I'll give you a lift to the station if you want?'

She nodded. 'Thanks.'

The silence was palpable. He wished there were some way that he could dispel the tension in the room. 'If you find her, tell her I'm sorry,' he said.

'Do you think that will be enough?'

'No. But it's all I can say, isn't it?'

Carmen stood up. She drained her coffee cup, and pulled twice on the cigarette before stubbing it in the saucer. He drank his coffee hurriedly, as anxious now as she was to be out of the flat.

In the car she didn't speak. The traffic crawled along the quays until he branched off for Connolly Station. He was glad it wasn't far. This was a side of Carmen that he hadn't seen before, a seriousness that had always been hidden beneath her flirtatious façade. He didn't dislike it, but her need to be away from him made him feel uncomfortable. It was a good thing that she was going away.

He pulled up outside the station and they both got out of the car. He took Carmen's bag from the boot, and they stood there for a moment saying nothing.

'You'll give me a call if you find her?' he said.

Carmen nodded. 'I'll let you know.'

He kissed her awkwardly on the cheek. She turned away from him and made her way hurriedly towards the escalator that would take her up to the station. A moment later she'd disappeared through the double doors without looking back.

Oliver sighed and got back in the car. He wondered how long Carmen would spend in Belfast looking for her sister. He felt a mild sense of guilt, knowing that he was the cause of this fruitless trip, but there was nothing he could do about that. He just had to hope that Carmen would decide her search was futile and that she'd give up after a few days.

He turned the car and drove back towards the house. He hadn't been alone for days and he found himself looking forward to the stillness which he had dreaded in the initial weeks of Mercedes's absence.

The house was as he'd left it. The bag that he'd taken to Belfast still lay beneath the stairs. He carried it up to the bathroom. He caught sight of himself in the bathroom mirror. He hadn't shaved, and he wondered what the neighbours would have thought if they'd seen him. He wondered if they'd noticed Mercedes's absence by now, or whether they had mistaken Carmen for her sister. He took out his razor, filled the sink and lathered foam onto his skin. Carefully, he dragged the razor along his jaw, then dipped it in the water, and repeated the movement. He remembered Mercedes shaving him once. He'd been nervous and she'd laughed at him.

'What – you think I'm going to cut you?' she said.

He didn't. Not on purpose anyway, but if he had moved unexpectedly it would have been easy for the blade to nick his skin no matter how steady her hand. He had felt completely at her mercy. It was a feeling alien to him and he hadn't liked it. He knew that Mercedes had liked the intimacy of it, but it had made him feel vulnerable and it was the only time he'd allowed her to do it. If she were here now, he thought, she would gladly cut him.

He towelled off his face and went into the spare bedroom. He had thought about moving into this room so that he didn't have to think about Mercedes. He looked at the double bed. The sheets had not been changed since Carmen had stayed. He decided that he would strip the covers and move his things into this room. He couldn't escape the memories in the house, not unless he sold up and moved somewhere else. It was a thought that appealed to him, but he knew that it would look odd to those who thought that Mercedes had so recently left him.

The house had never been in Mercedes's name. That was one thing he was glad about. He had bought it before they'd met, and she had never raised the question. When the time came he could sell it without her signature on the contract. But not yet. He would wait until a respectable period of time had passed and then he would think about moving to a place where no one knew him, and he could try to start anew.

He noticed that the red light was flashing on the answering machine by the bed. Someone had phoned while he was in the shower. He threw the towel down and walked round to where the phone sat on the bedside table. He picked up the receiver and punched in the code. A woman's voice told him that she was leaving a message for Mercedes Hernandez. She was from a bookshop and wanted to inform Mercedes that the books she'd ordered had now arrived. She could collect them whenever it was convenient for her to do so. Oliver erased the message and sat there looking at the phone. He wondered, briefly, what books Mercedes had ordered. It must have taken a long time for the bookshop to get them in. Perhaps he would pick them up the next time he was passing.

THIRTY-TWO

'How have you been?'

He was taller than she'd remembered. His skin dark from his time abroad, making him stand out from the pasty white faces that crowded the Luas stop. Joanna mumbled something about not having recognized him, which he ignored while gesturing towards her bag.

'Doing some shopping?' he said.

His attitude was casual, familiar; less like someone she'd met once and whose brother hadn't deigned to acknowledge her existence, more like someone confident of his ability to beguile. Immediately, she raised her guard.

'I've an exhibition in a few days' time; I was picking up some materials.'

A jingle in the distance: the Luas crawled into focus and the crowd surged nearer the line. Was that his hand on her back gently conducting her towards the doors? Deftly, he guided her onto the tram. There weren't any seats, and she had no option but to stand close to him as the doors closed.

'So you paint then?'

'What?' She clutched her bag of materials, and planted her feet apart to prevent herself lurching forward as the bell rang and the Luas chugged into motion.

'An exhibition, you said, I assumed it was paintings?'

'Oh, no, photography; I'm doing a degree. It's just a college exhibition.'

Thoughts whirling round her head. What if she were to tell him she'd seen him with her mother – what would he say? He was looking at her keenly, interest in his green eyes. He was handsome, there was no denying that. She wondered if Vince Arnold had had his magnetism.

'Where do you study?'

Genuine interest? Maybe. If not, he was good at feigning it. The tram stopped, doors opened and more people got on. 'The IADT, Dun Laoghaire.' Scent of cologne; his or someone else's? No direct questions – not about her mother, not yet. She'd suddenly had an idea.

'Would you like to come?'

Patrick looked at her, surprised. 'What – to your exhibition?'

Joanna held his gaze. 'Sure, why not? If you're interested … '

He paused, thinking. 'When is it?' he said.

'Friday evening. From about seven.'

A slow nod of the head. 'Maybe so – I might have something on, but if not, I'd love to. Vince used to take pictures, you know. He was bloody good too. If you come by the house, you can take a look at some of his albums. Rachel's got dozens of them.'

'Yes, she mentioned it before.'

The idea had come to her suddenly. If Patrick came to the exhibition, he would meet her mother there. Would they pretend they didn't know each other? She'd refrain from the direct approach until then, plan her next step based on their reactions. If they lied, then they were definitely concealing something. She'd confront her mother about it there and then. Confront them both if it came down to it.

'Rachel came by the house the other evening,' she said. 'I didn't know I was a beneficiary to my father's life insurance policy.'

Patrick nodded. 'Yes. I should have told you about that when you came to the house that evening,' he said. 'I didn't get a chance, it was all, well – rather awkward, wasn't it? I figured then it could wait till after the inquest when everything's sorted out. I must say, Rachel was surprised.'

'I can imagine. She was nice about it though – when she came, said she wanted me to have it.'

Patrick smiled. 'And why wouldn't she be? I mean, it's not like you don't deserve it.'

Another stop, they shifted to allow a group of passengers to get off. Two seats became available and they sat. Her guard was coming down. He seemed a straight talker, her father's brother, or had he honed it – this ability to make you feel like he was on your side? Is that what he'd done with her mother – and if so, to what end? Joanna looked at him closely.

'So Rachel said you live in Italy. What do you do there?' she asked.

'I'm in real estate. We buy and sell houses, land.'

'*Guilty of fraud, something to do with a land deal* … ' Oliver's words resounded in her head, reminding her not to trust him. 'Oliver says you used to practise law.'

This took him by surprise. 'Oliver Molloy?'

Joanna felt the colour come to her face. Maybe she shouldn't have mentioned Oliver, but she wanted to see how he would react. It might concern him that she should know about his dodgy past. But he answered, unruffled.

'That's right. I studied with him at the King's Inns back in the day. Couldn't believe it when I heard he was the one discovered Vince. How did you meet Ollie – at the funeral, was it?'

'Ollie'? He made it sound as though they'd been friends. 'Yes, Rachel pointed him out to me – said he was the one that … '

Patrick gave a short laugh. 'And he offered a listening ear, did he?'

'How do you mean?'

He shook his head, still smiling. 'Ah, just that he was always a good one for that … with the girls, you know. He'd work his way into their confidence and then … ' He laughed again. 'That was Ollie for you. Mind you, I heard he married a right cracker – she wouldn't be much older than you. Where was it she was from again – South America? No, Spain maybe. Yeah, I think that was it, Spain. Stunning-looking girl – I saw pictures of the wedding. They're still together, I suppose?'

Joanna felt her cheeks burn again. 'I don't know,' she said. 'I don't think so.' She must have looked flustered.

He leaned in towards her, his face serious now. 'Well, I'd be careful there, Joanna. Oliver's a nice guy, but when it comes to women … well, let's just say, the less proximity, the better.'

Joanna was about to say that he was just a friend. But then, what was the point? For all she knew her mother may have already told Patrick about her recent involvement with Oliver. Though, judging from his reaction to his name, she didn't think so. She just nodded and, face flaming, thanked him for the advice. Patrick shifted in his seat.

'Well, the next stop's mine,' he said. 'I'm glad I bumped into you. You should come by the house – have a look at those albums.'

'Aren't you going back to Italy?' she asked.

He stood up. 'Not for a couple of weeks. There are a few things I need to take care of first … for Rachel.'

Joanna nodded. 'So, I might see you on Friday then – if you can make it.'

Patrick took his phone from his pocket. The Luas was slowing down, preparing to stop. 'You'd better give me your number,' he said. 'I'll call you beforehand, let you know if I can come.'

'Okay.'

Joanna called out her number – watched him punch it into the phone. The Luas stopped at Blackhorse Avenue. He got off, smiled and waved before it pulled off again, and Joanna waved back. She was annoyed with herself for having mentioned Oliver. She was sorry she'd said anything about it to her mother, too. She'd been hasty. Patrick had intimated that Oliver was a womanizer. It had raised her hackles – but what if he was right? She thought of her mother disappearing into Tara Street station, dressed for the gym but clearly bound for someplace else. Everyone seemed to be in the know but her. And talking to Patrick, rather than enlightening her had served only to make her more confused.

THIRTY-THREE

Oliver sighed and shifted position, moving a step closer to the fat American woman who'd been holding up the queue for at least ten minutes.

'Maybe it's Reid with double e instead of ie. I know it's something like that,' she said.

The assistant, ever-patient, frowned and pounded on the keyboard. 'No, I'm afraid there's nothing coming up on the system,' she said.

The fat woman sighed. 'Oh well, that's a shame. Also, I was wondering, do you have any books by James Joyce?'

Oliver coughed and attempted to make eye contact with the assistant. She ignored him.

'Yes, if you go to the ground floor and look in the Irish Fiction section you should find what you're looking for,' she said.

Finally, the woman picked up her shopping bags and turned away from the counter. One of the bags knocked against Oliver as she passed, but she didn't apologize.

'Some people,' he said, as he stepped forward.

The assistant smiled briefly, but didn't comment.

'I'm here to collect some books for my wife. She got a call to say they were in.'

'Okay, what's your wife's name?'

'Mercedes Hernandez.'

The assistant stooped under the counter and took out two books. He could see a yellow Post-it stuck to one. It had Mercedes's name on it.

'Would you like a bag for them?' she asked.

'That would be great. How much is that?'

The girl told him the price and he handed her the money. 'Do you happen to know when my wife ordered these books?'

'One second and I'll find out for you.'

The girl went back to the computer and typed something. Oliver waited, curious to see what books Mercedes had ordered. He assumed that they were from one of the obscure Spanish writers that she liked to read and that they'd had to be tracked down.

'Yes, she ordered them almost two weeks ago. Sometimes it takes a while to get them in. Do you want to check and make sure they're the ones she was looking for?'

'No, no that's okay. I'm sure they're fine. And it was definitely two weeks ago?'

'Yes. February nineteenth.'

Oliver nodded. The assistant handed him the bag. 'If there's anything wrong, tell your wife she can return them, it's no problem.'

Oh, but it is he thought as he hurried out of the shop.

As soon as he was outside, he took one of the books from the bag, *The Prisoner of Heaven* by Carlos Ruiz Zafon. That didn't surprise him, but Mercedes couldn't have ordered the books only two weeks before. There had to be a glitch in the computer system. It was odd, the girl had seemed so sure when she'd told him. He imagined Mercedes browsing the shelves, her fingers trailing along the spines of the books. She would falter at the letter 'R', and then, not finding what she was looking for, would continue her search until the letter 'Z' confirmed the absence of the coveted writer.

He considered returning to the shop, asking her to check again, but the assistant already seemed curious and he didn't want to attract unnecessary attention, so he pushed on. It was beginning to rain. People hurried along, raising their umbrellas as they walked. He made his way down Grafton Street and decided to cut through St Stephen's Green Park in order to get back to the car.

He was walking fast, swinging the paper bag with Mercedes's books, when he saw her. He faltered. Her back was to him, and she was throwing bits of bread from her bag to the waiting ducks at the edge of the pond. Her name caught in his throat and he wondered whether he should turn and go as fast as he could in the other direction, but then it was too late. Feeling his eyes on her, she turned, and he saw that it was not, of course, Mercedes but Carmen. She was wearing the clothes belonging to Mercedes that he'd given her the night she'd got caught in the rain. He tried to recover himself, hoping that she hadn't seen the look of shock on his face just as she'd turned. He'd never thought that he would confuse Carmen with Mercedes despite their similarities. He guessed that it was the fading light that had tricked him. That and the fact that he'd not anticipated coming upon her so unexpectedly.

'I didn't know you were back,' he said.

Carmen eyed the bag in his hand, and then continued to feed the ducks with the last of the bread. They gathered round her as she shook the crumbs to them. 'I got back this morning. I was going to call you.'

'Did you see her?'

'Yes.'

The silence hung between them. He was aware of Carmen's eyes studying his face. He searched for the right words to say, but she was first to break the silence.

'You look surprised.'

'Well, Belfast is a big place. How did you manage to find her?'

'It wasn't so hard. I checked out the hotels in the city, decided which ones she was likely to stay at and then phoned them. I found her at only the fourth one.' Carmen knelt and clicked her fingers. The ducks gathered round scrabbling for the bread that they thought she was about to feed them. When they realized she didn't have any they dispersed. She straightened and met his eye. 'So, aren't you even going to ask me what she said?'

Oliver kicked at the ground. He wasn't sure what it was that Carmen was playing at but instinct told him to go along with it. 'Did you tell her I was sorry?' he said.

'She wasn't interested, said she's moved on, that she doesn't need you.' Carmen tossed her head as if they were her own words. She'd put a colour in her hair, a burgundy hue in the black waves making it more like Mercedes's.

'Is that so?'

Oliver took a step closer to gauge her reaction. He leaned in, removed an imaginary leaf from her hair and flicked it aside. Carmen ignored his proximity. He couldn't help admire this new coolness. It was studied, planned, and she was getting the reaction that she wanted without realizing that she too was being lured. She had probably spent time alone in her hotel room devising this new strategy. That was if she had been alone. He wasn't sure why, but he had a fleeting memory of the guy in the leather jacket that he'd seen leaving Carmen's flat that day, and it caused him a moment of doubt. Still, he didn't believe that Carmen was indifferent towards him. He knew her too well, and would confirm it before the night had ended.

Carmen stamped her feet and blew on her hands. 'Let's walk,' she said. 'I'm freezing.'

They began to follow the path towards the exit. There didn't seem to be anyone else in the park, and he hoped that the gate-keeper had not, unwittingly, locked them in. He quickened his step, and Carmen matched his stride. The rain was starting to get heavier; large drops fell in the pond sending ripples round the ducks, making them bob on the water.

'So what else did Mercedes have to say?' he asked.

'She said she doesn't want anything from you. All that she wants is whatever belongs to her.'

Oliver nodded. 'She took most of her things when she left, but the rest I'll pack and send them on.'

Carmen shook her head. 'She doesn't have a long-term address, and you can't send them to the hotel. She hasn't decided what she's going to do yet. Maybe she'll stay here; maybe she'll go back to Spain. She wants you to withdraw the money from your joint account and send her what's hers.'

He hadn't been expecting that. 'That's fine. I'll write her a cheque,' he said.

'No, she wants cash.'

'Cash? How can I give her cash when she won't agree to meet me?' he said.

'She wants me to meet her with the money next week.'

Oliver laughed. 'What? So she'll meet you, but not me? The last time I checked we were in this together. Why has she suddenly forgiven you?'

Carmen shrugged. 'We're sisters.'

The gates were open. They paused outside, and Carmen told him that her bus was in the opposite direction.

'It's dark. I'll drive you home,' he said.

She didn't object, so he put his hand beneath her elbow and guided her in the direction of the car. He wondered when she'd decided to concoct this story. Had she really gone to Belfast and, if so, how much time had she spent searching for Mercedes? He didn't care about the money. Carmen could have it if she wanted, but was that her motive for telling him that Mercedes never wanted to see him again, or had she decided that Mercedes's absence yielded more benefits than her return? Whatever her reasons, Carmen's lies could serve as a worthy alibi if anyone started to question him about Mercedes's sudden disappearance.

THIRTY-FOUR

When Joanna arrived home, she took advantage of her mother's absence. If she'd been getting the train somewhere, then chances were she wouldn't be home for another hour, not even if she'd simply got off at the next station. Joanna dropped her things in the living room, took off her coat and went upstairs.

Her mother's room was immaculate as always. She went in, sat on the bed and wondered what it was she was looking for, and where she might be likely to find it. She began with one of the bedside tables where she knew her mother kept some old photo albums. She used to love looking through those photos when she was younger, but she hadn't looked at them in years and she wondered if she might have missed something – some pictures of Vince Arnold secreted among her mother's things. She turned the pages. There were family snaps. Her mother pictured with a baby in her arms, Joanna's grandmother in the background. Her grandfather had taken that shot only days after Angela had taken Joanna home from the hospital. They'd been very supportive, her mother had told her, not once suggesting that she give the baby up. Joanna looked at those pictures of her grandparents now and wondered how much they knew about her conception. Had her mother confided in them about Vince

Arnold? She doubted it. Doubted that her grandfather would have let him away with it if he'd known who he was.

There were other pictures. Joanna's mother as a teenager, arm looped through a friend's, hair backcombed, lips ice pink. More of them making faces in a photo booth. Joanna had always loved these shots – the seventies hairstyles, big collar blouses and flares. She knew who most of the people were. Her mother had often told her about her friends and the antics they got up to. It was just a pity she hadn't told her the most important thing: that she'd felt she had to cover it up, bury it in the past. Several minutes and many photos later, Joanna had reached the end of her mother's albums. No pictures of him, no mementos hidden away, at least not there. She piled the albums back into the drawer where she'd found them.

Next she opened the wardrobe. There was a shoebox there where her mother kept important documents. She knew because when she'd asked her mother for her birth certificate a few years before, when she was applying for a passport, she'd gone to the wardrobe and taken it down. Joanna felt like a snoop searching among her mother's private things. She still didn't know what it was that she hoped to find – nothing, perhaps. Assurance that there were no more surprises waiting to ambush her. She looked through the papers in the box, her grandparents' birth and death certificates, her mother's and her own birth certificates, cards congratulating her mother on the birth of her baby girl, none from Vince, of course, and the deeds to the house they lived in: the house her mother had inherited from her parents, that she would inherit from her mother. Birthday cards, Christmas cards, tickets to concerts ... nothing that told her anything she didn't know about her family.

An hour passed. She didn't want her mother to find her rummaging in her room. The real question was not something that was going to be solved by looking through memorabilia. She took the box and climbed on the stool again to put it back on the shelf, but her foot caught on the rung as she did so and she tripped, the contents of the box spilling onto the floor. Shit. She got down to retrieve the papers scattered at her feet. She gathered the certificates, the documents. She hadn't looked through it all and her hand alighted now on a picture – her mother at a beach wearing a striped swimsuit. Joanna looked closer, Portmarnock was it? Sand dunes in the background, or maybe Brittas Bay. A natural shot, the girl, laughing, leaning to the side, hands supporting her in the sand. She turned it over – 'Angie, 1983'. Joanna gathered and straightened more papers, saw another picture and turned it over. It had been taken on the same day, only in this one a boy lolled on the beach next to her mother. Joanna peered at the shot. The boy was an adolescent – no more than fifteen. A cousin maybe? They were smiling like they'd just shared a joke, except he was looking straight into the camera. Green eyes, short hair, fringe sticking up, pushed to the side. Joanna gripped the photo as realization slowly set in. She turned over the shot – more writing in pencil – her mother's hand. 'With P.A. Brittas Bay. 1983.' Christ. She turned it over, stared at it again. Patrick Arnold. 1983. Old friends, why hadn't her mother said? And the photographer, the eye behind the lens, Vince? These were shots that wouldn't be found among the albums at Rachel Arnold's. Joanna searched for more, but there were none. She placed everything back in the box and, carefully this time, put it back in the wardrobe.

This changed everything. Her mother's association with Patrick was not something that had materialized on the death of Vince. Their meeting might have nothing to do with that, could simply be a revival of an old friendship, or could it? Joanna thought about the young Patrick Arnold in the photograph. Where did he fit in the grand picture? Had he been a willing accomplice to his brother's deceit – a decoy maybe? He was younger than her mother. He'd studied with Oliver – so that would make him what – forty-two? Not such a gap now. Had his sudden appearance awakened in her mother the feelings she'd felt for Vince? It wouldn't be uncommon to transfer these emotions to the brother she'd known since her youth.

Joanna was still puzzling over the situation when she heard her mother come in.

'Jo, are you here?'

'Yep.'

She came out of her room to see her mother coming up the stairs, gym bag in hand. She looked ruffled, face pink from exertion. Maybe she'd just power-walked from the bus stop. She dropped the bag in her bedroom, and stretched.

'I'm just going to hit the shower,' she said. 'Did you get much work done?'

'Not really, I had to go into town to pick some stuff up.'

No reaction.

'Well, never mind, you have the rest of the evening, haven't you? I picked up something nice for dinner by the way.' She sounded cheerful.

Whatever the reason she'd met Patrick Arnold, it had obviously gone well. Her mother went into the bathroom and closed the door behind her. A few minutes later, Joanna heard the shower. Quickly, she went into her mother's room. The gym bag was where Angela had left it. Joanna hunkered down, unzipped it and looked inside. There were clothes in the bag, not gym clothes, but good clothes, clothes she might wear going to meet someone, although she'd still been in her sportswear when Joanna had seen her with Patrick. Maybe she hadn't had time to change. She rummaged beneath the clothes, searching for anything strange, anything that might suggest why her mother had met Patrick Arnold. Deodorant, change of underwear, nothing she wouldn't have expected to find in a gym bag. Sometimes her mother showered there before she came home. She unzipped a small pocket inside the bag. Now there *was* something strange; her mother's old mobile phone, and what's more it was switched on and appeared to be working. Just then Joanna realized that the shower had stopped. She put the phone back in her mother's bag, zipped it up and sneaked out of the room just before the door opened and her mother emerged wrapped in a towel.

THIRTY-FIVE

Oliver sat on the edge of the bed and watched Carmen sleeping. She looked different when she was sleeping. Her face lost some of its fierceness and, bereft of make-up, she looked almost innocent. He stood up and eased his clothes on. He heard her breathing change and, for a moment, he thought she might wake, but she settled again, and he stole quietly from the room.

They hadn't pulled the curtains in the living room, and the greyness of the winter sky seeped through the net curtain and emphasized the starkness of the flat. He stood looking out the window at the jackdaws that picked at the fast-food wrappers in the street, and he wondered how long Carmen would stay in this place.

In the kitchen he made coffee and thought about Carmen's motive for having said she'd met Mercedes. What could she want the money for – and wasn't she taking a risk stealing her sister's money? But maybe it wasn't about the money; maybe her revelation had been intended to shock him into some kind of confession, to catch him unaware. How would she have reacted if he had just blurted it out, if he'd told her that she couldn't have seen Mercedes, that it was impossible? He had been close to it. He'd had to will himself not to speak. It struck him that Carmen might not be shocked. She was a woman capable of unscrupulous acts, but none as horrifying as murder. There were times when the weight of what he'd done became so intolerable that he thought he couldn't continue. He told himself over and again that it had been an accident. He repeated it until his instinct for self-preservation kicked in and propelled him forward, and he knew that he had no choice but to go on.

'I didn't hear you get up.'

Oliver jumped at the sound of Carmen's voice in the doorway. 'I didn't want to wake you,' he said.

She was in her dressing gown, hair tousled, her face clean of make-up. It occurred to him again how young she looked, so different from the dark-eyed, red-lipped temptress she liked to paint herself as.

'Go on, sit down and I'll get you a coffee,' he said.

She smiled and sauntered back to the living room. When he entered with the coffee she was sitting at the table by the window, and she'd taken one of the books from the paper bag that he'd left there without thinking.

'You picked up my books,' she said.

He placed the coffee carefully before her. 'The book shop phoned; they said they were for Mercedes.'

She nodded. 'I ordered them. When they asked me my name they found Hernandez on the system and asked me if I were Mercedes. It was easier to say yes; she had an account set up already. I hate all that red tape.'

Oliver had often ordered books from that store. He knew that you didn't have to set up any account. You simply supplied them with your name and telephone number, and they called you when the books came in, but he said nothing. Maybe masquerading as Mercedes gave Carmen some sense of worth, of satisfaction. Mercedes had always claimed that Carmen had been envious of her. He eyed her across the table. She had already opened the book on the first page and was reading. She closed it a minute later and held it up so that he could see the cover.

'I love this writer,' she said. 'He's so passionate. His words are like music.'

He thought of Mercedes, the nights that she had sat up late in bed reading and he'd complained about the lamp keeping him from getting to sleep. He'd bought her a reading torch, but she didn't use it. She said she didn't want to strain her eyes by reading in the dull light.

Carmen put the book on the table. 'Would you like some toast?' she said.

'Sure. I thought maybe you hadn't had time to get anything in since you came back.'

'I hadn't, just bread.'

She got up. He watched her move across the room. Her legs were bare beneath her short dressing gown. On her feet she wore pink furry slippers, the kind that Mercedes used to wear. He listened to her move about the tiny kitchen, and he wondered if this was what she had wanted – the two of them having breakfast like any couple.

She emerged a few minutes later with a tray of toast with jam and butter. The smell filled the room and reminded him of other winter mornings. Carmen sat opposite him. He looked at her and wondered: if he'd met Carmen rather than Mercedes on the train that day, would he have asked for her number instead? Something told him that he would have, but she would still have led him to Mercedes. The link between them could not be severed. The choices that he made would still have been the same, but perhaps it would have ended differently.

He looked at Carmen buttering toast opposite him. He ought to hate her. If it hadn't been for her, none of it would have happened. Mercedes would still be alive and they would be living as they had been, but as that thought crossed his mind, so too did the reality of what things had been like between he and Mercedes in the months leading up to that night. He remembered her coldness. How she'd moved away from him when he'd attempted to touch her. He'd given up out of pride. They were like strangers, only they lacked the chemistry that could exist between strangers – the curiosity about the unknown. No, if it hadn't been Carmen, it would have been someone else. Mercedes didn't deserve what had happened, but she wasn't blameless either.

'So, when will you see Mercedes?' he asked.

'Next week, whenever you have the money,' she said.

Oliver nodded. 'I should be able to get it for you tomorrow. We signed some cheques in advance so I don't need her signature on anything.'

'She doesn't want a cheque. She specified cash,' she said.

'It's twelve thousand euro, Carmen. You're hardly going to get the train to Belfast with twelve thousand euro in your back pocket now, are you?'

'It'll look strange though, no? Why would Mercedes make a cheque out to herself?'

'True. And I suppose she doesn't want any trouble cashing it. I'll tell you what – I'll make the cheque out to you. That way you can give her the money and there won't be any questions asked.'

Carmen nodded and bit into her toast. She didn't question his readiness to write the cheque, and he wondered again what the money was for. He figured it was something specific, that she hadn't just decided to rob her sister of her savings without good reason. Again he contemplated the possibility that she suspected the truth; that she knew that Mercedes was unlikely to turn up demanding to know where her twelve thousand euro had gone.

Carmen stood up to clean away their plates. When she spoke her voice was bright. 'Why don't I cook for you tonight?' she said. 'Paella, you like that, right?'

'Sure, I love it.'

'It's probably better if I make it at your place. This kitchen, it's impossible to do anything. There's no space.' She waved her hand in the direction of the kitchen. Her dressing gown fell slightly open. He wanted to reach over and tear it from her.

Instead he tried to concentrate on her words. He also thought of Joanna. He hadn't called her in the last few days. A part of him thought that he ought to let it fizzle, that it probably couldn't go anywhere and he didn't want to hurt her, but then neither could his tryst with Carmen, could it? That Joanna had mistaken Carmen for Mercedes was still vital should Mercedes be reported missing. For now, he had no choice but to keep both women on side.

'I have to go into the office today, not sure how late I'll get away. In fact, I ought to get moving, there are some things that I need to pick up from the house. How about we do dinner another night – Friday maybe?'

Carmen nodded. 'Okay. I'll hold you to that.'

Oliver stood up. Carmen walked with him to the door. Outside in the hallway another door slammed and someone shuffled past, a dark shape beyond the frosted glass.

'You ought to put a blind up there. People can see you moving about.'

He put his hands beneath her dressing gown, pushed it back until the belt loosened and she stood naked before him. She moved towards him, but he stopped her. He wanted to look at her. He put his hands under her full breasts and caressed them. Carmen moved towards him again and this time he let her. Her breath was hot, her tongue probed and circled his, toying with him. He breathed hard. She raised one leg and hooked it round him, pulling him closer. They were standing in the hallway still. He unzipped his jeans. He couldn't bear it. He stumbled, slammed her against the wall a little harder than he'd intended, but she didn't say anything. She was clawing at him, her hands beneath his shirt. She said something in Spanish, raised her legs so that they circled him and she cried out, her nails digging into this flesh as he pushed harder against her, only semi-aware of the pain.

175

She was waiting for him when he emerged from the bathroom.

'So, I'll see you on Friday then,' she said.

He kissed her and this time pulled her gown around her. She laughed. He didn't know what it was she was up to but he would enjoy it, and her objective would become clear in time.

He whistled as he walked down the hallway. He wondered if they'd been heard. He'd never lived in a flat and was surprised by the proximity in which people lived. You couldn't do anything in such a place without being seen or heard. No doubt Carmen was already an object of some curiosity among the tenants. He didn't like to think about the kind of looks she'd attract from the men, particularly from the kind of men that lived there. He must warn her to bolt her door at night.

THIRTY-SIX

Oliver had called Joanna the night before the exhibition. It had been three days since she'd spoken to him and she'd begun to think that maybe she wouldn't hear from him again. Her heart sped up when she saw his name flash on the screen, despite her reservations. He told her he was really sorry; he'd got tied up with a case and had been in the office until ten every night trying to prepare his files. She couldn't help but remember Patrick Arnold's words when they'd met on the Luas – but Oliver accepted her invitation to the exhibition, saying he'd be delighted to come along.

Now Joanna stood by her photos on the lookout for both men and her mother. Already the room was thronging. Most of the people were friends and relatives of the students, but there were others, too, who had seen the exhibition advertised and had wandered in from the street. It was an exhilarating and unnerving experience to move among the crowd and listen to their comments.

Next to her, one of the other students, Karl, was discussing his photos with two bohemian-looking girls who she'd seen around the college and believed were art students. They were hanging on to his explanations – and she wondered if it was the pictures or Karl that they were interested in. Whatever the attraction she knew their type – pretentious to the core. But he seemed to be enjoying the attention, and she turned away to check the door again, wondering, tensely, who would show up first.

She was walking around the room looking at the other students' collections while occasionally glancing at the door when she saw Patrick come in. She was surprised and a little taken aback to see Rachel Arnold with him. How would her mother react to Rachel's being there? She wondered that Patrick hadn't considered that. Or maybe he had. Maybe he had some kind of agenda in bringing the two women together.

They stood looking around the room, and rather than going to meet them Joanna made her way back to where her photos were mounted, observing them until they had noticed her. Rachel raised a hand in greeting and touched Patrick's elbow.

'Hi Joanna. I hope you don't mind my coming along. Patrick mentioned it, and I really wanted to see your pictures. Wow.' Rachel stepped closer to the display and studied the photographs in detail. 'They're wonderful. I love the atmosphere, the contrast between the bride and the graffiti in the street ... and the light in this one ... ' She pointed to the shot of the bride in the window. 'Her face, it's so full of yearning.'

When Joanna glanced at Patrick, she found him looking towards the door. Checking to see if her mother had arrived? When he looked up and found her watching him, he smiled and shrugged as if to say what can you do?

'Did it take you long to put the collection together?'

Joanna turned back to Rachel. 'I've been working on it since the beginning of the semester. I took literally hundreds of pictures. It was a matter of picking out the right ones.'

Rachel nodded. 'You've a real talent,' she said. 'Just like Vince. You really must come over to the house to see his albums.'

'Yes, I was telling her that,' said Patrick. Another glance towards the door. As if reading her mind, Rachel looked around the room.

'Is your mother here?' she said. 'She probably won't be happy if she sees me.'

'Not yet, but she should be along soon.'

Joanna looked at Patrick. No reaction. Why had he brought Rachel? Didn't he know it would annoy her mother to find her here? And besides, she'd probably think that she, Joanna, had invited her.

Rachel looked at Patrick. 'Maybe we'll just go and take a look at a few of the others before we leave?'

'No need to rush, is there?' Patrick said. Was he enjoying this – the potentially explosive scene that might unfold at the meeting of Vince's two women? If they left, of course, it would be worse. Joanna wouldn't get to witness how Patrick and Angela related to each other.

'That's right. Look, don't worry about Mum. She's always late; probably won't get here for another hour at least. There's wine and a few nibbles over there. Take a look around.'

Patrick smiled. 'Wine? Of course. What? – Did you think I'd come to see your pictures?'

That over-familiarity again.

Rachel nodded. 'If you're sure it's not a problem.'

'No, no problem.' Joanna watched as they made their way to where the wine was being served.

They had just left when Oliver came in. He looked around the crowded room. Joanna stood on tiptoe and waved to try to get his attention, but he didn't see her. She pushed her way through the crowd, circled round and crept up behind him.

'Ah, there you are. It's a good turn out,' he said. Joanna couldn't help smiling. 'Where are these famous pictures?' he said. 'It is the arty self-portraits portfolio you're exhibiting, isn't it?'

Joanna punched him in the arm. 'Of course. They don't call it an exhibition for nothing.'

She led him through the crowd to where her section of the exhibition was.

'Look – I really want to apologize. I had meant to contact you,

you know. You must have been annoyed?' He gave her a sheepish look designed to disarm her and it did.

Joanna shrugged. 'To tell you the truth, I haven't had much time to notice. I've been up to my eyes getting this lot ready.' *To tell you the truth. With all due respect.* How many other expressions meant the direct opposite?

He stepped back to look at the pictures. 'They look even better now that I see them like this. You must be very proud.'

Just then Joanna saw her mother come in. She hadn't had time to warn Oliver that she'd be there, nor had she had a chance to tell him that his old friend, Patrick Arnold, was there too. She put her hand on his arm. 'Listen, my mum is here. I hope that doesn't make you uncomfortable ... she knows about you, that we're friends ... '

'Ollie, what brings you here?'

Before Joanna could finish, Patrick had come from the opposite direction of her mother and slapped Oliver on the back. He turned, surprised.

'What do you think of our Joanna here? Talented young woman, isn't she? Of course, I believe you two have become friends.'

Joanna felt her face burn at Patrick's words. What else was he likely to say, to insinuate? She did a quick scan of the room. She couldn't see either Rachel Arnold or her mother. At what point were the two women likely to converge on the gathering?

'Where's Rachel?' she asked, to save Oliver from having to answer. Patrick waved a hand.

'Not sure. She went to the ladies; I'm sure she'll find us.'

'Not due back in Italy yet?' Oliver asked.

'No, I've a few bits of business to look after here first. Maybe we'll find time for a beer before I go back. We didn't really get to catch up properly, did we?'

'Maybe. I'm so busy these days, I've had to let a lot of things slide.'

'All work and no play, Ollie … we can't have that. The wife must never see you. Lovely girl, I heard – Spanish, is she?'

Oliver nodded, evasively. He wasn't about to tell Patrick Arnold his business. Still, he could have mentioned that they'd separated, not made Joanna feel like the woman on the side.

Just then, to Joanna's relief, Rachel appeared.

'You remember Oliver Molloy,' Patrick said.

Rachel looked surprised. 'Y … yes. Have you some interest in photography, Oliver?'

An awkward silence. 'Not exactly. Joanna invited me; I thought I'd take a look.'

'Oh, I wasn't aware that you knew each other. It really is a small world.' Rachel looked at Joanna, curious.

'We don't, well, didn't. Oliver showed me the spot where Vince's body was found.'

'Oh.'

Silence at the mention of his name. Patrick stood by looking amused at everyone's discomfort.

Oliver looked at his watch. 'I'd better be going,' he said.

But before he had a chance to do so, Joanna's mother appeared.

'Well, isn't this quite the party,' she said. 'Rachel, I certainly didn't expect to see you here.'

Joanna looked at Patrick, but his expression was unreadable. Rachel had coloured slightly.

'I expect not, but Patrick mentioned it and well … I thought it would be interesting to see Joanna's photos.'

Joanna felt sorry for Rachel; if anyone was innocent here, it was she. Patrick Arnold and her mother had failed to even look at each other. Joanna decided it was time to intervene.

'Oh, I'm sorry – you two haven't met before, have you? Mum, this is Patrick – Vince's brother.' She watched as her mother held out her hand stiffly.

'Angela,' she said.

'Of course,' Patrick took her hand, squeezing it briefly.

No admission of any prior acquaintance. If Rachel hadn't been there, she'd have called them on it right then, but she figured the woman didn't need to be embroiled in this particular showdown. And then there was Oliver.

'I'm sorry, but I really should get going,' he said.

Rachel looked slightly panicked. 'So should we, in fact.' She glanced at Patrick, and left her glass of wine, almost untouched, on a nearby table.

Patrick caught her mother's eye. 'That's a very talented young lady,' he said. 'You must be proud.'

Angela nodded, and put her arm around Joanna. 'She certainly is.' She looked defiantly at Rachel who refused to meet her stare.

'Thanks for asking me, Joanna. Great pictures,' Oliver said.

'Give me a second, I'll walk you out. Mum, there's wine and snacks if you want to get yourself something. I'll be back in a second.'

'Yes, we'll be going too,' said Rachel, desperate, Joanna thought, not to be left alone with her mother.

Patrick and Rachel walked ahead, then Oliver, with Joanna bringing up the rear.

Outside, a few smokers were congregated around the doorway. They said goodbye to the Arnolds and then walked in the opposite way.

'God, I'm so sorry about that,' Joanna said. 'Talk about awkward. I didn't know Rachel was coming; my mother's face when she saw her. And Patrick … is there some history between you two? He seems, I don't know … a bit … ' She cast around for the right word. 'It's like he's set on embarrassing you or something. But maybe he's like that with everyone?'

Oliver looked away. 'We've never exactly been friends. A few of the guys I knew were friendly with him, that's about it. I don't know where he gets off with the whole Ollie thing. My friends don't even call me that. Like you said, I think he likes to set people on edge.'

'They know each other.'

'Who?

'My mother and Patrick. I found a picture from years ago – and then a few days ago I saw them together in a café.'

'Is that unusual?'

'It is when both of them claim never to have met.'

Oliver looked thoughtful. 'Hmm, that is odd.' He looked at his watch again. 'Look, I'm really sorry, Joanna, but I honestly have to rush off; I've another few hours to do in the office. I don't suppose you're free tomorrow night?'

'I might be, why?'

He grinned. 'I thought you might like to come over; we could order in, watch a movie, see what happens? You can tell me what's been going on with the Arnolds.'

Joanna nodded. 'Sounds good. What time?'

'Say seven?'

He looked around to see if anybody was watching and then gave her a quick kiss on the cheek.

Joanna stood for a minute and watched him leave. Then she turned to go back inside and face her mother.

THIRTY-SEVEN

Oliver left the exhibition and hurried to the Dart station. In little over an hour Carmen Hernandez was to arrive. He checked his briefcase to ensure that he had the chequebook for his and Mercedes's joint account. There were two cheques remaining that bore her signature. He'd write a cheque to Carmen for twelve thousand euro, and backdate it to the day before he'd booked the Eurolines ticket. If she asked any questions, he'd tell her the date had already been written, that he'd started writing a cheque for something else. It was no big deal anyway; it would have no bearing on her cashing it. He still wondered what had inspired Carmen to ask for the money. It was a risk. How did she know that Mercedes would not contact him for that exact reason? Either she needed it badly or she didn't care what Mercedes thought anymore. He hoped it was the latter; it might stop her looking for her sister. On a whim he stopped off at a supermarket and bought chocolates for Carmen, as well as an expensive bottle of wine.

It was after seven o'clock when she arrived weighed down with bags.

'I had to go to two different supermarkets to find what I needed,' she told him. She went straight to the kitchen and emptied the food out on the counter.

He had a fleeting image of Mercedes doing the same thing and tried to erase it from his mind.

'I guess you know where to find everything?' he said.

Carmen shook her head. 'You can show me. You know how to make paella, no?'

'Me? No, I'm not much of a cook actually.'

Carmen raised an eyebrow. 'Five years living with a Spanish girl and you don't know how to make paella? So today you will learn. You can be my assistant, and next time you can make it for me.'

'Won't I be in the way?'

'Uh-uh.'

Carmen had been taking out cutting boards and knives as they talked. She spread the ingredients on the countertop, unwrapped three breasts of chicken and began to cut one into thin slices.

Oliver spread his hands and laughed. 'So, what do I do?'

'First you cut the chicken like this.' She indicated the slices that she'd already cut and gave him the knife.

He began to cut. 'Okay?' he said.

'Perfect.'

Carmen had taken a sharp knife and began to busy herself chopping tomatoes. He watched as she worked. Her hands were small. A gold bracelet glinted on her right wrist, and he wondered if it were a gift from a man. He didn't doubt that she had her admirers. She caught him looking at her and smiled.

'Okay. Now heat some oil in the pan. When it's hot, you start to fry the chicken.'

He had to admit he was enjoying himself. Mercedes had always cooked for him, but she had never asked him to help. When he'd gone into the kitchen when she was cooking, she'd chased him out, and he'd gone willingly. Carmen seemed at home in the kitchen. She was in command, and he guessed that was how she liked it. He'd begun to realize that he didn't know Carmen at all. He wasn't fooling himself. He knew that she was treacherous and that to get on the wrong side of her was a bad idea, but he figured there were many things that he didn't know about her. She was volatile and it was because of this that she excited him as no other woman had.

The chicken sizzled in the pan. He stirred it once. Carmen was arranging vegetables on a plate. He put his hands on her waist and kissed her neck. She laughed and pointed her knife at the sizzling pan.

'The chicken will burn,' she said.

'Let it.'

Oliver lifted her skirt and caressed her silky skin. She groaned and pushed his hands away. When he did it again she picked up the knife and pointed it at him, laughing. He wondered for an instant if she'd use it. Something told him that, in the right circumstances, she might.

They stood like that for a moment, and then Carmen let the knife fall. It clattered on the tiles beneath their feet shattering the spell. She put her arms around his neck and kissed him. When he lifted her, she said something about the food burning, and he reached out blindly to remove the frying pan from the hob before carrying her to the kitchen table.

Carmen curled her legs round him. He took her wrists and pushed her away so that she was lying flat on the table and then he ran his hands along her body. He unbuttoned her blouse. And with trembling hands he tore at the last few buttons that wouldn't come undone. She was lying on the table-top as he pushed his way inside her. He heard Carmen gasp and he pushed further still. She attempted to move, to manoeuvre herself into an upright position, but he didn't want her to. He was in control, not her. He thrust harder. Carmen cried out, and he wasn't sure if he'd hurt her and he didn't care. In all his years with Mercedes it had never been like that. Sex was contained to the bedroom. It wasn't something spontaneous – something rough. He withdrew almost guiltily when he was done. He glanced at Carmen's face, half-afraid of what he might see there, but she was laughing. She was laughing so hard that she couldn't sit upright. He helped her up and kissed her, still slightly guilty about how rough he'd been, but Carmen could take it. She was the antithesis of her sister.

Carmen buttoned up her blouse and finished cooking the paella. Oliver opened the bottle of wine he'd bought, poured two glasses, sat in his armchair and waited.

In the kitchen he could hear Carmen singing softly as she cooked. He took his briefcase from where he'd left it on the floor, snapped the locks open and took out his chequebook. He tore out the cheque that he'd made out to Carmen, folded it and put it in his shirt pocket. He would give it to her when they'd eaten. After that, it was up to her what she did with the money. He didn't care.

He looked up as Carmen entered with the food and, for a moment, her resemblance to Mercedes froze the smile on his face. What would she think, he wondered, if she knew what he'd done? Would she understand that it had been an accident – that he'd never intended for it to end as it had? He took a large mouthful of wine and swallowed back the wave of panic that threatened to wash over him. What had happened to Mercedes was a dreadful accident, and he had to move on.

Satiated after the meal, Oliver pushed his plate away and poured the last of the wine. 'I have that cheque for you by the way,' he said, reaching into his shirt pocket and taking out the slip of paper.

For a moment Carmen's face darkened, but she took it, looked at it and then put it in her purse.

Oliver swirled the liquid at the bottom of his glass and held her gaze across the table. He noticed how the wine had blackened her lips like blood.

'When will you see her?' he said.

'Maybe tomorrow.'

'Tomorrow? How did you know I'd have the money so fast?'

187

Carmen shrugged. 'I didn't. But now that I've got it, I can meet her. I'll take the train to Belfast in the morning, spend the weekend.'

Oliver nodded and said nothing. He looked at Carmen and wondered if that's what the evening had been all about. Had she simply been waiting for him to hand over the money?

Carmen stood up and began to clear the table.

'It's okay, you can leave that,' he said.

He took the plates from her, put them back on the table and kissed her. 'In the morning when you've gone it will remind me of what a nice evening we had,' he said.

He saw Carmen's face soften. He kissed her again, took her hand and led her towards the stairs. He still hadn't worked out if her motive was one of love or if it was something more cunning than that. But he knew that he would constantly have to remind himself that Carmen was not an ally – not when it came to her sister and what he had done.

THIRTY-EIGHT

Joanna braced herself for her mother's outburst when she went back inside. She hadn't been outright rude to Rachel Arnold, but the undertones were there. She hadn't flinched when Joanna introduced her to Patrick; the years of lies had made her an expert in the art of deceit. Joanna would say nothing about it until she got home. It wouldn't do to make a scene at the exhibition, nor did she want to give her mother an excuse to wriggle out of it; she could easily storm out leaving Joanna without any explanation.

She scanned the room for her mother and saw her talking with the head of the photography course. He hadn't delayed in introducing himself. Joanna was amused at the attention her mother still drew from men. She imagined the man, Bernard, awkwardly praising her work. He wasn't big on people skills but it didn't stop him. She and the other girls used to laugh about him arriving at the college on his bicycle, his socks up over his trousers secured with a set of bicycle clips. He was the eternal bachelor – but they figured not through any lack of trying on his part.

Her mother looked at her and smiled in relief. 'There you are. Mr Byron was just complimenting you on your work.'

Joanna smiled.

'Bernard. Call me Bernard, please. Mr Byron sounds so … Anyway, Joanna, I was just saying to your mother, you'll be starting to look for a job soon I imagine. I'd be delighted to give you a reference … your portfolio is exquisite … simply exquisite.'

They suffered a few more effusive comments before Bernard Byron, receiving nothing more than polite nods of the head, decided to try his luck elsewhere.

The moment they were alone her mother's smile vanished. 'What was Rachel Arnold doing here?' she asked in a low voice.

'She came with Patrick.'

'You didn't invite her?'

'No.'

'But you invited him?'

Joanna shrugged. 'Yes, I met him in town – we talked about my pictures, he seemed interested. Why – is it a problem?'

'No. No, it's fine. I'd just prefer to have been told about it instead of walking into them like that.'

'Yeah, sorry. I didn't get a chance. You're out a lot these days.'

No response to that. 'Well, look I'd better be getting along too. I'm meeting an old school friend this evening. I suppose you'll be late home yourself?'

'Probably, I think they're planning on going for drinks afterwards.'

Joanna watched her mother leave. Saw Byron's eyes follow her to the exit. So – another evening out. She was half-tempted to call by the Arnolds' when the exhibition ended. Would Patrick, by coincidence, be out too?

She looked around the room. The crowd was starting to thin now. They'd be wrapping up in the next half hour or so. Karl came along, glass of wine in hand.

'You going for drinks later?' he said.

'Probably, I have to pop home first, but I imagine everyone's out for the night?'

He nodded. He was quite attractive. It wasn't any wonder those girls had been interested. If she wasn't so interested in Oliver, she may have been tempted to make more of an effort herself.

Her mother had already left when she arrived home. Maybe she had gone straight to wherever she was going. Patrick could have dropped Rachel home and made his excuses. Where were they now – and why? If she knew, she'd go there and confront them both, find out, finally, what was going on.

She was going upstairs when she heard something – a familiar whistling sound. She stopped and listened. Hadn't that been the message alert on her mother's old phone? Since Joanna had spotted it in the gym bag that evening, she'd been waiting for her opportunity to seize it. She hurried down the stairs, cast her eye around the hall. One of her mother's jackets was hanging at the end of the banister. She searched the pockets, her hand alighting on the rectangular object. She pulled it out. Dear God, don't let her discover she's forgotten it, she thought, watching the front door. The screen was lit up – a message alert, no name, just a number.

Joanna took the phone and hurried upstairs. She went into her room, leaving the door open to listen for any sound in case her mother should return. She clicked on the incoming message.

On your way?

A simple message. Nothing to give away the identity of the sender. Still, she doubted it was from the old school friend that her mother had mentioned. Why would she have given her a different number, or he: it could be a man. Joanna's mind kept turning. No, it wasn't simply a new relationship that her mother was hiding. She'd gone to the trouble of buying a new SIM card so it was something bigger than that, something that required absolute secrecy – that she was not willing to run the risk of being discovered on her own phone. Almost in dread, Joanna clicked on the previous message.

All arranged. Not long now.

It had to be Patrick Arnold. If only she'd taken his number that day when she'd given him hers she'd know. She scrolled through some of the other texts, equally obtuse. There were a few that requested that her mother bring things to their meetings, books mostly, biographies and factual texts. That was strange. Joanna looked for a pen, wrote down the number that the messages had been sent from and the titles of two of the books. She would look them up; find out what they were about.

When she'd scrolled through enough of the messages and still not gleaned anything about who they were from or why she went downstairs to put the phone back in her mother's coat pocket. There was no way to mark the last text as unread so she deleted it. It wasn't anything important; whoever it was had sent it they were unlikely even to mention it. Joanna took her own phone and changed the settings to withhold her caller ID. She dialled the number, heart thumping, finger poised to end the call should someone answer. She simply wanted to see if she recognized the voice. It rang on and on until eventually an automated voice told her to leave her message after the tone. Almost relieved she hung up.

THIRTY-NINE

Oliver had changed the bedclothes and made sure that there was nothing that belonged to Carmen lying around the house before he called Joanna. That morning, when he'd woken, he thought that Carmen might have backtracked on her plan, but she asked him to take her to the train station. It was Friday and she said that she intended to spend the weekend in Belfast. She would call him on Monday when she returned.

As Oliver sat waiting for Joanna to arrive, he wondered where exactly Carmen had gone. Despite the time he'd spent with her she continued to surprise and intrigue him. He had watched her ascend the escalator into the station with her bag and had toyed with the idea of parking the car and following her to see where she went, but then he'd decided against it. Carmen was likely to see him entering the station, and he wouldn't be able to explain his presence there. Instead, he'd parked the car along the street where the escalators were in sight. He'd sat there for over half an hour watching for Carmen to reappear with her bag, but she failed to do so and, finally, he'd given up and returned to the house.

He wondered now if Carmen had taken the train to meet someone. The thought evoked in him a feeling of jealousy, which he tried to dismiss, but it continued to nag him. He was glad that Joanna was coming over to distract him. Carmen could play her games, but he wouldn't waste his time puzzling over her motives. She was probably spending the weekend at the flat, but perhaps there, too, she had company. The thoughts continued to whirl round his head until the doorbell rang, and he chided himself for allowing Carmen to dominate his thoughts.

'Hey, good to see you.' He stepped back to allow Joanna into the hall and then quickly closed the door before he kissed her. 'I'm sorry I had to rush off the other evening. How did the rest of it go?' He wound a handful of her auburn hair round his fist and pulled her closer to kiss her again, trying to dismiss the voice in his head that told him that it was nothing like kissing Carmen Hernandez.

'It was fine, wound up shortly after you left. Sorry about the drama.'

'Drama?'

'Well, tension then. My mother and Rachel Arnold – I wasn't expecting that. I'd asked Patrick along but … '

'Yeah, you said something about him and your mother; what was that about?'

Joanna sighed and flopped down on the sofa. 'I'm not sure. I asked Mum before if she knew him and she said no, then the other day I saw them together in a café. Not only that, I went searching through some old photos and came across one of Mum and Patrick from years ago. There's something going on there. I don't know if they're seeing each other or if it's something else – but Mum's been acting very peculiar. She has two phones – she said one of them was broken but then I found it. She's using it to dial only one number.' Joanna paused. 'You don't have his number by any chance – Patrick's?'

Oliver took out his phone and began to scroll through his numbers. 'As a matter of fact I do.'

Joanna jumped up and took her phone out. 'What is it?' Oliver called the number out, but it didn't match. Not unless Arnold had a second phone too. That would be strange. 'I was thinking; you know how you can ping a number to get its location?'

'Ye … s … s … s?'

'I know it's not exactly legal, but do you know anyone who could do it? And how accurate is it – does it give you the exact location of the phone?'

'It depends on the technology; if the owner is using an iPhone, you can track it to within fifty to a hundred feet because of the GPS apps. Otherwise, you're talking several square miles.'

Joanna nodded. She put her arms round his neck and pressed against him. 'So, do you know someone who could ping this number for me? I'd be … *very* grateful.'

Oliver laughed. 'So you want to inveigle me to break the law? I might need some convincing.'

He pushed her away, put his hands on her shoulders and marched her towards the stairs. The door to the room that he had shared with Mercedes remained closed. He hadn't gone in there since he'd moved his things into the other room. It seemed to resonate with her presence. He tried not to think about it every time he passed, but as soon as his feet hit the landing he could sense her. Now, he hurried Joanna along the landing and towards the light in the other room. She laughed, and the sound of her laughter kept the ghost away; at the least, the ghost in his mind.

Outside, a wind had picked up. It rattled the glass and they shivered beneath the covers. Joanna lay with her head on his chest, and he could feel his own heart beating as her hands travelled over his body. She was a different kind of lover to Carmen. Her love was about giving, and he felt that if he were to come on rough like he'd done with Carmen it would frighten her away. Carmen had created an urgency in him that both excited and frightened him. It was too similar to the way he had felt that night with Mercedes, appalled and exhilarated by his own strength. Sometimes he wondered if he could take it too far. If he'd lost control once there was every possibility that it could happen again. Sex was just another form of violence.

Joanna's gentleness was almost taunting. She seemed to need to be the one in control. She lay above him, caressed his body and made him ache. Then she withdrew and started all over again. When it was over it was almost a relief because he wasn't sure that he could refrain from taking her as he'd taken Carmen. It took all his will to restrain himself until the moment when she'd seemed happy to end it.

He must've fallen asleep almost immediately after because when he woke it was still dark, and he could hear Joanna breathing by his side. He lay on his back and wondered what had woken him. He thought that he'd heard something, a noise downstairs, but now it was silent, and he told himself that it was nothing and began to fall into a slumber. He jumped when, a minute later, he heard someone at the handle of the bedroom door. It was eased down gently, and he sat bolt upright trying to think what was to hand to hit the intruder with. The curtains were drawn tight blocking out any shred of illumination that might filter in from a streetlight. He made a grab at the lamp on the bedside table, but he knocked it over and felt Joanna move beside him. Next he heard a voice.

'It's only me. I didn't mean to scare you.'

Carmen Hernandez was standing feet away in the dark.

She hadn't yet seen Joanna, who had frozen in the bed beside him. He felt Joanna's hand on his arm, and he guessed that she was silently asking him what she should do next.

'Carmen? Jesus, what are you doing creeping around in the dark?'

He had pushed Joanna's hand away, hoping that she would take it as a signal to ease herself from the bed and make some attempt to hide. It hadn't occurred to him that he had used Carmen's name. If he'd only said nothing, Joanna would have mistaken her for Mercedes as she had done before.

Joanna was still beside him, but sitting upright with the covers pulled round her when Carmen switched on the ceiling light and exposed them all. Carmen's look of shock quickly turned to rage.

'I should have known … ' she said.

Oliver jumped out of bed before she could make a lunge at him. Joanna had jumped up, too, and was shouting at Carmen, demanding to know what right she had to go barging into people's houses in the middle of the night. Carmen sneered at her.

'Is this what you replace me with when I'm out of sight,' she said.

She spat at Joanna, who moved back, scared.

'I should have known you'd do this. You made a fool of Mercedes, but you'll never do it to me. I know you, Oliver. I know what you're capable of. Maybe now you'll tell me what you've done to my sister. Maybe you'll tell her, too, because soon everyone's going to find out.' Carmen had moved closer to Oliver.

'Don't be stupid, Carmen. You've seen Mercedes. You told me yourself you met her in Belfast. That's where you're supposed to be now. Did you say that just so you could come back and spy on me?'

Joanna was putting her clothes on as quickly as she could. Carmen turned to her.

'Don't believe a word he tells you. You mean nothing, just like the rest. Ask him where he was last night.'

'Working, he—'

Carmen bellowed with laughter. 'Wrong. He was with me – that's where. Tell her.'

Joanna looked at Oliver. He could see the look of hurt on her face and, in that moment, he decided that he couldn't let her believe anything that Carmen said.

'Is this true?' she said.

'Of course not, she's crazy. She's my wife's crazy sister. I think it's time you left, Carmen, before I call the police.'

'Oh, you'll be talking to the police all right. And you're going to tell them what you've done to my sister. I'll never forgive you for this. Never.'

Carmen stepped closer to Oliver. She swung at him and her fist connected with his jaw. He stumbled backwards at the unexpected blow. She attempted to hit him a second time, but he caught her by the wrists and she kicked and screamed at him. He twisted one of Carmen's arms behind her back, and she shouted out with pain. He'd forgotten that Joanna was in the room until he heard her voice.

'Stop it, for God's sake. Just stop.'

He loosened his grip on Carmen, and she squirmed away from him.

Joanna stood there, shaking.

'Get out of here,' Oliver said. He attempted to put his hand on Carmen's shoulder to usher her from the room.

'Get your hands off me,' she screamed.

She walked down the stairs in front of him.

'How did you get in here anyway?'

Carmen took a set of keys from her pocket and threw them at him. He ducked and they landed with a crash on the stairs.

'I took them back last week, but I guess I won't need them now!'

'You didn't really think you meant anything to me, did you? What we had – that was just sex, Carmen. I'd never get involved with someone like you.'

'And you think I'd want to be involved with someone like you? You must be crazy.'

Carmen picked her coat up from where she'd left it on the banister. She made her way towards the front door without stopping to put it on. For a moment she paused with her hand on the lock, and then she turned towards him. 'You'll regret this, Oliver,' she said.

She spat the words like venom and then she was gone, leaving him staring at the closed door.

Immediately he crossed to the door and bolted it. There would be no more surprise visits tonight. He put his hands to his head. His mind was racing. Would Carmen call the police before the morning? He wouldn't put it past her. She was mad enough to do anything. He had to be ready. He had to get the story straight in his head before they started asking questions. He heard a noise and looked up. Joanna was standing halfway down the stairs staring at him over the banister.

FORTY

'Is it true what she said, that you were involved with her?'

Oliver nodded. 'Yes, but not now, it was before. Please, just come in and sit down. I want to tell you everything. I had hoped I wouldn't have to.'

Joanna hesitated, not sure anymore that she wanted to hear anything, but how could she condemn him without first hearing the evidence? He didn't speak for a moment, shaken still by his confrontation with the woman. Carmen, is that what he'd called her? It certainly hadn't been Mercedes anyway. Not this time.

'Before Mercedes left, our relationship hadn't been the same. I don't want you to think I'm using that as an excuse, I just want you to know how things were. The physical side of our relationship had become non-existent. We were like strangers living in the same house. There was no warmth between us, and yet Mercedes didn't want to acknowledge that. Every time I tried to bring it up she just got angry, and every time I attempted to get close to her she pulled away. I guess what I'm saying is it would have ended sooner or later regardless of Carmen.'

Joanna averted her eyes as he took a breath and went on.

'Carmen had been staying with us for a couple of weeks. She and I did and didn't get on. Mercedes had told me to be nice to her and I was trying. From the moment I'd met Carmen, she'd made it clear that she was interested. She was blatant about it, had tried it on a few times when Mercedes wasn't around. I'd mentioned it to Mercedes before and she'd laughed and said that was just how Carmen was and that she didn't have any real intention, but I knew otherwise. Anyway, usually it annoyed me when Carmen acted like that, but things were the way they were between Mercedes and me, and I have to admit that I started to enjoy Carmen's attention, encouraged it even.'

Joanna shifted in her chair but said nothing.

'Mercedes had to go to a conference for work. Carmen and I both knew this and things had already gone further than they should in the odd moment when Mercedes was out of the room. It was exciting ... I mean Mercedes would go upstairs and Carmen would—'

Joanna put up a hand to stop him. 'I don't want to know about that,' she said.

'I'm sorry. Anyway, you can imagine. Carmen didn't care about anything, and Mercedes and I hadn't been physical for months. I didn't even feel like I was cheating on her. Anyway, she went away for the night, and Carmen and I finally slept together. When she came back, we acted as though nothing had happened, and I thought that that was an end to it. I didn't want to pursue anything with Carmen. It wasn't like that; it was just sex.'

'And Mercedes found out?'

Oliver nodded. 'It wasn't until a couple of months later. Carmen had gone home. I thought it had been forgotten, that Carmen had got her way and now she wasn't interested, but I was wrong. She told her everything.'

'What did she say?'

Oliver stood up and paced the floor, face contorted at the memory. 'She went crazy, started attacking me. She said she never wanted to see me again, that she couldn't believe I'd betrayed her like that, and with Carmen of all people ... She took her things and left.'

He sat down again, leaning forward in the chair trying, she thought, to gauge her reaction. He spread his hands.

'And that's it, that's what happened. I'm sure *you* feel the same about me now as Mercedes did. I know only too well how women feel about … about *that*.'

Joanna was silent for a moment before she spoke. 'And Carmen, did you and she continue—?'

'You must be joking. I didn't want anything to do with Carmen. You've seen what she's like. I couldn't understand why she'd told Mercedes … she knew that it didn't mean anything. It was her twisted way of trying to get one up on everyone. Look I just want you to know, I'd never done anything like that before. I'd never cheated on Mercedes. If things hadn't been the way they'd been at that particular time, I don't think any of it would have happened.'

'You don't think?' Joanna stood up, she couldn't think straight. She needed to get away from him.

'No, it wouldn't have happened. Look, Joanna—'

She put a hand out to ward him off. She didn't want him to touch her, not now. 'I'm sorry, look I have to go, I can't … I can't be around you right now.'

'Okay. I understand. But just so you know, I have told you everything. I know I was weak, stupid, but Mercedes had her hand in it, too. I mean things were over. We just didn't want to face it, not after four years of marriage. If it hadn't been Carmen, it would have been something else.'

Joanna felt sick. If she didn't get away from him soon, the nauseous feeling would overwhelm her. She grabbed her coat and bag from the chair. He followed her to the door.

'Is it okay if I call you in a few days?' he said.

'I'd rather you didn't. I need time to think.'

'Okay. I'm sorry, Joanna, sorry I didn't tell you everything from the start. But I liked you, and I didn't want to spoil it. I won't call, but I hope once you've had time to consider everything, you might … I hope it's not the last time I see you.'

They stood awkwardly. He put out a hand but she turned from him, said goodbye brusquely and hurried out the door. At the car she fumbled the car keys, dropping them on the ground. She stooped to pick them up and hurriedly sat in before having to lean over the pavement to vomit. She glanced at the house, thankful to see he'd gone back inside.

When the episode had passed, she drove away from the house, but she didn't feel like going home. Her mother would wonder what had made her return in the middle of the night. She drove out of the estate and then pulled the car in by the canal. The water shone slick beneath the garish glow of the streetlamps. She lowered the window to feel the sting of the cold night air and breathed in deeply. Oliver said that he had told her everything, and she wondered if he had. He'd been frank in his description of his relationship with Mercedes, if it was true. The fact that the relationship had perished long before may have been nothing more than an excuse, and what's more, he knew it was the sort of thing she'd want to hear.

Carmen Hernandez was a different story. If she hadn't made her dramatic entrance, Joanna would never have known she existed. And in turn she wouldn't have found out why Oliver's marriage had ended. She thought about his betrayal of Mercedes, and wondered if it was true that Carmen had tempted him at a time when his resistance was low, or whether he'd have succumbed anyway despite the fragility of his marriage.

Joanna got out of the car. She needed to walk, needed to breathe the cool air. She thought of how shocked Carmen had looked to find her there. But there were several things, apart from the obvious, that bothered her about Carmen's intrusion. The first was Carmen herself. Did she bear such a remarkable likeness to her sister that she couldn't tell them apart, or was it Carmen and not Mercedes that she had seen that first night coming out of the house? The woman she had seen undressing before the fire, that had been Carmen surely? And, in that case, had she ever seen Mercedes?

She thought of the way that Oliver had grabbed Carmen's arm, twisting it behind her back so that she couldn't move with pain. It was like a badly choreographed tango where neither partner knew which step to take next, and so they'd stood – frozen – each unwilling to concede. She, the forgotten spectator, had watched until she couldn't bear to watch any longer, and it was the thought of what might have happened if she hadn't intervened that bothered her most.

Oliver said that Mercedes had attacked him when she'd found out about his betrayal. What had he done to defend himself? Had he taken hold of her wrists as he'd done with Carmen or had he simply allowed her to beat him? There was no one there to stop it, no one there to see what had happened between them. Had Mercedes simply packed her bag and left without returning? What if she'd never left at all?

Joanna had been walking briskly. She found herself now near the place where Oliver had found her father's body. She walked onto the lock and stood peering into the water. There was no one around, no one to hear the screams of a person drowning. She thought about Vince Arnold. What had he been thinking as he crashed through the ice? As his body was sucked under without hope of escape. About Rachel, or Angela, or the daughter whom he'd failed to acknowledge, but who would inherit fifty thousand euro on the event of his death. Did he think that was enough to make up for what he'd done? It was ironic that he, the absent father, had been the catalyst – the reason for her meeting Oliver Molloy. At the beginning she'd seen it as fate, but now she wondered if their relationship hadn't been doomed from the start.

Joanna took a coin from her pocket, raised her arm and threw it into the water. She heard it hit the surface with a plop and imagined it sinking slowly to the bottom of the canal. She remembered a park she'd been to with her mother. She must have been about four years old. There'd been a big fountain, its base filled with hundreds of coins. Her mother had opened her purse and given her a penny to throw in, telling her she should make a wish. She wished now: not that she hadn't met Oliver Molloy but that he was telling the truth. She wished that Mercedes would turn up to dispel the suspicions that Carmen Hernandez had stirred up. Mind churning, she turned and walked quickly back to the car.

FORTY-ONE

Oliver couldn't get back to sleep after Joanna had left. Instead, he sat in his armchair in the living room and wondered whether there was substance to Carmen's threats. She had extorted money from him on the pretence that she'd seen Mercedes as recently as a week ago; could she afford to go to the police? It would be impossible to do so without getting herself into trouble. Then again, she was livid. Logic might not come into it if she was hell-bent on revenge. He couldn't afford to take a chance, and so at eight o'clock in the morning he called the guards.

They arrived a little after ten: the same two men that Oliver had met at the canal bank the morning he had found Vince Arnold's body. What were the chances?

'Mr Molloy?' the older man asked as soon as Oliver had opened the door.

'That's right. Come in.' He opened the door wider and stepped back allowing the two men to enter.

They waited in the hallway until he invited them to follow him into the living room. He saw them take a quick glance around. Sweeney's shrewd eyes rested momentarily on the framed photo of himself and Mercedes that he'd replaced on the mantelpiece after he'd made the call.

'When was the last time you saw your wife, Mr Molloy?' Sweeney crossed to the picture and picked it up.

'About two weeks ago.'

'About two weeks ago? Why did you not report her missing right away?'

Oliver thought of Joanna. Had she realized by now that the woman she'd seen at the house that night was Carmen? He decided he'd take his chance and hope that she'd back him up if he needed her to.

'We'd been living apart; she came by to pick up some of her things.'

'You and your wife are separated? When did that happen?'

'Close on two months ago.'

The younger garda was taking notes while Sweeney asked the questions. He put the photo back on the mantelpiece and looked at Oliver with piercing blue eyes.

'And what were the circumstances of the separation?'

Oliver ran a hand through his hair. Stick to the truth as closely as possible, that way there would be less probability of mistakes. That way, he would paint Carmen black without even mentioning the money.

'Mercedes found out that I'd slept with her sister. We had a big row and she left.'

A raised eyebrow. 'And do you know where she's been staying since she left you?'

'No.' He'd been about to tell them about the message – the one that placed her in Belfast – but let them find out; it would be better that way. The trail he'd left using Mercedes's debit card would lead them straight there.

'And you've had no communication with her?'

'Well, yes, there was a message she sent from Facebook, but that was a fortnight ago.'

'What did it say, this message? Was there any talk of a reconciliation; had you arranged to meet?'

'No. Nothing like that. She said I wasn't to contact her, that she doesn't want anything to do with myself or Carmen – her sister.'

Sweeney looked at him, impatient. 'And so, what makes you think that your wife is missing, Mr Molloy, if she's expressed a wish not to communicate with you?'

'She's not answering calls – not just that but her phone is powered off the whole time. She hasn't updated her Facebook page or Twitter.'

'Surely, there's nothing strange in that, unless your wife is a daily user?'

'Well, no, not necessarily. I'm sorry, obviously you think I'm over-reacting here – but I'm concerned. I just need to know that she's all right. She'd been suffering from stress, had been on prescribed medication before we'd split, so I'm concerned about – about her state of mind.'

'What kind of medication was she taking? Would you say she was depressed?'

'Maybe, yes. It was more anxiety. The doctor prescribed anti-anxiety tablets.'

'I see. And you and your sister-in-law, Carmen, have you continued this … relationship?'

'Relationship? No, there is no relationship. Carmen just arrived from Spain a couple of weeks ago. She became concerned when Mercedes failed to answer her calls. She was desperate to sort things out with her – after what had happened.'

'Right, well we'll have to talk to your sister-in-law, see if she can verify what you've told us. Would you have a contact number for her? How long does she intend staying in Dublin?'

Oliver gave them Carmen's number, only, he changed one digit; he had to be sure he had a chance to talk to her, to set her straight about what he had and hadn't told them before she got the call. He said he didn't know how long she would be around, but that he suspected she'd stay until they had some news of Mercedes.

Sweeney looked at him, serious. 'Your concerns are probably premature, Mr Molloy, given the situation, but every report of a missing person has to be taken seriously irrespective of the circumstances. We'll need some personal details about your wife: date of birth, description, that kind of thing.'

Oliver described Mercedes. He pointed out the photo on the mantelpiece, and they asked whether it was a recent shot. He said that it had been taken two years ago, but that he could show them a more recent photo if they needed one. They said they would: it would be uploaded on the Garda website.

'Could you tell us what your wife was wearing the last time you saw her?'

He thought for a moment, tried to exorcise the image of Mercedes in the clingy blue dress she'd been wearing the night it had happened. 'I'm not sure. Like I said it was a few weeks ago. I think she was wearing a skirt, boots – maybe a black leather jacket. It was raining the night she came. She usually wore a leather jacket.'

'And you said that she came to collect some possessions. Did she leave any documents, her passport, for example?'

'No, I think she's taken everything like that. She had a file where she kept her documents, and it's gone. What happens now? I mean how will you go about finding her?' Her passport, he'd have to find that – destroy it and any other documents she'd have been expected to take with her if she'd planned on leaving the country.

Sweeney sighed and shifted on his stubby legs. 'We'll put her details on the website, see if anything turns up. We'll need to speak to family members, friends who may have seen her recently. Were there any places that she went to regularly, hang-outs or haunts?'

'Nowhere regular, no. We liked to eat out, go to the cinema. I guess you could say we'd had a fairly quiet social life in the last few years.'

He was aware of the young garda taking note of everything he said.

'Was your wife working, Mr Molloy?'

'Yes. She's a translator.'

'And you've tried to contact her at work?'

'No, she'd taken time off before any of this happened. I doubt she'd have gone back; like I said, she was suffering from stress.'

'Okay, well we'll need to contact them too. What's the company name?'

'ITS. International Translation Services.'

'Right. That's enough for the time being. We'll get your wife's profile up on the website. We're going to need a copy of that photograph. Here's my email address, Mr Molloy. I'd appreciate if you could get it to me this afternoon. We'll talk to your sister-in-law and, in the meantime, if anything turns up, we'll be in touch.'

The young garda put his notebook away, rose from his seat and followed Sweeney to the front door.

'What do I do in the meantime?' Oliver asked.

'You could contact Mercedes's friends if you haven't already done so; see if anyone's heard from her. We'll be doing that anyway, but it might be better coming from you, less alarming.'

Oliver nodded. 'Thank you – I'll send the photo on to you, straightaway.'

As soon as they were gone, he went upstairs. There was a drawer where Mercedes had kept most of her documents. He pulled it out and began to search through the papers. He found a copy of her birth certificate, a few old car insurance certificates, pay slips, bank statements, but no passport. Where could it be? While he searched he thought of the questions Sweeney had asked him. Had there been any suspicion in the older man's face, in his tone? He didn't think so. Not yet anyway. It was more likely that they thought he was wasting their time.

It was after they had traced Mercedes's movements that the

trouble would begin. He knew that, as the husband, he'd come under suspicion. There was no avoiding that. There had been too many cases in the last decade and, if he were caught, he would be no more than another statistic – a husband who wanted his wife out of the way.

He thought of the money he'd given Carmen. It placed her right at his mercy. If he told the police that she had claimed to have seen Mercedes, that she had extorted twelve thousand euro from him on the pretence of giving it to his wife, he would succeed in taking any spotlight off himself and placing it firmly on his sister-in-law. It was an ace he was prepared to play if she attempted in any way to incriminate him. He gathered the papers and put them back in the drawer, trying to think where Mercedes could possibly have put her passport. He would search again later; right now, he had to talk to Carmen before the police discovered he'd given them the wrong number.

FORTY-TWO

In the darkroom, Joanna searched through the recent photos she'd taken until she found the one of Mercedes – or was it Carmen? – Hernandez. She held the picture under the spotlight and stared at it. Certainly, if she'd known only of Carmen she'd have had no doubts that it was her, but sisters could be remarkably alike, couldn't they? The figure was the same, the tangled black hair, the full lips painted red. It was a shame she had never seen any pictures of Mercedes when she'd been at Oliver's house – then she'd know for sure, then she would not be plagued by these awful doubts.

There was only one way she could find out and that was to go back there. She couldn't do it right away – she still felt sick over Oliver's revelation – nor did she want him to think that everything between them was okay when it wasn't. She had told him not to call her, but she figured he would. If he didn't, she could call him – ask him if he'd found out anything about the number she'd asked him to trace. Besides, if he managed to do that it would be a huge step in finding out what it was her mother had been planning these last few weeks. She would take the risk to discover the truth. Joanna pinned the photo of Mercedes/

Carmen on her picture board, turned out the light and closed the door on the darkroom.

'Mum, what has you up so early?'

Joanna had been nursing her coffee, staring out the window, when her mother appeared in the doorway in her dressing gown looking as tired as she felt. Joanna looked at her watch: she'd have to leave in five minutes if she didn't want to be late for class.

'I wanted to catch you before you left to ask if you had any plans this evening.'

Joanna drained her coffee cup, stood and looked around for her rucksack. 'No, why?'

'Good. I'll make dinner for us both, I … I have a bit of news for you.'

Joanna looked at her mother; the search for the bag instantly forgotten. 'Oh, what kind of news?'

Her mother smiled, but looked uncomfortable. She pulled her dressing gown tighter round her, closing the belt. 'I'm not telling you now; you'll have to wait till later.'

'Well, should I be worried or is it something good?'

Her mother looked away. 'I think so,' she said. 'Anyway, look you'd better be off. I don't want to make you late. I'll tell you everything this evening.'

Everything? That would make a change. Joanna's already knotted stomach twisted further in anticipation. All of a sudden she wasn't sure that she wanted to hear her mother's news.

The day passed in a haze. Joanna made mistakes in simple tasks – mixed up the solutions when she was developing shots – managed to get a rise out of Lord Byron for wasting college materials. She didn't care; all she wanted was to get home and find out what it was her mother had to tell her. She also checked her phone several times throughout the day to see if she'd received any messages from Oliver Molloy, but he'd respected her request and the phone remained stubbornly inert.

Her mother was home when she got in from college. She'd already begun cooking; the aroma of garlic and other herbs wafted from the kitchen. The radio was on, and her mother was singing along with an eighties pop song. The table had been laid, and a candle burned in its centre. For a moment Joanna wondered if someone else were joining them, but no, there were two places set. Whatever it was Angela had to tell her, she was certainly making it an occasion. Joanna wandered into the kitchen where her mother was stirring sauce in a pan.

'Whatever it is, it smells great,' she said. 'I'm starving.'

Her mother smiled. 'Roast potatoes, garlic chicken and roast veg,' she said. 'There's a bottle of white chilling in the fridge, if you want to open it. I'm almost ready to serve up.'

Joanna took out the wine. Her mother's tone was too bright, a forced gaiety. She took a corkscrew from the drawer. 'So what's this big news then?' Her tone equally bright to match her mother's.

'I'll tell you in a few minutes, just let me dish this lot out – and pour me a glass, would you?' She stooped to open the oven.

Joanna took two glasses from the press and poured the wine. She took a long swallow of the liquid; it was bitter but it warmed her insides. Her mother placed the food on the table and sat opposite.

'So what's it all about then?' Joanna leaned in to scoop some roast potatoes onto her plate.

'The job.'

'The job?' She paused – disappointment like lead in her insides. What – had her mother decided to take early retirement – was that it? No big revelation after all.

'I've been offered a new position in the company.'

'Oh – that's, that's great. Congratulations.' Joanna raised her glass. A celebratory meal then. Nothing about Patrick Arnold. Nothing to explain the spare phone. Nothing of any great consequence.

'It is; it's great. The thing is, Joanna, it's in the head office in … Milan.' Her mother exhaled, as though on that breath she'd let go of a great worry. Joanna put down her knife and fork.

'Milan? What – you don't mean permanently?'

Angela took a sip of wine, lowered her eyes. 'I don't know. The contract is for six months initially, but if it worked out … I could use the change, Joanna. I've been here in this house all my life, the office more years than I want to count, and to tell you the truth the idea of a new place, new faces, it's very appealing.'

'But what about the house? What about … what about me?'

Her mother leaned forward. 'Oh, Joanna, I wouldn't be abandoning you. It mightn't even work out – I might go for six months and hate it. Look, you'll be finished your course in a few months – you could come out, maybe you could even find a job there? We could rent out the house – short-term – until we'd decided it was what we wanted to do. No matter what happens this house will be yours. You don't need to worry about that.'

'You're talking like you've made up your mind already. Have you accepted the offer?'

Her mother nodded. 'Yes. I didn't want to tell you, not until I was sure that it was going to go ahead. It's all arranged – I leave in a month's time.'

'I see.'

'Come on, Joanna. Don't look like that. It's six months – and besides, you're not a child anymore. You've got your own life. How are things going with that man you're seeing – Oliver, isn't it?'

Joanna didn't answer. Milan. Not unrelated after all then. Isn't that where he lived, where he would return to in a few weeks' time – Italy?

'Is that the only reason you're going?'

'How do you mean?'

'The job. Did they really ask you to set up in Milan, or did you request a transfer?'

'They asked me – why?'

Her mother looked nervous now. This time she'd follow it up. What did it matter if she had to admit she'd been snooping through her mother's things? What did anything matter? She'd waited long enough to hear the truth.

'This wouldn't have anything to do with Patrick Arnold, would it?'

'Patrick Arnold … what are you talking about?'

'Yes, Mother, Patrick – your old friend. Look, we've both done enough skirting round the matter. The thing is, last week I was looking for my birth certificate – I took down the box in your wardrobe, the one you keep those things in, and a picture fell out. A picture of you and Patrick Arnold taken at the beach years ago.'

Silence. Then admission. 'Yes, I knew him then.'

'And then, by coincidence, I saw the two of you in town together having coffee.' She decided to jump right in, reveal all. There was no point in listening to her mother's further excuses – of how she knew him then, but hadn't seen him for years.

Her mother put down her glass and nodded. 'You're right. I was going to tell you. We are, like you say, old friends; but Rachel Arnold doesn't know that, and Patrick thought she'd been through enough – that it was better to keep it from her. That's why we had to pretend not to know one another at your exhibition. She invited herself along at the last minute.'

'And it's a coincidence then that you're moving to Italy, is it?'

'Actually yes, but Patrick's been helping me. You know he works in real estate – so he's been trying to find an apartment for me to rent. That's what we were discussing that day that you saw us.'

'And you're not – you're not involved with him?'

'With Patrick?' Her mother laughed. 'No. He's been nothing more than a friend.'

What she said could be true. It made sense given that he worked in real estate. But Italy – it seemed too much of a coincidence. Her mother could easily have requested the move. And if it was all that innocent, what about her mother's second phone – the one used to contact one number only? There was something else that her mother was hiding – and she couldn't ask her about it without looking like she'd been carrying out some Nancy Drew-type investigation. No – she'd leave that one for now, give it a few days and then run it by Oliver. If she was never to see him again, this could be the most important thing he could do for her.

'So has he found a place for you?'

'Possibly. There's a two-bedroom apartment on the outskirts of the city, reasonable rent.'

Joanna nodded. 'And you leave when exactly?'

'Four weeks' time. What do you say, will you come when you've finished your course – spend a bit of time in the sun?'

'I don't know, maybe. Will he be there?'

'Patrick? He works in Milan. It will be good to know someone there – he can help me settle in. There's nothing between us, Joanna, if that's what you're thinking. Besides, he is your uncle. If you come out, it will give you a chance to get to know him – in a different environment, away from Rachel and from the past.'

When they'd finished their meal, Joanna excused herself on the pretence of having an assignment to complete. She spent the rest of the evening in her room going over her mother's revelation and thinking about Oliver Molloy. Maybe her mother was right to make a fresh start in a new country. She was still a young woman, and Joanna wanted her to be happy. In a few months' time, she would finish her photography course and it would be time to make decisions about her own life. It wasn't like her mother was leaving her homeless, or penniless for that matter. Things with Oliver were not going to work out now, and she had

217

no ties once her studies were done. Milan didn't sound like the worst option provided it was as her mother said. But there were other questions to be answered – chiefly, the mystery surrounding that second mobile phone.

FORTY-THREE

Carmen Hernandez refused to answer his calls. Several times he had tried and got through to her voicemail. Finally, he withheld his caller ID and tried again. 'Carmen, don't … ' As soon as she heard his voice she hung up. Damn that woman and all the trouble she had caused. He took his car keys and drove to the apartment where she was staying.

The door to the complex was shut this time, so he buzzed the intercom. No answer. She clearly knew it was him. He put his finger on the button and left it there, imagining the shrill sound reverberating through the apartment. Finally, she picked up and uttered an expression in her native tongue which he knew was far from polite. There was a click and the connection was cut. He put his finger on the buzzer again. This time when she picked up he didn't give her a chance to say anything.

'The police want to talk to you.'

No reply, but the door clicked open this time. He hung up and, two steps at a time, climbed the stairs.

'What do the police want with me?'

She was carefully made-up, wearing a blue dress that reminded him of the one Mercedes had worn that night. She was barefoot, and a book lay where she'd left it face down on the table. It was one of the ones he'd picked up from the bookstore.

'I called them this morning to report Mercedes missing.'

She looked surprised. 'Why would you do that?'

'Because, Carmen, you told me she is. Up until last night, I was made to believe that you'd found her up in Belfast. Which reminds me, you've got twelve thousand euro belonging to me – anyone might call that extortion.'

'Don't threaten me, Oliver.'

'Don't worry, I haven't said anything to the police about it: not yet. Despite what you might think about me, I have no real wish to land you in that kind of trouble.'

'How considerate of you.' An arch of the eyebrow, a sardonic smile – but the worried look hadn't left her.

'I told them what happened.'

'What do you mean?' Curiosity in her dark eyes.

'That you and I had slept together, that Mercedes had left because of it.'

'Surely, there was no reason to tell them that?'

'What's this – not ashamed, are you? They wanted to know why I hadn't reported her missing immediately. I explained that we were separated, that I'd only seen Mercedes once – the night that she returned for her stuff. They asked what the circumstances of the separation were. I could hardly go making it up now, that would be inviting trouble.'

'She came back for her stuff? When?'

He thought for a moment. 'A night or two before you turned up.'

A shift in her expression. The cogs of her mind turning. 'You didn't say that before.'

He shrugged.

Carmen stepped closer to him. She was wearing that scent again – the Chanel that he associated with Mercedes. She looked directly at him. 'Where is she, Oliver?'

'I don't know.'

'And the other one – how long has that been going on?'

'Does it bother you?'

'What – that you think I'm out of the city for one night and you have some … some girl in your bed? Familiar tune, isn't it, Oliver? Maybe I wasn't the only one, eh? Maybe Mercedes had more to worry about.'

'Come on, Carmen, we were hardly an item, you and I? The girl … that was nothing – a friend who stayed the night. And I hate to admit it, but she was nothing compared to you, not in that respect anyway. Still, I paid good money, didn't I? I'd say you owe me a lot more for twelve thousand euro.'

The slap came like lightning. He lifted a hand to his jaw, which stung and burned from the impact.

'You bastard,' she said.

He fought to stay calm. 'Where's my money?'

'It's gone.'

'What do you mean it's gone? You spent twelve thousand euro in a matter of days?'

'Not exactly, I … invested it.' She smirked.

'Invested it? And would you mind telling me what you invested my money in?'

'It wasn't your money, it was Mercedes's. And besides, it'll be worth it, you'll see.'

He was beginning to wonder if he ought to be concerned. What could she possibly have done with that amount of money in so short a time? He shook his head.

'That's what worries me,' he said.

Carmen circled the room, 'And what exactly will the police want to know when they talk to me?' she asked.

Oliver shrugged. 'They'll ask you when you last saw Mercedes, I suppose. How she had seemed to you in the last few months, and if you've heard from her.'

'And thanks to you, they'll look at me as the whore, the one that slept with her sister's husband,' she said, sulkily. 'I suppose you gave them my number.'

'Not exactly. I gave them a number – but not the right one. I wanted to talk to you first, let you know what to expect. I'm sure they'll be in touch again once they've discovered it's the wrong number.'

'So you decided to dump me in it, and then protect me, is that it? You are so many contradictions, Oliver. Besides, they might not get me. I have to go to Spain in a few days' time.'

'Oh?' He wasn't expecting that. 'And are you coming back?'

'That depends … ' She stopped pacing and stood before him. 'Why? Would you miss me, Oliver? I think, maybe, after the last few weeks the least you could do is give me a send-off, no?'

Flirtation – blatant, the Carmen of old. The girl changed mood so often it was impossible to keep up. She reached a hand round the back of his neck and pulled him towards her. He didn't resist, why would he? Whatever it was that Carmen was up to – what was on offer was too good to resist. In a few days she would return to Spain to do who knew what – and he would contact Joanna to try to get her back on side. The fewer enemies and more alibis he had, the better. It wouldn't be long before the guards discovered that Mercedes's was a legitimate missing person's case, and the groundwork he'd laid had better pay off.

FORTY-FOUR

Two days later, he called. Joanna saw his name flash up on the phone and debated whether to answer it or not. If she didn't, she'd have to ring him back anyway, and so she picked up before it cut off.

'Joanna, hi. I'm sorry for ringing. I know you said not to, but I have the information you were looking for.'

'You have?'

'Yes, look I don't want to talk about it over the phone, could we meet?'

She thought for a moment. 'Okay. I'll meet you by the canal at the place where you found Vince.'

She didn't know why she picked there, but she knew she didn't want to meet him anywhere crowded, or, worst of all, at the house. She wanted to see him first somewhere neutral – somewhere she could easily escape should that nauseous feeling overpower her.

She arrived before him, sat in the car until she spotted the familiar figure walking up the bank. Then she got out and went to meet him.

'Hi. How have you been?' His tone, uncertain, penitent almost.

'Okay.' She kept her hands firmly in her coat pockets. No

physical contact; if he touched her she couldn't be sure she wouldn't give in, that she wouldn't make herself believe he was sorry. 'So you were able to trace it – the number?'

Oliver nodded. 'To the exact place and, this is the surprising part, the location is a boat – a barge – docked at Grand Canal. Any ideas?'

Joanna shook her head. She thought of her mother going into Tara Street station that day, after she'd left Patrick Arnold. Is that where she'd been going – to Grand Canal dock – and to see who? Not Patrick, but somebody else, somebody unknown.

'You have the location?'

He gave it to her. 'It won't be any more than fifty yards out if it's anything. What are you going to do?'

'Find out who owns that boat.'

'Do you want me to? I will – if you want. I don't want you getting involved with anything ... anything that might be dangerous.'

Joanna gave a short laugh. 'It's hardly dangerous, Oliver. This is my mother we're talking about – I doubt there's anything criminal in what she's doing.'

'So what *do* you think?'

'I don't know. You know she's thinking of emigrating? She told me last night. I'm not sure it's even sunk in to be honest. I can't imagine her not being here. The job is sending her to work in the head office in Milan – a promotion of sorts, she says – six months to begin with. She's suggested that I join her as soon as my course is done in the summer.'

They'd begun walking. It was still so easy to talk to him despite what had happened. She found herself making excuses; it was Mercedes he'd cheated on, not her. At least that was how he'd told it. Carmen claimed the affair had been ongoing – but then she had seemed unhinged. Was it Carmen she had seen through the window that night – was there any possibility that it had been Mercedes?

'And will you?'

'What?'

'Milan – do you think you'll go? There are worse places you could start a photography career I'm sure.'

'Maybe. A change might be good. I don't have to decide just yet anyway. Mum leaves in a month's time. That'll be strange.'

Oliver stopped walking to look into the water.

'We should go back,' she said, sensing a shift in things.

He turned towards her. 'Joanna, I *am* sorry. I know I've said it already, and I should have told you everything from the start, but I thought you'd run as far as you could if I told you.'

'You'd have been right there.' She started walking back the way they'd come.

'I know. I don't expect anything, and I couldn't blame you if you want nothing to do with me at all, but I do like you; we could be friends. That would be good enough for me.'

Friends. Could she do that? She was so attracted to him it would be hard. On the other hand, if she agreed she might have the opportunity to find out the truth – to discover finally if the woman she'd seen undressing at the house that night had been Mercedes. And what then? She didn't know – but at least she could rid herself of any outrageous notion that something had happened to his wife.

'I'll be honest with you. I don't know if I can. I want to – I'd like to. What we've had has been great – and I'm not ruling that out either – so yeah, I suppose what I'm saying is, let's try. Let's give the friends thing a go.'

She put out her hand and he laughed and shook it.

'As long as you know, I am really sorry.'

They'd almost reached the car now. 'Can I give you a lift back home?' she asked.

'If you don't mind.'

'No. Come on, sure it's on the way anyway – friend.'

She laughed, and tried to fight down the nervous feeling she

225

had when they got in the car. If she could spend enough time in the house just to locate a picture of Mercedes, then she could decide whether or not she ever wanted to see him again. As far as he was concerned she still believed that the woman she had seen was his wife. She would do nothing to make him suspect otherwise.

She pulled up in front of the house. He hesitated, hand on the door.

'Will you come in for a cuppa?'

She pretended to consider. 'Okay, but no funny business.'

He spread his hands. 'You have my word. As long as you're sure you can keep your hands off me?'

'Ha! You're not all that, mister,' she said.

After they'd had tea, she excused herself on the pretence of going to the bathroom. When she'd listened on the landing for a few minutes for any sounds from downstairs, she crept into the bedroom and looked around. Where might Mercedes keep her photos? She opened the top drawer in the dressing table – there was nothing there but underwear. She closed the drawer and then quickly looked in the other two – again just clothes. Damn it.

She heard movement downstairs, quickly crept to the bathroom, flushed the toilet and ran the tap. He was on the phone when she went back downstairs.

'Yeah, just give me one second, Colin, and I'll check … ' He covered the mouthpiece. 'Work,' he said. 'Give me two minutes.' He left the room and went into his adjoining office.

Through the door, Joanna could see him booting up his desktop computer. A few papers lay on the kitchen table; she flicked through them. There was a bank statement addressed to Mercedes. Joanna glanced at the office door before turning it over to see when the last few payments had been made. There were two transactions for the tenth of March. One was for forty-seven pounds sterling made payable to Eurolines, while the other was a transaction for ninety-six pounds spent in a Spar shop – again the amount was in sterling. Joanna stared for a moment at the statement before taking it quickly and putting it in her bag. Oliver was still on the phone. Her mind raced. Two transactions made on Mercedes's debit card – the very date that they had been in Belfast. There were two possible explanations – one unsavoury, the other unthinkable. She found herself hoping that rather than attending a business meeting in Belfast Oliver had in fact arranged to meet his wife. His coat hung on the back of a chair. She put her hand in one of the pockets and her fingers closed round his wallet. Quickly, she took it out and searched the contents, debit card, credit card – nothing to arouse suspicion – nothing but that statement in his wife's name.

'Yeah, okay – I'll do that. That's fine – okay, no worries, Colin …'

She put the wallet back in the coat, stood and placed her mug in the sink. She was putting on her jacket when he entered the room.

'Sorry about that. Ah, you're not going already, are you?'

'Afraid so; I've stuff to do for tomorrow, and besides, it *was* just tea.'

'It was good. Thanks – for the lift and the chat. I hope you have some luck finding out what or who's behind that mystery number. If you need anything, you know where I am.'

She thanked him, forced a smile and managed to stop herself from running to the car.

FORTY-FIVE

Oliver hadn't heard from Carmen since he'd been to the flat. He wondered if she was back in Spain and the reasons for her returning. The guards had phoned asking him to confirm the number he'd given them; said that they'd got through to a man who claimed he'd never heard of any Carmen Hernandez. Oliver repeated the number, correcting the one wrong digit he'd given them. A clerical error, that's all, committed by the fresh-faced guard. He'd probably got a bollocking from Sweeney.

Had they talked to Carmen then, before she'd left? Probably. He was glad he'd got to her first, let her know that he hadn't dropped her in it. Who knows what she might have told them if it had been sprung on her – if she thought he'd told them about her having claimed to have seen Mercedes, about the twelve thousand euro. What had she done with that – taken it back to Spain with her? Carmen. He'd been thinking about her a lot recently. He told himself it was her similarities to Mercedes that had him thinking about her, but it was more than that. Somehow, she'd managed to get under his skin. The Arnold girl, she was sweet, a bit too curious for his liking though. He'd keep her on side for the moment, then cut her loose when it was safe to do so, if it were ever safe to do so.

Since he'd reported Mercedes missing, he'd been on edge. They weren't taking it seriously at the moment, but he knew that, once they'd failed to locate her, they'd be crawling all over him. The husband – victim, suspect, always suspect. He comforted himself with thoughts of all those missing women, of the thousands reported every week who were never found, of all the bogland, waste ground, and forested areas across both the Dublin and Wicklow mountains that failed to yield their grizzly secrets.

Oliver switched on the television. He'd enjoy the peace until the circus began. Tired from sleepless nights, he was dozing in front of the screen when he heard it: 'A woman's body has been found in a shallow grave in a forested area near Glencree. A man came across the partly decomposed body when out walking his dogs.' Christ. He'd opened his eyes as soon as he'd heard the word 'body'. Glencree. His heart hammering – was that what the area was called, he wasn't sure. He grabbed the remote control and turned up the volume. Gardaí; yellow tape cordoning an area of woodland. Was that it, was that the place? Maybe not; he couldn't be sure. It had been dark – he'd not seen his surroundings, wouldn't have noticed much if he had. It could be someone else. One of the thousands missing. He prayed to God it was.

'The partly decomposed body.' How long did it take for a body to decompose? He didn't know, but clearly this one had not been in the ground long. What state would Mercedes's be in by now? Would she be recognizable? How long would it take for them to identify the remains? Questions whirled round his head – but what if it wasn't? If it wasn't her and he was in the clear … what if? It was still possible. If the body was decomposed, he assumed they would try to identify it through dental records. They wouldn't find any for Mercedes, not here. She always went home to Spain for any dental or medical check-ups. As for DNA, there was no database in Ireland; of course, they'd come round asking him for her personal belongings to get a match: comb, toothbrush. If only he hadn't reported her missing – if he'd waited. The first thing they would do, of course, was run a check on missing persons. It was a wonder they hadn't called by now. He checked his phone – nothing. Maybe he should call them – the distraught husband, having seen the news report, demanding information. No – that would be walking right into it.

A man appeared on the screen, fifty-odd, weather-beaten, wellington boots over his jeans. He explained how his Jack Russell terrier had gone missing. He'd been shouting and shouting for the dog, had followed its barking into the woodland. The dog had been pulling at the corner of something – 'blue fabric'. Christ, it was her all right. The blanket – why the hell had he left the blanket? His own DNA, his prints all over it. He'd been quick-thinking enough to remove her wedding ring, but he couldn't bear to lay her in the ground without some protection, couldn't bear to shovel the earth on top of her. His DNA would be on the blanket anyway; sure wasn't it from their house, but then why the hell would Mercedes have been wrapped in something from the house if she'd been killed elsewhere? Why would she have been buried in the Dublin mountains if someone had killed her in Belfast? It would take some defence lawyer to get him out of this. He began to think – okay, there was the blanket, damning enough to probably send him down. What else was there? Joanna – if she testified that they'd been in Belfast, he was finished. He had to ensure that that wasn't about to happen – had to keep her on side, now more than ever: give her a reason not to talk. The man was still talking. The camera panned round him, zoomed in on the dog, a small white terrier with a brown patch.

What about Carmen? The lies she'd told about seeing Mercedes in Belfast – but that was just his word against hers. There was the twelve thousand euro, but that could have been for anything – could have been a pay-off for her to keep quiet. Joanna was the one who put him in the most danger. What would keep her from talking? Stupid, bringing her to Belfast like that. At the time he thought it'd be a nice little cover-up. But no, it put him right in the frame. Idiot. Unless, unless … he started to think, what was it that mattered most to Joanna? There was the whole Arnold thing – shame he'd already given her the location of the boat. He could have withheld it – offered it quid pro quo. He thought about what she'd told him about the mother emigrating to Italy, about Patrick Arnold setting the whole thing up. Arnold – he had no conscience, had no qualms about breaking the law. There were some who studied law to just that end. Why the boat? Arnold was staying with the sister-in-law, Rachel, wasn't he? There was no need for him to have hired a barge – not unless they were hiding something. He'd been concerned about the policy – why? Because he was afraid his brother's death may have looked like a suicide? Natural enough under the circumstances. But the boat?

Oliver took out his phone. He checked his emails – looked up the location that his friend from the telecoms company had sent him. Grand Canal Dock. What if he was to go down there, do a bit of investigating of his own?

A sudden ring at the bell jolted him from his thoughts. *Jesus, was it them? Had they found out already?* He could pretend he wasn't in, but then the TV was on; they might have seen its glare through the window. Maybe it was better to answer – could be they just wanted to inform him that a body had been found. It was too soon for them to have discovered the identity. Reluctantly he rose and made his way to the door.

FORTY-SIX

Joanna took out the statement and looked at it. 'Spar, Charlestown Plc'. She opened up her laptop and typed in the address. Immediately her suspicion was confirmed – the shop was in Belfast. She checked the calendar – tenth of March, the Friday they had gone to Belfast. How long had he been missing that day: two hours? Long enough to have met his wife, to have had lunch and a long conversation, but why would he have invited her along? It didn't make sense.

She looked at the name on the statement. Mercedes Hernandez. She typed it into Google and clicked. Several websites came up bearing the name. She clicked on a LinkedIn profile, and found herself looking at someone who bore a strong resemblance to the woman she had seen at Oliver's house that night. But was it her? Her hair was different; she couldn't be sure. It could be an old shot. *Find Mercedes Hernandez on Facebook.* Joanna scrolled through the list – looked carefully at each thumbnail, eliminating the ones that were definitely not her, clicking on those that might be. She opened up a profile that was definitely the same woman who was on LinkedIn. She clicked on an album and found the answer to her question.

Mercedes and Carmen Hernandez were strikingly alike. Joanna

stared at a picture of the two sisters, arms round each other, standing on the deck of a boat. Both wore large fashionable sunglasses – their hair was the same. In size and stature, you couldn't tell them apart. They could have been twins. Joanna guessed that the picture was several years old. The girls – she couldn't separate them by name – looked much younger in the shot than Carmen Hernandez had when she'd burst into the house that night. Joanna clicked through the album – in more recent years it was easier to tell the sisters apart. Mercedes had changed her hair: rather than the mad waves of Carmen it hung sleek in a V-shape, and she'd had a side fringe cut that hung over her left eye. Mercedes was not the woman she had seen that night – she was not the one that Joanna had seen at all. It had been Carmen coming out of the house that first time she had called by Oliver's house; Carmen who she had seen undressing before the fire that night. She continued to click through Mercedes's album. There were shots of her and Oliver, both of them dressed up – at a wedding, maybe. One of him carrying her on his back, arms round his neck, him laughing. Joanna stared; her fears confirmed. She had never seen Mercedes Hernandez. Her card had been used in Belfast that Friday – and to book a Eurolines ticket. Had he gone there to see her off – to try to persuade her not to go? And if not, if not. There was only one thing she could do – confront him.

The house was in darkness when she arrived. She stopped the car, relieved, almost, that he might not be home. It occurred to her that she should have told someone where she was going. She had no idea what she was walking into. No idea how he might react when she challenged him. Hastily, she took out her phone and texted her mother his address. She didn't say anything, didn't indicate why. If she was in danger, if something happened, her mother would know why she had sent it – she could inform the police, telling them that the last text she'd had from her daughter was to give her this address.

She got out of the car, chiding herself for allowing her imagination to run wild. She walked up the path and rang the bell; the sound of it echoed inside the house. She waited, shivering. Her heart leapt when she heard movement inside. She was tempted to turn and bolt, but she forced herself to wait. A light came on in the hall.

'Joanna, hey.'

She must have woken him. His hair was tousled, his feet bare.

'Come on in.'

She followed him to the door of the living room, waited for him to turn on the light.

'I was watching a film; I think I dozed off. What time is it?'

'About eight.'

He looked at her, curious. 'I hadn't expected to see you so soon. Is everything all right?'

'I saw her statement earlier on the table: Mercedes's I mean; the last two payments made on her card were in Belfast.'

'So?'

'So they were made on the same date that we were there. What's going on, Oliver?'

'What do you mean what's going on? What is it you're getting at, Joanna?' His expression had changed to fury.

She persevered, despite the fear. 'Why did you take me up there? Had you arranged to meet her, is that it? Is that where you disappeared to – not a business meeting at all, but a meeting with your wife?'

He didn't answer. 'I don't like all this cross-questioning, Joanna. It's none of your concern what I was doing. I'm not even sure what it is you want me to say.'

'Simple – if you didn't meet her, then what were you doing using her card?'

Fury changed to incredulity. 'I don't believe this. Are you saying … ?' He shook his head. 'You think I've done something to her, is that it? Christ, Joanna, you have some cheek coming into my

234

house accusing me … you know what, I'd like you to leave. I'm not even going to have this conversation. Will you just go?'

He walked back out to the hall, stood with his hand on the lock.

She could do it – just leave, forget about him, remove herself from danger. 'No,' she said.

He opened the door. 'Get out.'

She didn't like the look in his eyes. If she were wise, she'd take his advice and leave, but she stood her ground. 'Not until you've told me what's going on. Where is she, Oliver?'

'Belfast, I assume. Isn't that what it said on the statement?'

'Did you see her there?'

'As a matter of fact, yes. She wanted some of her stuff. I took it to her. Satisfied?'

Was he telling the truth? He didn't look at her when he said it. Fury filled him, barely repressed, making his hands shake. He seemed like a different person from before.

'What stuff?'

He sort of guffawed and spread his hands. 'What business is that of yours?'

'None, I suppose. It might have been nice if you'd told me the truth at the time, but then I suppose the truth is not your strong point, is it, Oliver? Look what you did to Mercedes, to her sister … '

'Ah, it was only a matter of time, wasn't it, till you threw that at me? Look, it would never have worked. I don't have to listen to this.' This time he opened the door wide. 'You'd want to sort out your issues, Joanna. All this daddy stuff seems to have messed up your head.'

'Go fuck yourself,' she said, brushing her way past him and out the door.

It took some time before she stopped shaking.

FORTY-SEVEN

He shouldn't have lost it with her. He knew that. There was nothing to say that she wouldn't go to the police as soon as she heard the news. And clearly, she hadn't heard yet. When had it been announced? Was this evening's broadcast the first? If so, she might not hear it until tomorrow, and that gave him time to find something on the Arnolds.

He took his coat, put a hat on so that no one would recognize him – there was no point in sitting here waiting for the guards to arrive, one false alarm had been enough – he'd go down to the dock and see what he could find out about Arnold and the boat he had hired. That way he may have something to trade for Joanna's silence.

He drove out, parked down a side street and made his way towards the prominent red lights. There was a show on at the theatre, crowds milled around the foyer. He made his way towards the jetty and down towards the boats. Most of them were in darkness. He'd typed the location he'd been given into Google Maps and had zoomed in to take a look. If it was accurate, then what he was looking for was a low black and blue boat. He walked slowly, keeping an eye out for it. Dim light shone from a few of the cabins, and somewhere in the darkness he heard the faint sound of music playing.

In all, about twenty boats were moored there. He found it quite easily – on either side of it two other barges, one red, the other green. At first he thought there was no one on board, but then he spotted a light through a chink in the curtains pulled across the small square windows. He crept closer, walking right to the edge of the jetty to try to gain a better view. Movement behind the curtain – definitely somebody there. He looked around for a better vantage point, a place from which he could spy without being noticed. He glanced at one of the boats next to Arnold's, the one with a view of the window. It seemed to be deserted; certainly, there was an absence of light.

Carefully, he stepped onto the deck and then walked round to the other side to cup his hands against one of the windows. Uninhabited. Inside, the cabin looked sterile, a houseboat for summer rental probably. He doubted they got much activity in wintertime, which made Arnold's choice all the more strange. He tried the door. Unsurprisingly, it was locked. He wondered what it would take for it to give; if he could break in without causing a racket, he could settle down to watch the neighbouring boat incognito. He stooped down to examine the lock. As he did so, he heard movement – the sound of men's voices. He dropped to the deck without a sound, lay flattened against the cold wood. They were just two or three metres away; light spilled from the open cabin door. He listened – they were speaking in low voices – he recognized one of them immediately as Patrick Arnold, and he strained to hear the other man, but he couldn't figure which of them it was that was speaking.

Cautiously, he pushed himself up slightly on his hands to raise his head above the deck. What he saw was two men standing smoking in the night air. Patrick had his back to him. The other man was nearer the cabin door, his face partially lit by the cabin light. He was bearded, hair grey: he wasn't as tall as Patrick; a few years older maybe. It was his voice that really caught Oliver's attention. If he hadn't been looking, hadn't known there were two men, he'd have thought Patrick was answering himself. The tone, the timbre was identical. Vince Arnold – it had to be.

'Maybe she shouldn't come round so much. If anyone sees her … we can't afford any slip-ups.'

'Sure who'd see her?'

'I don't know. Joanna, maybe, and she's become fairly friendly with Rachel from what I can see.'

'How is she?'

'Bright. Resourceful. A lot like her mother.'

'I meant Rachel.'

'Ah. Hardly the time to develop a conscience now, is it? She'll be all right. People keep going, don't they? Not much choice.'

Oliver was relieved when they stubbed out their cigarettes and went back inside. Cramped in position, he lowered himself prostrate back onto the deck, and then slowly, cautiously – when he heard the cabin door close – he rose, took a quick look round and hurried back down the jetty.

Patrick Arnold. Oliver had known something dodgy was going on – all that concern about the insurance policy. No wonder Patrick was jumpy about it. Oliver walked briskly back towards the car. An insurance scam – but then, who was the dead man in the canal if it wasn't Vince? Whose body was it that he had come across frozen beneath the ice? Clearly the Arnold brothers had committed more than straightforward fraud. His trip to the boat had given him more than he could've wished for. How would Joanna feel when she discovered the father she'd thought dead was hiding out on the boat? Furious, at first – but then … she'd want to protect – if not Vince – certainly her mother. There was no way she could tell the police about Belfast now, not when he had enough information to put both her parents in prison.

He took out his phone and called up her number. Then he paused – if she saw his name, she wouldn't answer, would she? Not after the words they'd exchanged. He changed his settings to withhold his caller ID and then rang.

'Hello?' Her voice, weary.

He felt bad doing this to her – she'd been through a lot, but he couldn't afford to take a chance on her going to the police. If only she hadn't been so damn inquisitive.

'Don't hang up – it's important. It's about your father.' Silence at the other end. 'Joanna?'

'What do you want? I told you not—'

'Listen to me for a minute. It's about Vince; you need to hear this.'

'What about him?'

He hesitated. It would be better to tell her in person, wouldn't it? And besides, if she was with him she wouldn't get a chance to see the news. 'Look, could you meet me somewhere?'

'What's this about, Oliver?'

'Your father is alive. I've seen him.'

'That's ridiculous. You're the one who found the body—'

'Look, I don't want to tell you over the phone. What I'm saying is true, I swear it.'

She was hesitant; clearly she didn't believe him. Probably thought it was some kind of trick. But why? To harm her? Jesus, if that was what she thought about him, then she'd certainly believe that he'd killed his wife.

'There's a bar next to the theatre. I'll meet you there in about a half hour. And Oliver … this had better be true.'

It had begun to rain, wind blowing it in sheets beneath the lights of the square. He crossed to the theatre – the crowd from earlier had disappeared – immersed by now in whatever was showing. He found himself wishing it were a normal night, that he were meeting, if not Joanna, then some other girl for a date at the theatre, and not to blackmail her with the fact that her father had faked his own death.

The bar was quiet. It was a Tuesday night and he guessed most of their clientele was the pre-theatre crowd. Joanna arrived before she'd said. He guessed curiosity had quickened her pace. He wasn't sure how to greet her after their earlier argument, and he felt the anger rise again when he thought of how she'd come round accusing him, but he swallowed it back; now wasn't the time.

'What's all this about?' She sat down opposite him without taking off her coat.

If he'd had any thought of apologizing, which he hadn't, she looked in no mood to hear it. He scanned the room, lowered his voice. 'The boat, the address I gave you – your father is hiding out there.'

'How do you know this?'

'I saw him – they're there now, or at least they were thirty minutes ago: Patrick Arnold and his brother.'

'Are you sure? I mean, what makes you think it was him? Did you talk to them?'

'I heard them talking. I was on the next boat.'

She stared at him, incredulous. 'I don't get it. What were you doing there?'

'Maybe I wanted to protect you, see what it was you were getting yourself into.'

'Ha! What, after the way you behaved? Don't try to make me believe that.'

He spread his hands, irked by her bad temper. What was the point now in trying to get her on side? He had the information he needed to prevent her from saying anything. 'All right, so maybe I was curious – you're not the only one capable of spying on people, Joanna.'

She stood up, ready to leave. 'Why should I believe anything you say?' she said.

He sipped his drink, looked at her calmly. 'Because it would be in everybody's best interests.'

'What do you mean?' She sat again.

He leaned in close to her. 'You're not going to tell anyone about our trip to Belfast because, if you do, I'll tell the police about your little family plot. Your father is pretending to be dead in order to fake an insurance claim – both your mother and Patrick Arnold are party to this crime – and if you say one word to the guards about me, all three of them will wind up in jail. Fraud is taken very seriously, Joanna – particularly when there's a body involved that turns out to be somebody else.'

'You're lying,' she said, but she'd turned pale.

He'd as good as told her that he'd killed his wife, and there was nothing she could do about it.

'Go there, and you'll see for yourself,' he said.

Before she had a chance to answer, he drained his glass and left.

FORTY-EIGHT

It was five minutes or more before Joanna moved from the table. She watched Oliver, head ducked, striding through the driving rain across the square in the opposite direction of the marina. The boat – could what he said be true? She stared out the window to where the rows of barges were moored not one hundred metres away and wondered if it was a trap. What if all he had told her was a lie – a ruse to get her down to the jetty and onto one of the boats? Women disappeared all the time. Mercedes had disappeared. She, Joanna, knew too much – she had proof that he had used his wife's card in Belfast. Maybe she ought not to go near the boat, but instead, go straight to the police, dismissing what he'd told her. It was, after all, Oliver who'd given her the location in the first place when she'd asked him to ping the number. There was every chance he'd made the whole thing up.

'Can I get you something?'

Joanna looked up to find the waitress looking at her, curious. 'No … thanks.' She took her bag and stood. 'I've changed my mind.'

She stepped outside, stood in the semi-shelter of the doorway and stared out at the deluge. She'd seen him walking in the opposite direction, but could he have doubled back around and made it to the barge, where he now lay in wait for her? Christ – what to do! Her head told her to go straight to the nearest police station, but his words paralyzed her. If what he'd said was true, she'd throw all their lives into chaos. The thought of her mother in prison, no matter what lies she'd told, was unthinkable.

Her father. Rachel had said he owed money. It would be the perfect way out – escape the debtors and receive the one hundred thousand – although that wouldn't be the case, would it? It was she and Rachel who would receive the money, unless … unless Rachel was a party to it – but then why give Joanna anything at all? It was a lot of money to sacrifice for a guilty conscience. No, she didn't believe that Rachel was involved; her grief was too genuine – her sadness too real.

Suddenly, Joanna saw movement: a figure, hunched against the rain. Instinctively, she shrank back into the doorway. No, it wasn't him, not Oliver – too short to be Oliver. As the figure grew closer, there was something familiar in its gait. Joanna pulled up the hood of her coat – but the person wasn't coming towards the pub; they were heading for the marina, for the barges. Long black coat, boots, a white woollen hat with a large bauble on top. Her mother passed not thirty metres away and failed to notice her secreted in the doorway. Paralyzed, for a moment, by surprise and indecision, Joanna let her go. It was true then, was it? Vince on the boat all this time – Vince, not Patrick, who her mother planned to abscond with. Unless … could Oliver have somehow orchestrated her mother being here?

Fear made her spring into action. Her mother was not far off the marina by now, and Joanna set off after her, running as quickly as she could. At the sound of the running footsteps behind her, she turned, startled. Joanna caught up with her, breathless.

'I know,' she said. 'About Vince, the whole set-up. I know.'

Her mother stared at her. 'What? What are you doing here?'

'Is it true? Is he there?' Joanna pointed towards the marina. Her mother cast about her, looking for something to say, but she was out of excuses. She nodded. 'How did you find out? Was it Patrick?'

Joanna glanced round. 'No. I'll explain, but not now. We have to move. It's not safe here. Which one is it?'

She followed her mother to the barge – so distracted by thoughts that Oliver might be lurking somewhere ready to spring that she didn't have time to consider the fact that she was about to meet her father.

Carefully, her mother stepped onto the deck. It was in darkness save for a shred of light that showed through a small gap in a curtain. Her mother put out a hand and helped Joanna aboard, and then gave a knock – a soft rat-tat-tat on the cabin door. Joanna heard a noise – a key turning – and she almost knocked Vince Arnold off his feet in her hurry to get inside.

'What—?' In his panic, he'd reached for some kind of metal bar.

'Vince – stop. It's Joanna. She … '

Joanna had locked the door on the inside. She looked at the man in front of her and spoke in a hurry. 'You have to get out of here. It's not safe.'

'We know that. It's just another few days, until everything's died down, until everything's ready,' her mother said.

But the man had heard the panic in her voice. 'What do you mean?' he said. 'What is it?'

Joanna stammered – awareness finally hitting her that the grey-bearded man in front of her was her father. 'I'm not the only one who knows.'

'Who else?'

'Oliver. Patrick knows him. I know something about him – something really bad, but he's said if I tell the police he'll report you. You have to get out of here as soon as it can be arranged. Otherwise, he'll walk.'

'But he can't go to the police right away – he knows that you have this, this information about him?' Vince ran a hand through his thinning hair. His voice was soft, almost identical to how his brother spoke.

'Well, yes, but it's not just that … I'm afraid of what he might do.'

Her mother interrupted. 'This is the man you've been seeing, the solicitor? What's he done?'

There was no point in keeping anything back now; they had to know the danger they were in, all of them. 'I think he killed his wife. And if he did, there's every chance he'll want me out of the way.'

Vince Arnold didn't hesitate. He took out his phone – *the phone*, Joanna guessed, and made a call.

'Yeah, look something's happened; you'll have to get over here – and make it quick.' He looked at Angela. 'Patrick's coming back. We'll think of something,' he said.

She bit her lip and looked at Joanna. The three of them suddenly alone together.

'So, you've been here all along?' Joanna said, softly.

Vince nodded, avoiding her eye. 'There were some very dangerous people … I had to.'

'Does Rachel know?'

'No – and don't you go telling her,' Angela said.

Joanna looked at her – then at Vince – anger replacing her fear. 'When did this start? Had you no intention of ever telling me? Were you just going to go to Milan and disappear, pretend you were dead too?' Reproach, she was due that much.

Her mother put a hand up to silence whatever Vince was about to say.

'We were going to tell you,' she said. 'But not yet. There was the inheritance money; I'd have had to explain it – but we couldn't tell you everything until Vince was safely out of the country, until we were settled in Italy and he had a new identity.'

'And in the meantime, I'd have thought that my father was dead?'

'It was the only way,' Vince said. 'I'm sorry.'

Joanna sat down, trying to work everything out – all the mysteries, the subterfuge of the last few weeks, only to end like this. 'There was a body – Patrick identified it as you … ' Fear's cold fingers creeping round her insides as she said it.

Vince looked at Angela. 'A homeless man,' he said. 'Died in the freeze.'

'Jesus. And nobody knows – he's buried in your grave … Where? Where did you find him?'

'It sounds too fantastical to be true, but it's what gave us the idea. The garden shed – I went out one morning, found that the lock had been tampered with. The man had crept in out of the cold – minus twelve degrees that night … '

'Didn't Rachel know?'

'She never went out there. I called Patrick; it was him that thought of it. I'd been talking about disappearing but a body … if there was a body … he could identify it; the insurance money wouldn't be stuck in limbo.'

'So you took the body – the man – and dumped him in the canal?'

Vince nodded. 'We didn't do it immediately. I had to disappear first, then Patrick came to take care of things. I put a new lock on the shed, left the keys for him. We made a patch in the ice – we'd put my coat on the body, my wallet in the pocket, so that they'd contact Rachel without any DNA being done. We knew the freeze was to last until the end of the week – that within hours the ice would have formed again, covered him over. It would look like an accident, like I'd slipped and fallen into the water.'

'Christ. Had you no conscience? How do you know that man hadn't a family, a wife out looking for him? And Rachel, what about Rachel?'

'Rachel and I … I'd met your mother again, and the feelings were still there.' He took Angela's hand, she looked at Joanna, eyes pleading. 'This was our chance to make it work, and she won't know it, but it's better for Rachel this way. I put her in danger – got myself in a situation I couldn't get out of – they were calling the house, making threats.'

'And what's to stop them from doing that still? With you dead, they can be sure that she's about to come into some kind of inheritance. What makes you think they won't go after her for the money?'

Vince shook his head. 'We've seen to that. Patrick's going to pay them off with Rachel's share of the money. She was happy to do it, to live in peace. It just about covers what's owed.'

'And you're happy to do that, leave your wife with nothing?'

Vince looked away. 'Rachel will be okay; her family will see her right.'

Joanna took a step closer to her father forcing him to look at her. 'You don't care who you implicate, do you? You don't care about putting us in danger ... about ... '

'I won't, I swear it.' He gave her a long, penetrating look – a look that said 'you can trust me'; the look he was probably used to giving her mother but would hold no weight with her.

'But you already have, don't you see that? My mother is complicit in your crime – if you're found out, we'll all go down. If Oliver—'

'You're the one who brought him into it'. Her mother snapped, fear making her forget who was really in the wrong.

Joanna was about to make a sharp retort when they heard a noise outside, and the same rat-tat-tat her mother had tapped out on the door. Vince Arnold moved to open it.

'Well, well,' Patrick said when he saw Joanna. 'Is this what all the panic was about?'

'Not quite. Tell him, Joanna.'

Joanna looked at Patrick – apart from the beard, the two brothers really were alike.

'Oliver knows,' she said. 'You have to get him out of here.'

'Oliver? What's he doing sticking his nose in for – ah, I get it – you two are involved, aren't you? I knew he wouldn't let that chance pass him by. What about the wife, does she know?'

'She's missing – I think he did something to her – he practically admitted it. And now he's blackmailing me – saying if I go to the guards about him, he'll report all of you.'

'How did he find out? Did you tell him?'

'No – he told me.' Joanna turned to her mother. 'You wouldn't tell me what was going on. I found the phone – your old phone – and had Oliver ping the number you'd been calling. It gave him the location of the barge. That was before I knew anything about his wife being missing. He was here tonight spying on you.'

'Whoa – back up a minute. What are you saying? What exactly do you have on Ollie?'

Joanna took a breath – she felt dizzy with it all. 'We went to Belfast, Oliver and me. While we were there he used his wife's debit card. I know because I saw her statement at the house. When I asked him about it, he got really annoyed – then he pretended to have met her in Belfast – but I discovered her profile on a website for missing persons. He's killed her. I'm sure of it – that's why he's trying to prevent me from telling the guards about him being in Belfast. He went there to leave a trail, make it look as though she'd been there when she disappeared.

'Jesus. Ollie – a killer? Maybe you're getting a bit carried away here—'

'Why else would he care if I said anything?'

'I don't know. But look, whatever about Oliver, I think it's time we got you out of here.' Patrick had turned to Vince. 'I'll check flights – whatever flight is going out in the next two hours, you're on it. It doesn't matter if it's going to Milan or not. You can use my passport, just in case – then send it back to me. I'll give you enough cash to get you through the week. Your documents should be ready by then. And I'll join you.'

Patrick booked Vince onto the last flight to London. He would travel on to Milan – to Patrick's apartment – on the first flight the following morning. It was decided that Vince would leave alone. He borrowed Patrick's coat and scarf, and put on a cap to hide his face. They didn't know if the boat was being watched: if Oliver was still out there he might phone the police with an anonymous tip-off. Without that threat over Vince there was nothing to ensure Joanna's silence. Patrick gave him the keys to the four-by-four he'd hired; he could leave it at the airport, hide the keys some place and call him from a public phone to tell him where they were. Vince would leave the mobile phone on the barge – Oliver had already had it traced once, it would be easy to do it again.

Joanna and her mother left shortly after Vince had departed.

Her mother began to speak. 'So now you know why I couldn't say anything. I'm so sorry, Joanna, I … '

Joanna cast her eyes round the marina. 'Sssh. Not here. Somebody might be listening.'

They walked in silence the rest of the way to the car.

'I'm sorry, Joanna … it was never meant to turn out like that; if Rachel Arnold hadn't turned up at the house that night … ' Her mother turned to her as she put on her seatbelt.

Joanna looked at her. 'Are you sure you're doing the right thing?'

Angela nodded, eyes teared over.

'And what if he's caught? If someone recognizes him in Milan? It could happen. The world is pretty small.'

'We'll take our chance. You won't say anything, will you, to anyone?'

Joanna had started the car. 'What and have you locked up?' She shook her head. 'I'm doing this for you, not for him. You might have fallen for his charm but you needn't expect me to – nothing changes the fact that for the past twenty-six years he failed to recognize that he even had a daughter.'

'I know that. I hope you'll give him a chance though, in time – if only for me.'

For the next two hours Joanna watched the clock. Vince Arnold's flight to London was scheduled to depart at a quarter to ten. He'd have touched down in Luton at half past and would be safely out of the jurisdiction. All he had to do was keep out of sight, in so far as he could, until he reached Milan.

It was approaching midnight when Joanna stole from the house, got in the car and made her way to the police station. With her father safely out of the country, there was nothing to stop her from reporting Oliver. He had no proof that Vince was alive. The only thing she had to fear was for her own safety, and she'd take that chance and hope they brought him in before he could come anywhere near her.

There was no one at the desk when she arrived. She stood there going over what it was she wanted to say. Five minutes passed. She could hear voices in an office somewhere beyond the desk. Then laughter.

'Hello?' she called.

A few minutes later, a garda appeared and asked gruffly what he could do for her.

'I have some information about a missing woman: Mercedes Hernandez.'

'Oh yeah?'

'Her husband was in Belfast on the tenth of March; it's the last date that Mercedes used her debit card – I … I have evidence.' She took the statement from her bag, put it on the desk in front of him.'

The garda looked confused.

Joanna ploughed on. 'I saw her name on a missing persons site – it said that she's been missing since the beginning of March, but her husband was in Belfast on the tenth of March and claims to have seen her, so why would he report her missing?'

The garda peered at the statement. 'Where did you get this?' he asked.

'I took it from their house. I'm ... a friend of the husband. I was with him in Belfast.'

'Wait there for a moment.' The young guard disappeared in the back again.

Joanna waited, she hadn't made herself very clear. She was nervous. A few minutes later an older, heavy-set man appeared.

'You have some information on the Hernandez case?' he said.

Joanna began again. 'I have reason to believe that Oliver Molloy – her husband – has harmed her.'

'Oh?' He stared at her, sharp blue eyes curious.

'I was in Belfast with Oliver Molloy on the tenth of March, the last date that Mercedes Hernandez's bank card was used. I questioned him about it, and he claims that he met Mercedes there, but I've since seen that he reported his wife missing from the beginning of the month. I think he's lying about having seen her in Belfast– and that he used the card to place her there.'

The garda didn't look too excited by her information. She showed him the statement. He didn't say anything for a moment. The he folded it and handed it back to her.

'I can see why you're concerned, but Mercedes Hernandez has been found safe and well. In fact, she turned up in a police station in Belfast to identify herself just a number of hours ago.'

'What? Are you sure?'

The man nodded.

'I'm sorry, I ... I didn't mean to waste your time.'

Joanna left the station, dazed. Mercedes had turned up. So why had Oliver made that threat? It didn't make any sense. 'Tell the police about Belfast and I'll tell them about Vince Arnold', that was what he'd said – and now he could. She had nothing on him. But no – there was something – something that didn't add up. If he'd met Mercedes in Belfast, if she had used her card there, why would he care if the police knew about their trip? In fact, why hadn't he told them about it himself – had them call off the search for a woman he'd reported missing?

Joanna started the car, and the radio came on. She paid no attention to it, caught up in her thoughts, until she heard the newscaster's announcement. 'The body of a woman has been found in a wooded area near Glencree.' Quickly she reached for the volume. The reporter described how a man out walking his dogs had come across the body, which had yet to be identified. All they could say for the moment was that the body was believed to be that of a woman in her early thirties. Joanna thought of the Hernandez sisters – and the physical similarity between them. Vince Arnold had used Patrick's passport to get on the flight. Too risky, Patrick had said, to use his own. They bore a strong enough resemblance to get away with it. Was it possible that the woman Joanna had thought was Mercedes Hernandez had pulled a similar trick? With Carmen on side, maybe even an accomplice, Oliver could get away with it – unless there was, of course, something to link him to the woman who'd been found in Glencree.

FORTY-NINE

Oliver had seen Joanna running through the rain towards the marina. Then he'd turned and headed for home. They'd all be there now – on the barge. He could make a call and have the lot of them brought in, but he wouldn't. In truth, the girl had been through enough. She wouldn't do anything to put her family in jeopardy, whatever she thought about him.

When he'd left the house, he'd forgotten to take his mobile. He picked it up to find that he had three missed calls, but he didn't recognize the number. He was about to dial into the voice-mail when it rang in his hand; the same number flashing up on the screen. The guards, probably the guards. He could just ignore it. But wouldn't that be worse – a man desperate to find his wife not even picking up the phone? And besides, he couldn't avoid it indefinitely, not if he wanted to make a plea of innocence.

'Mr Molloy, we have some news for you. Could you come down to the station?'

Sweeney's voice was clipped, staccato, and he wasn't sure if he imagined it but he sounded almost upbeat.

'Is it Mercedes?' His mouth had gone suddenly dry. 'Have you found her?'

Sweeney ignored his question; he clearly didn't believe in giving away information over the phone. 'How soon can you get here?' he said.

'I'll come right away.'

He hadn't even had a chance to take his coat off. He picked up his keys and headed back out in the rain. If they'd discovered it was Mercedes – if they'd identified her so fast, wouldn't they have called to the house in person? Wouldn't he be on his way to the station in the back of a patrol car rather than driving there willingly? Maybe it was nothing. Maybe there had been a sighting since the ad went up on that website and someone had mistaken some other woman for his wife. It happened all the time. People swore blind to a positive identification only for it to be proven untrue.

That wouldn't happen in his case. Nobody would see Mercedes in some crowded street. She wouldn't be caught on CCTV in a big department store. She was gone. Her body had, according to the news story, already begun to decay. He didn't like to think of that – maybe that's what Sweeney had called him in for – he wanted him to take a look at the body, see if he could positively identify it as his wife. He shuddered at the idea. How could he ever look at her face again?

When he pulled up outside the station, it was still raining hard. He sat gripping the wheel, delaying the moment. What was it Sweeney wanted from him? – Would he walk out of there a free man? He killed the engine, made a dash for the doors; one way or another he had to face whatever lay ahead.

The desk was unmanned when he entered. He stood tapping his fingers on the counter. In a room in the back he could hear voices. A few minutes later the young garda that had been with Sweeney the first time they had paid him a visit appeared at the desk. From the blank look on his face he seemed not to remember who he was or why he was there.

'Garda Sweeney's expecting me.'

The young garda made some noise that could have been an acknowledgement. Then he disappeared into the back room, presumably to locate Sweeney.

Oliver looked around the station. There wasn't even a seat for people waiting, not that he wanted to sit. He felt like pacing, but he didn't want to appear nervous and so he stood with his hands in his coat pockets where no one would see the tremor that had crept into his fingers. He heard before he saw Sweeney's bulk emerge from the innards of the station.

'Mr Molloy, how are you?'

'Have you found Mercedes?' *Have you found her body rotting in the earth?*

Sweeney didn't answer right away. He simply led the way to a small room at the end of the corridor.

'It seems your wife walked into a Garda station in Belfast and identified herself last night.'

Impossible. Sweeney picked up a remote control and aimed it at a flat-screen television high on the wall opposite. He pressed a button and the screen turned blue. Oliver didn't respond. He couldn't respond. He waited, eyes fixed on the screen.

Sweeney was no whizz with technology. He fumbled with the buttons and grunted in exasperation when he knocked off the wrong button and the blue screen turned to millions of scrambled pixels. He moved his arm and kept pressing until finally an image of a Garda station, not unlike the one they were now in, appeared on the screen. The camera was directed at the double glass doors. There was a timer in the corner of the screen that read 18.10.

On screen, the door opened and a woman appeared. She made her way to the desk. Oliver leaned forward in his chair. Sweeney paused the shot and zoomed in on the woman who claimed to be Mercedes Hernandez. Oliver nodded. He was aware of Sweeney's shrewd eyes assessing his reaction. In the close-up it was still difficult to differentiate. To the untrained eye, it would be almost impossible. She had changed her hair. It made her face look thinner, her mouth less full. He peered closely at the screen, and Sweeney pressed another button and the woman reached the counter, smiled at the young garda on duty and leaned forward at the desk. She reached into her bag then and pulled out what looked like a passport. She placed it on the desk for the garda to see. The woman on the screen was a modified version of Mercedes Hernandez. She had the same figure, and the same hairstyle and, if he hadn't known that it wasn't possible, she may even have fooled him. He wasn't sure what she had done, and hadn't even begun to fathom why she had done it, but Carmen Hernandez had almost metamorphosed into Mercedes.

'Is that your wife?'

Oliver nodded.

'Beats me why a man would want to cheat on a woman like that.' Sweeney shook his big head and turned off the television.

'Sometimes we don't know our luck,' Oliver said.

Sweeney ignored him. 'We tried to get in touch with her sister, but her phone seems to be powered off. Maybe she's out of the country?'

Oliver nodded. 'She went to Spain to see if she could find out anything from friends there. I'll try to get in touch with her. What do I do now?' he asked.

Sweeney looked at him and shrugged. 'Nothing. Just wait for her to cool off I guess. Whether she decides to get in touch with you is her decision. Nothing much you can do once a woman's made up her mind.'

Oliver looked at Sweeney, at his almost wistful expression, and wondered what lay behind the words of advice that he hadn't asked for. 'I meant do I have to sign something or ... ?'

Sweeney shook his head. 'No. You've confirmed that it's Ms Hernandez. That's all we need to close the case.'

Ms Hernandez. Mercedes had never changed her name. It was the name on all her official documents, the name on her passport, which Carmen had obviously taken from among her things when she'd been in the house. He wondered when she'd had an opportunity to do it; maybe on that first night when he had arrived to find her in the living room. What else had she seen as she'd gone through Mercedes's documents? What else had she stolen?

Oliver looked at his watch. It wasn't yet ten. He wanted to go round to the flat to talk to Carmen. He got into the car, drove out of the car park and veered left for the city. Carmen had ended the search for Mercedes, but why? Had she finally decided that the best thing was to remove Mercedes from the picture? A myriad of thoughts spun round his head as he made his way across the city towards Carmen's flat, wondering if she'd returned yet from Belfast.

When he arrived a girl with a stroller was struggling in the door of the apartment block. He hurried to hold the door open for her and then took the opportunity of slipping into the dimly lit hallway without having to alert Carmen to his arrival. As he climbed the stairs to her apartment, he wondered if she had stayed in Belfast.

She must have known that he'd have seen the footage by now. He wondered what kind of reaction she expected. She had no guarantee that he wouldn't tell the police that the woman caught on CCTV was not Mercedes. The thought had occurred to him as he'd sat in the interview room with Sweeney. If he'd told Sweeney there and then that it was Carmen, he could have had her arrested for impersonation, for perverting the course of justice and who knew what other crime. Carmen had put herself in the firing line, but she had done it for him. That was the thought that had been going through his mind since he'd seen the tape. It had curtailed any thought he might have had of trying to fit Carmen up for Mercedes's disappearance, for her murder. He didn't want to think of it as that. It wasn't murder. At most it was manslaughter. Slaughter – he hated that word. He hadn't slaughtered anyone. Slaughter suggested bloodshed and violence, and that was not what it had been. What it had been was an accident, and he had to put it out of his mind.

He paused outside Carmen's door and listened for any sound within. He thought he could hear voices – a radio, perhaps – but he wasn't sure. It might have been coming from another flat. He rapped on the door with his fist. The wood rattled under his knuckles, and the voices died. He tried again, put his mouth close to the keyhole and called her name.

'It's me,' he added.

The last was redundant. He knew that. She would know his voice, know that he would be round to ask her why she had done what she did, what she hoped to gain from it; though he thought he already knew the answer to that and it made his pulse quicken.

At last he heard a noise, saw a movement beyond the glass, and knew that she was there. The form grew. He knew it was Carmen, knew from the way she walked, the sway of her body even through the thick glass. Suddenly the door opened and she stood before him. Despite seeing the video footage, he hadn't been expecting her to look the way she did. She stood back, and he stepped into the hallway where they stood facing each other, saying nothing. He felt the nausea that accompanied episodes of panic seize him and he tried to swallow it back. He could see how she had tricked the authorities into thinking she was Mercedes. The likeness was stronger than he'd imagined it would be now that she was standing before him.

'What have you done?' he said.

Carmen smiled and shrugged. Her smile was not the smile of Mercedes. There were differences still, but only those who had known them intimately would recognize the inconsistencies that made it possible to tell them apart.

Carmen turned and walked into the living room. Oliver followed, watching the sway of her hips and feeling the blood course through him.

'It's better this way, no?'

'For who?'

'Everyone.'

'What if Mercedes comes back?'

'She's gone. She's not coming back, Oliver. You know that.'

Her dark eyes looked directly into his, and he knew that she knew. And that it didn't make a difference.

He put a hand to her face, traced the outline of her lips.

'Why did you do it?'

'You know why.'

'Where?'

'Spain. First I went to see my mother. I told her about Mercedes, what I'd done. I said that she'd come back, that you and she would probably work things out. On the way back I used Mercedes's passport, and I knew that it had worked – that I looked just like her.'

'Carmen—'

'No. From now on you must call me Mercedes.'

'I don't know if I can.'

'I did it for you. That girl, I know she didn't mean anything, but you and me – we're the same.'

Oliver thought of Joanna. She'd have met Vince Arnold by now. He felt a pang of regret about her. Now that Carmen had claimed to be Mercedes, the information Joanna could give the police about Belfast meant nothing. But Carmen was right, they were the same. He looked at her, and realized that he loved her madness. She would do anything for him, anything to get what she wanted. He knew the danger involved, but he decided that he was willing to risk it. Carmen had saved him. The only way he was going down was if she decided to do it. In a way she had him under her power, and he respected her for that. If Carmen took him down, he would take her with him. She was complicit in his crime. And he no longer had to feel alone with his guilt.

She didn't ask him what had happened that night. Maybe she didn't want to hear it put into words. It was easier to be with him this way. He would never tell her, he decided. Let her assume what she wanted. A confession would never come from his lips, no matter what the nights brought.

He put his hand beneath Carmen's chin and turned her head from side to side. She had had her lips reduced, her teeth straightened. She was more beautiful, not the imperfect version of her sister that she used to be. Carmen had wanted to be Mercedes and now she was. He wondered if it would make a difference to her, or if she'd regret it in time.

Carmen took his hand and drew him nearer. She kissed him and her lips felt the same. Her mouth was hot and tasted of cigarettes. She pressed her treacherous body against his, and he knew why it was that he couldn't get her out of his head. It was her unpredictability, her almost masculine aggression that he loved, that drew him to her. Carmen would never be Mercedes. She was bolder. She was the kind of woman that saw what she wanted and took it.

As she led him to the bedroom, he'd forgotten about Joanna. Mercedes was the name he uttered when they made love. If she were to become Mercedes, they had better start now. In the future there would be no room for mistakes.

FIFTY

Joanna couldn't sleep. She lay there thinking about Vince Arnold, and about Oliver's wife having turned up in a police station in Belfast, until she thought she'd go mad. At about three in the morning she got up, unable to lie there any longer, and went down to the darkroom. She took down the picture of Carmen Hernandez to look at it again. Tangled dark hair – slim figure. How much engineering would it take to turn herself into her sister? Not much, going by those earlier pictures when they were so much alike.

She went online to see if any more details had been released about the woman they'd found in the Dublin mountains, but she found the same scant information. More would follow, she supposed, if nobody claimed to know who she might be. The Hernandez case was closed. Would the police have any reasons to DNA match it to Mercedes? She doubted it; they seemed satisfied that the woman that had turned up in the station was Oliver Molloy's wife. But what of Carmen? If Joanna was right and it was actually Carmen who was impersonating her sister, then the old Carmen was gone for good. Her family, her parents would want to know where she'd gone, wouldn't they? Her friends in Spain would surely report her missing if she simply vanished –

unless Carmen managed to keep up the difficult, not to mention risky, task of playing the role of both Hernandez sisters. No, that would never work. Whatever she'd done to herself was, most likely, irreversible.

Joanna took the photo and looked at it again. She was right, she had to be. She'd been too late in getting to the police with the information about Belfast, but she had another idea. She would send a tip-off to the police, an anonymous letter telling them the identity of the woman. She'd send them the picture of Carmen that she'd taken through the window that night – tell them that all they had to do was do a DNA check against her sister, Mercedes, to find out for sure. DNA: Christ – why hadn't she thought of it before – the brush; the one she'd taken from the bathroom in Oliver's house was upstairs in a handbag. She hadn't cleaned it and, apart from her own hair, there were long dark strands caught between the plastic bristles – Mercedes's hair, maybe even Carmen's. That would be enough, wouldn't it? She'd heard that the DNA for siblings was an almost one hundred per cent match. If Oliver could walk free for Mercedes's murder, she'd have him questioned about Carmen's.

She took the stairs two steps at a time, opened the wardrobe and took out the bag where she knew the hairbrush still lay. She'd meant to bring it back, but then she'd forgotten about it. Now she pulled it from the bag, held it beneath the light and pulled a few loose strands of her own auburn hair from it leaving the mass of dark hairs caught at the base of the bristles. She opened the drawer of her desk, pulled a writing pad and a jiffy envelope from it. She scribbled a quick note, saying that she had reason to believe that the woman's body that had been found in Glencree was that of Carmen Hernandez, that the photo enclosed was taken at the house of Oliver Molloy three weeks before, and that the brush enclosed belonged to the deceased. She finished by saying that she believed that Oliver was responsible for the woman's death. She folded the note, unsigned, and placed everything in the envelope. Then she scribbled a quick note and left it downstairs on the table in case her mother should wake to find her gone.

Joanna pulled on her coat, took the envelope and stepped outside. An icy wind stirred the trees and she shivered, closed the door behind her and hurried to the car. She couldn't shake the feeling of being watched, not since Oliver had made that threat earlier at the dock. She locked the car doors and started the engine. She would post the envelope; she knew that Oliver would guess as soon as the police had shown it to him that it was her who had taken it – but for now she'd remain anonymous. After the police had received the evidence, he could do nothing to her – not while he was being investigated for his sister-in-law's murder. That was a risk he'd be far too clever to take.

Joanna found herself turning the car in the direction of his house. She knew she wouldn't see anything, but she felt compelled to look anyway. She slowed as she approached, parked on the opposite side of the road and turned off the lights. In the garden, his four-by-four was parked. The house was in darkness as it had been that first night when she'd seen Carmen Hernandez come out. And now, was she in there sharing his bed, pretending to be his wife? He had said it was what she'd always wanted. Was he foolish enough to think that her madness had saved him – rather than provided him with a short reprieve?

Joanna pulled away from the kerb, turned on her headlights. She stopped again a couple of blocks away when she spotted a post-box at the side of the road. She stood there for a moment, looking round the deserted street, before she dropped it in and heard it hit the bottom of the near empty box. The letter would be picked up in the first post, but it wouldn't reach the station until the following day. Vince Arnold would be in Milan by then, ready to begin his new life. Joanna thought of her father's deceit, of the tramp that had died in the freeze, and how the Arnolds had used his body to fake her father's death. If it weren't for her mother, she'd have been willing to report Vince too, but as it was, she knew she couldn't. She thought of Rachel Arnold, unwitting victim, as she was, to it all. When the insurance money came through, she'd return her half to Rachel, and hope that she could do some good with it. She wanted nothing to do with money got by such foul means. She wasn't sure she could ever have anything to do with him – the father she'd wanted so desperately to know. Doing so now would mean being party to all that duplicity.

Joanna turned and walked back to the car. She drove down to the canal, past the spot where Oliver Molloy had shown her where he'd found the body. Two people were dead, one an unknown man, the other, Mercedes. At least now one death would be vindicated. She would have to live with the legacy the Arnolds had passed on to her, doing the utmost to put it from her mind.

Acknowledgements

A big thank you to Lucy Dauman both for her enthusiasm for this novel, and her intuitive editorial suggestions. Thank you to Ian Gregson who supervised an earlier draft during my studies at Bangor University. For their invaluable feedback and suggestions, I would like to thank my husband, David Butler, as great a writer as he is a man, and also Arlene Hunt and Faith O'Grady who read previous drafts. For his expertise in the field of photography, I'm indebted to David Hussey, and also to Gosia Walczak whose beautiful photos inspired Joanna's *Runaway Brides* collection. For his guidance in the formative years of my writing career, I'd like to thank Martin Devaney, course facilitator. Huge respect and thanks to Alan Hayes of Arlen House, not only for publishing my book *When Black Dogs Sing*, but for all that he does. Big love and thanks always to Tom, Trevor, and Dani, and to the Butler and Hussey clans. Also to my great friends Antoinette and Adrianna. Above all, thanks to my mother, a creative force, whose beauty and kindness we will never forget.

Printed by RR Donnelley at Glasgow, UK